ABOUT THE AUTHOR

Kathy Rodgers lives in Longford with her two sons. Her debut novel, *Misbehaving*, was a national bestseller and was published by Poolbeg in 2003. Her second novel, *Afterglow*, was also published by Poolbeg in 2004. Kathy is currently working on her fourth novel.

Acknowledgements

A very big thank you to my parents for all their support and help, to my sister Ann, her husband Thomas, and the girls, Kate, Aine and Maeve. To all the O'Sullivans overseas, Conor, Oisin, Finn, Erin and Emer, not forgetting the Rodgers, Maeve, Eimear, Caroline and Louise.

Thanks to Gaye Shortland for her eagle eye and great editing skills. Thanks to the great team in Poolbeg and for all your hard work. Thanks to all the booksellers that I met – you did a brilliant job in promoting *Afterglow*. A very special thank-you to all those who bought a copy of my book. I hope you enjoyed it.

Thanks to Stephanie, a great pal, who always reads my work. Thanks to Ann for always being so encouraging. Thanks to Eamonn for reading an early draft and making some great suggestions. Thanks to Lil for the field trips.

Mary Carelton-Reynolds and all the staff at Longford Library have given me immense support and encouragement in my writing.

The Longford Book Club, the Cavan Literary Festival especially Elaine Lennon and indeed my agent Dorothy Lumley have helped to sustain my faith when, at times it wavered.

Thanks to Mayor Peggy Nolan and Longford Town Council for presenting me with the Mayor's award; I was deeply honoured.

While my sons, Kevin and Shane, were sleeping one night, my mind was drifting and the seeds for this novel were sown. This book is for you two and I hope you like it.

For Kevin and Shane

Chapter 1

"I wish, I wish, my wish come true."

"I wish I were in control again," Sophia reflects, as she considers events of the past twelve months, events that have disturbed and undermined her sense of safety, composure and well-being.

'Being in control' has brought Sophia to a point where she wears all the societal badges of success, aged thirty. Own apartment shared with the man she loves, own car, career, good looks. Today, however, she is miserable, panic-stricken and paranoid.

"You're the next patient," Dr Moran's secretary responds when Sophia points out that her appointment is running late. "Twenty minutes at most, I would say."

1

Sophia sits back down, leafing through the selection of magazines on offer, out-dated issues of *Hello!*, *Oprah*, *Woman's Way*. Nothing at all for the men, she thinks – maybe that's why that unshaven chap has been staring at me since I came in – he has nothing to read and nowhere else to look.

"Sophia Jordan . . ." Dr Annette Moran at last appears smilingly at her surgery doorway, inviting her to come in.

Dr Moran has been running a private practice near Monkstown for near twenty years. She is much respected and her clientele is predominantly female. She sees each of her patients as unique and does not allow their conditions to lead her into categorizing them as objects.

"Well, Sophia, how are you since we last met?" she asks kindly. Dr Moran's greying hair is swept back off her round face by a hair-band.

It seems to Sophia she is the only person who has truly listened to her. She is about to speak when Dr Moran continues.

"You were run down and not sleeping well. You also felt a lot of remorse over your dad's death. How long is it now?"

"Nearly four months. It gets no better. I find . . ." The words fade, dry up in her parched mouth.

Nervously she starts to shred the sodden tissue in her hands.

Dr Moran tilts her head slightly. "That's natural, but you need to acknowledge to yourself that you are carrying too much guilt. Yes, he was doing the good Samaritan for you, taking your car to the garage – but, poor Alan, he had significant quantities of alcohol in his bloodstream."

Sophia nods. She knows, yes.

"So, Sophia . . ." Dr Moran hesitates, "what are your feelings now about those break-ins and other unexplained events?"

Sophia grips the sides of her chair, like she is holding on to a lifeline. Minutes pass and Dr Moran waits patiently.

Sophia forces herself to speak. "It maddens …" She stops to take a breath and feels tears spring to her eyes.

"Take your time, Sophia." Dr Moran hands Sophia a box of tissues, then leans back in her chair as if she has all the time in the world.

"Thanks," Sophia mutters, grabbing a tissue and dabbing at her eyes. Then she leans forward and starts to talk. "Doctor, I still believe – I am *certain* that somebody is trying to cause me harm. Two break-ins! With nothing taken! And then those items disappearing at work – things important to me but of no real value to others."

"The photographs?"

"Yes – of me, of Matt – but, since I last saw you, my address book has gone missing too."

Dr Moran raises an eyebrow, then lowers her gaze and seems to ponder.

Sophia waits, with bated breath.

Dr Moran looks up. "And the Gardai?" she asks abruptly.

"Sympathetic at first, but losing interest."

"And Matt? How is he in all of this?"

Sophia's face brightens at the mention of his name. "Oh, he has been great to me, but I don't think he really understands or believes that – that someone is harbouring a grudge against me, trying to undermine me, maybe harm me."

"And you still have no idea who it could be?"

"It can only be someone at work," Sophia says weakly.

"Did you do that job interview in Sligo?"

"God, did I tell you that, last time? I'd forgotten I'd told you – I was so upset. It still disturbs me deeply – to come home and find someone had broken in and used my bath! I'm afraid to sleep, Doctor, and I'm so exhausted."

"And Sligo?" prompts the doctor.

"Oh, yes, I did the interview and I've been offered the job. Must let them know within the next ten days or it goes to the next person."

"Will you go?"

"I really don't know. It was an impulsive thing, a type of cop-out. Nobody knows about it. But, Dr Moran, I can't continue to live like this. It's hell."

Dr Moran reached for her pad and pen. "OK, Sophia. I'll prescribe some sleeping pills for you, purely to get you over your present difficulties. But – you cannot continue to live under this cloud. Something's got to give."

Sophia sits alone in a coffee shop sipping an espresso coffee. Normally, she would be preoccupied with preparing to brief the management team but, just now, it seems unimportant. She drifts back to thinking of Alan, her dad. Arrogant, insular, self-absorbed, occasionally charming. Now resting in Templeogue graveyard. Tears run unchecked down her pale drawn face. Since her father's accident she just can't stop crying. It was her fault, she reasons . . .

On that dreadful day, her father had come into town to see her and during lunch she told him that she had to take her car to the garage – the brakes weren't working properly. She had moaned about how stressful her job was and how she had no quality time to herself. This was partly true, but it was also her excuse for not visiting her parents as often as she should.

"I'll take the car into the garage for you," he had said. "I'm at a loose end today. I'll have it back by the time you finish work."

She didn't want him to do it but he insisted and she was too tired to argue with him.

A few hours later she got a phone call from the Gardai. Her father had been in an accident. She rushed to the hospital casualty ward, but he was already dead.

"He lost control of the car and hit a wall – he would have died instantly," the female Garda told her. The words, though gently spoken, seemed to vibrate in her head.

"He wouldn't have felt any pain," the doctor said.

Sophia was overcome with grief and guilt. But she was also frantic with fear for herself. Her father's death was further evidence that someone was planning her demise.

Matt came as quickly as he could when she called

him from the hospital. They drove out to Templogue to tell her mother Carmel and sister Christina.

"Alan, my Alan, dead, in your car . . . I don't understand ..." Her mother's voice trailed off in a quiver, her eyes shifting across the pictorial evidence of their union that lined the walls of their sitting-room – a large wedding-day portrait, christenings, first communions, graduations, weddings. It was as if she was carrying out an instant review of their life together.

Sophia nodded, tears spilling down her cheeks. "Yes, Mam . . . it was an accident . . ."

At the funeral service, Father White had whispered words of comfort to her. "You can't blame yourself," he'd said.

Sophia couldn't explain to Father White; he wouldn't understand. He'd just look on her kindly and privately think that she needed some therapy.

She knew her father's death was no accident. He had died in her car when it really should have been her. Who was going to be next? Her beloved Matt? Her sister? Or perhaps her grieving mother?

"God, the time!" Sophia suddenly exclaims. She jumps up and leaves the café.

"The MD is waiting in your office, Sophia," her colleagues, Brian and John, chime in unison as she arrives. They seem to enjoy her discomfort at being late for the Managing Director.

He is sitting at her desk, in her chair, when she enters.

"Sophia, come in, sit down," he says deliberately, making no effort to vacate her chair.

She is aware of his tone – it tells her everything: he is pulling rank.

"Where are the others?" Sophia asks, sitting down opposite him.

"Not coming. I wanted to talk to you alone, give you an opportunity to explain things."

To compensate for his widening girth Donal Brentworth always wears well-tailored suits. The top button of his shirt is opened, telling her that he's under pressure. He probably spent his lunch hour rehearsing his lines for this meeting. He is a very vain man and she has always used this to her advantage. In the old days she would have changed his tone with a bat of her eyelashes but not today.

"Explain things … I don't understand." Her mind starts to back-pedal furiously. She was going to use this meeting as an opportunity to bring some sinister events to his attention; with one sweep, her opportunity to place her concerns centre-stage has been sidelined.

"Sophia, I'll cut to the chase. You have given us several years of good service, but the last twelve months have not been nearly as impressive. You already know that, I've shown you the figures. Now, this week, I get bullying allegations about you from a clerical worker, Genevieve Dalton. Genevieve has gone on sick leave."

Sophia recalls her run-in with Genevieve last week. She caught her rummaging in her office and reacted like a coiled puma, heaping accusation after accusation regarding her missing files and photos. She also went to Genevieve's desk in the open-plan office, emptying all of her drawers in front of shocked colleagues.

She found nothing.

She tunes back into what Donal is saying.

"I'm giving you copies of her complaint, Sophia. Company policy. I would ask that you take the rest of this afternoon and Friday off – paid leave, of course – and come back to me by Monday. This is very serious, and I hope you have a good explanation. Genevieve is the filing clerk here. She has every right to be in your office."

He gets up and leaves immediately.

Sophia sits in a trance-like state, ignoring the calls coming through on her mobile.

"I wish, I wish, my wish come true."

Back in control, that's where I want to be.

Ironic, she thinks, as her life disintegrates around her. Intruders, stalkers, a suspicious death, sleeping pills, bullying allegations.

And four missed calls on the mobile. All from Matt.

Sophia returns dazedly to her apartment. It's five thirty. She is about to open the door when she hears voices inside. Matt is home early.

Who's he talking to? Claire, her best friend.

She slips into the apartment, almost holding her breath.

"Claire, I don't want to press you on this, but you're my last hope. She has had a bad run of luck over the past six months. Her dad's death was particularly difficult for her but her reaction to the other stuff is off the wall. Do you know anything?"

"No, Matt. I've been through thick and thin with Sophia over the years, but I've never seen her like this. It must be hard for you watching it."

Sophia can imagine the sincerity in those ice-blue eyes. She feels like an outcast, standing in her own

10

hallway eavesdropping.

"Sophia might have made herself some ene-
mies," Claire speculates. "I'm sure lots of her work
colleagues are envious of her success, but I doubt
they would go to extremes like stalking her or inter-
fering with her car."

Sophia hears a mug being replaced on the coffee
table. She is honing in, listening for his footsteps,
terrified of him walking out and catching her.

"We've been together for six years, Claire. Six
years! And they've been great until this. I think I'll
go in and see her boss next week, see if he can
enlighten me or help in any way."

"Jeez, Matt, talk to Sophia before you do that. She
won't thank you for it."

Soundlessly, Sophia slips into their bedroom.

When she listens again, she hears Claire coaxing,
"Come on, Matt, let me buy you a drink!"

"I should call Sophia – see what her plans for the
evening are."

Sophia watches through a slit in the bedroom
door. She hears the click of Claire's high heels.

"Why don't you let her call you?" Claire
suggests.

Matt walks into the hall. He's pulling on his
leather jacket. Claire is following him. He turns to

11

look at her. "Thanks for coming round," he says, smiling at her.

Once upon a time he used to look at Sophia with just such warmth and affection.

Having waited in the shadows while Matt and Claire leave the apartment, Sophia walks heavy-footed into their living-room. She sits quietly in the darkness, seething with rage that Matt could cap a dreadful day by talking about her to Claire like this.

Sophia cannot put an exact date on when it all started to go wrong but the past year has been hell. On two occasions their flat was broken into – or, rather, simply entered, as the locks weren't damaged – and the scary thing was nothing had been stolen. On the first occasion, the intruder had a glass of mineral water and looked through their photo albums. Matt was reassuring and appeared unconcerned; nothing had been taken and his treasured stereo system remained intact. They had got their locks changed in case the intruder somehow had got hold of a set of their keys and had them copied. A few weeks later, someone visited again – again without damaging the locks – on this occasion even helping him or herself to a bath. Sophia returned to their apartment after work to find the air perfumed with her

expensive oils. Her scented candles had been lit.
She made her way into the bathroom, hoping that it
was Matt home early. Tentatively she pushed open
the bathroom door. The room was empty, the bath
full of warmish soapy water. She rang Matt on his
mobile and he contacted the Gardai.

Again, nothing was taken. Again, they got their
locks changed though by now they knew that was
futile.

Sophia wanted to sell their apartment and move.
Matt kept his thoughts to himself. He trusted
Sophia but occasionally pondered over her reluc-
tance to share her past with him. He was so open
himself; his love was unconditional and he would
not allow his loved one's reticence about yesteryear
to be a barrier between them. But he could also be
firm; selling the apartment was just not on.

Sophia's fear and panic would not go away, but
she did not push further about selling the apartment. At times she gave way too easily on issues
that might bring up the past.

Matt told her that she was suffering from too
much pressure at work, that she was suffering from
fatigue. Their holiday to Lanzarote was coming up;
this would give her a chance to calm herself.

After two weeks of sunshine they came back to

Dublin, refreshed. She had almost forgotten about the break-ins when things started to happen all over again. Her wallet went missing and then turned up a week later – in her mother's kitchen of all places. Her filofax and address book went missing and she never found them again. Files that she had organized alphabetically at work were all jumbled up and moved from the filing cabinet where she had put them. She kept a photo of her nieces Sarah and Amy on her desk at work and this was also missing. Are my family at risk also, she asked herself, trembling. She felt she was being stalked and she wasn't sure if this was a real person or some ghostly presence. One evening, while walking home from work, she felt certain that a man was following her. She hurried into a newsagent's. He came in, bought a newspaper and then left again. Peering out the newsagent's window she noticed him getting onto a bus. Her feeling of fear intensified when she later noticed the same man being shown around a vacant apartment in the same block as hers.

She tried to ignore these events. She attempted reasoning with herself that she was reading too much into them. No one was following her, no one at work was out to get her.

At times, she wanted to scream but didn't dare. She simply held it in. She imagined the scream ballooning up inside her, making it almost impossible for her to breathe. She couldn't bear to be on her own in the apartment.

She wanted to suspect that it was someone in the office that was jealous of her most recent promotion. This was easier than looking further back. It almost made it acceptable, less scary at least.

Then, she would go over the death of her father while driving her car. Her gut instinct suggested foul play but, with car accidents commonplace, her fears seemed irrational without proof. Another dead end. How could she possibly explain all this to her mother or even Matt? They'd all think she was crazy.

After her father's funeral, Sophia returned quickly to work. At least, in work she could function. Act out her role, pretend that everything was OK.

"I wish, I wish, my wish come true."

Today's events convince Sophia that she needs to escape this hell. Six months, indeed! Matt isn't even aware how long she is suffering. She showers, puts on her black party dress and make-up and awaits his return. They are eating out and she will act out her role tonight. Tomorrow, she will stir herself to action. *Take control back.* Pouring herself a large gin and tonic, then another, Sophia feels a manic sense of conviction that she is going to determine her own destiny from here on.

'Taking back the power, that what's needed,' she smiles to herself.

Chapter 2

"Let go," a voice whispers as Marianne pushes open the glass doors. She stops, unable to move. The pale lined face that is reflected in the glass belongs to her and yet she hardly recognises herself. Normally, Marianne walks around in a daze but these words have such an effect on her that she's eager to see who has spoken them. She looks back. In the hotel foyer two men are standing by the reception desk, waiting to check in. An elderly woman sits on a Queen Anne leather chair, reading the paper – on the table beside her is a cup of coffee. Marianne looks enviously at the woman and thinks, 'That could be me. Her husband is probably gone to play a few rounds of golf and she'll sit here waiting for his return.' A man in a check shirt with rounded

17

shoulders walks purposefully towards the door.

Marianne steps out onto the pavement. It is a crisp bright September morning. A smile flitters across her face and then dies. She replays the words in her head: 'Let go.' It seems they were carried on the breeze from some distant place and deposited here just for her. "Let go," she whispers the words, echoing the hushed voice she has just heard. It sounded like a woman's voice, though she couldn't be sure. But she is sure it wasn't her mind playing tricks on her. She tilts her chin defiantly and pushes strands of silver hair off her face.

'If only I *could* let go,' she thinks.

She feels it must be the Universe warning her to stop what she is doing but she cannot bring herself to do that. She feels the gentle breeze caressing her cheeks and closes her eyes to savour the moment. The smell of the sea is carried towards her and she opens her eyes and looks across at the bay.

"It's a beautiful morning," she hears herself say.

She crosses the road, not caring about the traffic. Someone beeps a horn at her but she walks on indifferently. Once upon a time men whistled and beeped at her when she was young and pretty and had shapely legs. Now men hardly notice her except when, like now, she's an obstruction.

"Watch where you're going!" she hears a man shout.

She smiles mischievously to herself. At least I got his attention, she thinks, and feels a slight tingling running up her spine. It's a long time since she has felt this good and the feeling propels her to walk even faster towards the sea.

She pauses in her stride when she thinks of her late husband Stephen. He loved Westport. Not for the first time, she wishes she could share this thought with someone. She walks on, thinking to herself that there is something magical about the place. Here she can just *be*. Here she can be Marianne. A woman on her own. To her friends she has other labels that are edged with sympathy. "Poor Marianne!" How often has she heard those words and how she has grown to hate them! Here, in this place, she's anonymous. Here she can escape herself. She feels her heart swell with something, some emotion that she cannot quite name. Is this grief or sorrow or anger or a mix of all those feelings?

She starts to walk towards Rosbeg. Two young women are pushing prams and their loud chatter is carried back to her on the wind. "Yes, I told him so," she hears one of them say. She looks up at the conical shape of Croagh Patrick. It looks magnificent in the morning light, the summit shrouded in clouds. Marianne feels she is in a vacuum, the only annoying noise the relentless drone of cars on the road. The women have gained some distance on her; she doesn't mind. This time on her own is perfect. She feels Stephen is by her side, just walking along with her, sharing the moment.

"Oh, Stephen, I wish you were here!" she says aloud, acknowledging her sorrow. Her eyes fill with tears as she turns once again to face Clew Bay. She looks skywards, searching for gannets and gulls but sees nothing. Everything is quiet, the stillness is tangible. It's like the place is holding its breath.

Stephen died last September. For thirty-two years she was known as Mrs Taylor. A lifetime. She nursed him until the very end. She was determined that they would beat the cancer together but Stephen had given up on life. He didn't have it in him to go on. She once heard Dr Phil state as one of his Life Laws that there is power in forgiveness. She wonders if he would say the same thing if he was walking in her shoes. Someday she just might sit down and write to Dr Phil. Let her letter pile up with all the other desperate letters. But not now; the time isn't right.

Life is fragile: she considers this the great law. All too quickly a family can become extinct. That's the lesson she has learned.

Suddenly she feels the full weight of her pain as she walks along. It is solid and almost unbearably heavy. She imagines it is like a metal pellet that has got lodged in her stomach, multiplying in size just like Stephen's cancer. She pauses for breath. Has she the energy to continue walking? She closes her eyes and inhales deeply.

'Today is a gift,' she thinks and her eyes spring open as she wonders where such an absurd thought has come from – certainly she has made no conscious effort to think of anything positive. Why should she feel any gratitude for the fact that this day is heavenly?

Every day is just another emptiness. She's aware of her solitude and loneliness. She feels she's not travelling on the same path as her friends any more. They all have families. Once she had belonged to that 'club'. Now she feels like an outsider. Granted she wasn't ostracized; she chose to isolate herself. The coffee mornings, the shopping trips, the occasional trip to the health spa hold no enjoyment for her any more. The feel-good factor is gone. Slowly, she pulled away from her friends, leaving them as part of her past. Letting them enjoy their simple little pleasures. Some day it might be their turn for a little misfortune.

As she thinks of misfortune, it reminds her of Kathleen, her best friend in Kells. She feels a guilty pang. She left without saying goodbye to her when she moved to Dublin. She considers this the most cowardly thing that she has ever done.

She shakes her head to stop her train of thought.

"You silly woman, stop this nonsense," she mutters to herself. She is unaware that she has developed a habit of talking to herself.

She is just an ordinary woman, aware that she has no great wealth or talent to distinguish her from any other woman. The one thing that had distinguished her and which gave her life meaning was her family. Her husband Stephen and son Liam. Her life revolved around them. A lump of emotion grows in her throat and she has to swallow past it. They were a strong, solid family, the Taylors. She is now the only survivor.

She imagines that her son and husband aren't dead but spirits hovering around her, taking care of her. She believes that they approve of what she is doing. It is this knowledge that gives her the will to go on. Nothing is impossible; this is what she has discovered. She has set herself a task and she feels it is within her capabilities to accomplish it.

It is when her stomach starts to rumble that she realises that she hasn't eaten any breakfast. She turns her back to the sea and walks back towards the hotel.

"Good morning, Mrs Taylor," the receptionist says as Marianne walks past.

Marianne is surprised that she has noticed her. This morning she has been feeling quite invisible. "Oh," she says and smiles apologetically at the pleasant-faced girl. "Good morning."

After taking the elevator to the fourth floor, she goes into the dining-room. She fills a glass with orange juice and selects a table facing the sea. She notices it is starting to rain. Her companions in the dining-room are mostly older people like herself. She guesses that the men sitting together are all golfers: they have that outdoor look to them. A blonde woman is sitting on her own, her back to the other diners.

'At least I'm not the only one dining on my own,' Marianne thinks to herself. This is a good omen. Just then a man pulls out a chair and sits down beside the blonde woman. 'Ah, well,' she thinks with some resignation, 'that's the way the cookie crumbles.' She can't help noticing his plate piled high with rashers, sausages and at least two fried eggs along with a small mound of mushrooms. She finds herself staring at the couple. They look to be in their fifties or early sixties.

After the death of her son Liam, Marianne took to watching the TV with the volume turned down. She isn't an expert at lip-reading but she can figure out most of the time what people are saying. And so, from a little distance, she can tune into their conversation. She moves her chair so that it is at the perfect angle to observe them. It is a wonderful pastime. One can well and truly become the fly on the wall.

"You should have the fry," says the blonde woman's partner.

"Oh, I couldn't face it," she replies and waves her hand dismissively.

"We're not eating until this evening," he says. He starts to eat with unrestricted gusto.

"You should have seen the rainbow," the woman is saying, a cup of tea held up to her mouth.

He grunts and continues to eat. "You should eat," he says as he munches away.

"I told you I'm not hungry. I'll have soup later for lunch."

"Eat now," he persists.

Marianne notices that he's got egg yolk on the corner of his mouth.

"Value for money," he says as he shovels a full sausage into his mouth. Marianne sips her orange juice and is thankful that he isn't her companion.

"Tea or coffee?" a foreign-looking waiter asks, interrupting her thoughts.

He startles her. Marianne takes a few shallow breaths and smiles at the young waiter.

"Tea, please."

"Full Irish Breakfast," the waiter is saying as he indicates the self-service area. He smiles at Marianne and she believes that it is a real smile, a genuine smile from his heart. As if he knows that she is a lost soul, like he possibly is in this country.

"Thank you," Marianne replies.

"Would you like me to get it for you?"

Marianne looks at his rounded childish face and she thinks his eyes don't belong in that face. His eyes are too weary-looking. She wonders what pain and hardship have taken him here to this cold climate. "That won't be necessary." She can't help but stare at him. She knows it's rude and possibly hurtful. But he is a young man. He is a son and she is a mother though they are strangers to each other. She marvels at the delicate colour of his olive skin. She wonders what it would be like to touch him, to caress his face, to hold him for one quick hug before he made his escape. She is thinking of her son Liam now; the thought stabs her with its bare-bladed realness. The waiter looks Asian; she is tempted to ask him where he is from.

She gets up and makes her way towards the self-service. A man stands with his newspaper open. He is reading the sports page, oblivious to the fact that he is in her way. She has to walk around him. Once again she has donned her invisible cloak and it thrills her. She decides not to have the fry, choosing the healthy option of cereal. As she makes her way back to her table she cannot help but hear the man telling his blonde wife to relax.

"Chill," he commands, pausing to munch loudly on a crispy piece of bacon. "You're on holiday."

"Stop bossing me," she replies.

Marianne fixes her chair so she can observe the couple again. It looks like he has no neck. His head just sits on his shoulders.

Biting her bottom lip, she looks out the window. A rainbow arches across the sky. Her eyes fill up with tears and it makes the rainbow shimmer and look even more amazing. The young Asian waiter returns with her pot of tea.

"Thank you," Marianne says and avoids looking up at him.

She butters her toast and fills her cup with tea. You can cry later, she says to herself. The dining-room starts to fill up with more people, mostly couples. The women haven't put in much of an effort with their appearance. Why ever not, she wonders.

The man stops a waitress passing by his table. "Do you serve soup for breakfast?" he bellows and then laughs, his whole body shaking.

"Sorry, did you say soup?"

The blonde woman hits her companion's arm affectionately. "Stop it!"

He chuckles to himself.

"Don't mind him," she says to the waitress.

To Marianne with warmest wishes . . .

Paul Durcan signs his name and dates a copy of his book.

"You read beautifully," Marianne says.

"Thank you," he replies as he hands her back her book.

The day is over and Marianne is glad.

After breakfast she had intended retreating to her bedroom; there she would stare out at Clew Bay while she cried.

But she had surprised herself today. Things had turned out different than what she had planned. Sure, she had cried and sure she had spent a lot of time just staring out at the sea – but the day had been eventful. First she had a massage, then she retreated to her bedroom and slept a deep comforting sleep. She dreamt about making daisy chains like she did when she was a little girl. After dinner where she tried Clew Bay mussels for the first time, she attended a poetry reading by Paul Durcan. She sat with her eyes closed, imagining that Stephen was by her side. She listened to the soothing timbre of the poet's voice as he read from his work.

"Wasn't he wonderful?" a woman says as they line up to get their books signed.

"Yes," she replies, a little taken aback that someone wants to talk to her, that someone has noticed her, that she's no longer invisible.

Chapter 3

Slowly and very reluctantly Sophia becomes aware that it's morning. Beyond the comfortable haven of her bed, she can hear the sluggish sound of early morning Dublin traffic. Matt has already gone to work and she misses his comforting presence beside her. As she thinks about Matt, a tiny smile flickers across her parched lips and then dies. She surrenders to the heavy thud of a headache because she knows there is no point fighting it. She moves to Matt's side of the bed. Every muscle, every sinew, every cell in her body is fermenting from the after-effects of too much alcohol. She regrets drinking so much last night. She is tempted to open her eyes but she stops herself. Against her closed eyelids, she can feel the glaring morning light stream in through the curtains, summoning her to get up. She is determined to ignore it. She would much rather stay in her suspended hazy state.

In her mind's eye she can see herself rushing around their apartment. Her routine is etched on her brain. About this time, she should be having her first cup of black coffee while applying her make-up. In the living-room her briefcase and mobile are on the coffee table ready for take-off.

With her eyes still closed, Sophia hears a single piano note. She realises it's in her head. Then another. It's a memory from another time and place that she has allowed to surface. She can picture a woman with long graceful fingers playing the piano. The notes come together easily. Unfolding effortlessly. Locked in her memory, she's aware that she knows this particular piece, the haunting sound. Only the title of the music eludes her. The notes play on. Gently they invite her to take a trip back in time to her home in Templeogue. Sophia imagines the piano player to be her sister Christina. She is sitting at their piano. Sophia can picture the late evening sun filtering in through the living-room window. She can see tiny particles of dust dancing in the shafts of golden light. She has discovered from her science class that dust is made up of dead body cells. Every seven years we shed our old selves. Isn't the world an amazing place? In the kitchen her mother is cooking dinner and their father *might* be home later. Though he had a family, he didn't exactly show that he relished spending time with them. He had other interests like work, golf and the pub to occupy his time.

Sophia hears the notes rise again in her head. Expertly, Christina plays each note with just the right amount of feeling to make the notes soar into something more. Sophia is amazed at how clear it sounds. She has allowed herself to remember and now she hates herself for being so stupid, for being so weak. She quickly represses the tears that well in her eyes. She turns in the bed as she wrestles to smother another unpleasant thought that has surfaced from some dark recess in her mind.

She gets out of bed. She slowly looks around their bedroom, her eyes trailing over each object to see if anything has been moved or taken. Everything seems in order. She looks down at her black party dress that lies crumpled and discarded on the floor. A remnant of a smile comes to her face as she picks up the dress, going back over the wonderful night they had spent together. "Matt," she whispers. She hugs the dress close to her.

She rings Donal Brentworth, and is put through immediately.

"Mr Brentworth, Sophia Jordan here. I have been thinking about our talk yesterday and have decided to offer my resignation." She is surprised at the firmness in her voice.

"You've read the allegations – you're not even going to defend them?"

"You probably won't believe it, but I haven't read them. I did a job interview in Sligo recently and mentioned you as a reference. If they contact you, will you send it on to them?"

"Of course. Recent events will not be mentioned. We will not need you to work out your notice. Company policy, as you well know. Thanks and best wishes in the future, Sophia. Oh, will you put your notice in writing?"

"Yes –"

He hangs up.

"That's it with the soulless multinationals! Rising star one day, forgotten lady the next," she rants furiously to herself.

Her second call is to confirm her acceptance of the college's offer. Shortly she will be Sophia Jordan, part-time lecturer.

She glances at her digital clock and sees that she

has a lot of packing to do. She takes down her largest suitcase and throws it on the bed. She flings open her wardrobe doors and looks inside. Quickly she dumps clothes into the case, not giving any consideration to what she is taking with her and what she is going to leave behind.

Sophia met Matt at her sister's wedding. Christina's husband-to-be Tony introduced them. Sophia stops packing as she tots up the number of years Christina and Tony are married. She and Matt have known each other for six years. Imagine: six years.

"I'm glad you're not the bride," Matt had said.

At the time of Christina's wedding, Sophia wasn't seeing anyone. Matt wasn't the type that she was normally attracted to. She liked taller men with dark complexions. Matt was shorter with light brown curly hair. He didn't make her heart race but she noticed the way he carried himself, how comfortable he seemed in his own skin. When he spoke to her, he made eye contact and was not looking over her shoulder to see was there someone more attractive he could be talking to. She was the centre of his attention, his universe. She noticed he had really nice blue-grey eyes.

Matt is different. Not just testosterone on legs. He

is considerate and charming, which are more favourable characteristics, when she ponders some of the predators and opportunists who have hurt her in the past. Now, events are tearing her away from her soul mate, her gift from God.

Her luggage packed, Sophia continues to ponder the dreaded return of Matt to the apartment later in the evening. Last night while they were having dinner, he had asked her again to marry him. Such timing! 'I shouldn't be encouraging him,' she thought, but drinking too much wine had weakened her resolve. She hates herself for being so weak. Why couldn't she have been honest with him and told him there and then that she was leaving him? But how do you announce this quite suddenly, and after six years? She cringes again at her cowardice and deception. She had led him to believe that they had a future together while, all along, she was planning her great escape. Matt, on the other hand, was making his own plans. He suggested that they might buy a house in the Templeogue area. That way, she'd be beside her mother and sister.

"We're going to have children," he said with a twinkle in his eyes.

She wanted to tell him to stop but she couldn't; she loved hearing it. This was the life she was supposed to lead, this was the life she really wanted to lead but an invisible force was stopping her.

Now she knows how ridiculous those plans really are. They belong to someone else, not to her. She knows she has to leave Dublin, make a clean break and start fresh somewhere new.

Sophia closes her eyes and takes a few short shallow breaths as she tries to stop herself from shaking. The silence of the apartment is unbearable; she feels the living-room is closing in on her.

"Please, leave me and my family alone," she whispers, almost inaudibly.

She glances at her watch. "God, look at the time!" she says, remembering that there are other people to be told.

Sophia stops first at Eason's in O'Connell Street to pick up a copy of the *Sligo Champion*. Getting accommodation in Sligo is on her "to do" list. She walks up Grafton Street, noticing the shops full of trendy autumn wear. She is aware of what she is doing but shuts down on the implications. She is going through the motions. She catches a glimpse of her reflection as she walks past a shop window. Her clothes are last season's but she doesn't care any more. Now she is dancing to a different tune.

She walks down the few steps to the basement restaurant on Stephen's Green and takes off the sunglasses that shielded her eyes from the bright autumn sunlight. Christina has been curious about this particular restaurant for some time. Sophia had let her make the choice; it only seemed right with the news Sophia is bringing.

"Sophia!" Christina says, arriving just at the same time.

Christina is thirty-four, Sophia four years younger. Christina has her mousy-brown hair high-lighted. She looks different wearing make-up and high heels. Normally Sophia sees her in jeans and runners with her shoulder-length hair scooped up off her face.

"Good timing," Sophia says, giving her sister a quick hug.

Christina clutches her sister's arm. "Don't look now," she says in a conspiratorial whisper, "but there is a man over there that can't take his eyes off you."

Sophia finds herself stiffen. "Oh, God," she whispers. Simultaneous feelings of fear and affirmation run through her. At last someone else has noticed what she has suspected for months.

Christina sees the panic in her sister's face.

"What's the matter?" she asks.

"Nothing," she replies.

"Men are always ogling you," Christina says in a resigned voice. "It's something I have learned to live with."

"Where is he?" Sophia asks when they have sat down.

"At the bar."

Sophia glances quickly at the bar. "Which one?"

"Blue shirt."

"There are at least three men at the bar with blue shirts." Her voice is tinged with impatience.

"They are all admiring my beautiful sister!" Before Christina opens her menu she says across the table, "I was lucky to get Tony before you saw him." She laughs. "I feel like a new woman. I got my hair done this morning and I got all dressed up to come into town to have lunch with you. This is the life. I could get very used to all this pampering." She looks closely at Sophia. "You look tired. I hope you're not working too hard."

Sophia says nothing and picks up the menu to read from it. Her stomach is gurgling, but she figures it's more nerves than hunger.

"Mammy is picking Sarah up from school, so I have the afternoon to myself."

"That's nice," Sophia says and she wishes she wasn't the bearer of such bad news.

"I can't make up my mind. It's so long since I've eaten out."

Sophia knows Christina isn't complaining. She is all too aware that she is happy to teach music part-time and to take care of her two girls.

"There's a house for sale just two doors up from me," Christina says.

The words are said lightly and they hold no meaning for Sophia. She is past caring about a mortgage and getting married to Matt and having children. This is something she can no longer visualize. She is envious of Christina's obvious contentment with her domestic lot but Sophia is on a survival mission.

This is going to be much harder than Sophia had imagined. She regrets not having hinted at a possibility that she might be splitting up with Matt and leaving Dublin. It occurs to her as she gazes at the menu that Christina and her mother are anxiously awaiting some developments between herself and Matt. Now that their father is dead, they are looking to her to bring some joy back into their lives again. A lump grows in her throat. She feels like she is suffocating, desperately gasping for each breath.

Her insides quiver and shake and she feels like she isn't a body, contained and solid any more. At any moment now she will crumble, yet her sister appears not to notice. So, she carries on, determined to get this over and done with.

"I'm going to have the onion soup," she announces and closes her menu. She has become accustomed to looking around her; she can never truly relax.

Christina makes a face. "What has happened to your appetite?"

"I've lost it," Sophia replies and turns her attention to her sister.

Christian looks at her seriously. "Sophia, I'm worried about you. Is there anything wrong?"

"I keep thinking about Daddy, I should never have told him that I was taking my car to the garage." She laughs nervously. "I only said it to make conversation."

"Please, Sophia . . . we've been over this so many times." Christina's pained expression makes Sophia feel guilty.

"Sorry," she mumbles.

"You haven't been yourself in a long time, Sophia. Mammy is really worried about you. So much has happened to you – Daddy's car-crash, the break-ins – maybe you need to make some changes, maybe the stress of your job is getting to you."

Sophia shudders as she remembers the fear that gripped her when she entered the apartment to discover that someone had been there. The smell of scented candles and expensive bath oil. She shakes her head vigorously to block out the memories. Soon this nightmare will be over.

She squares her shoulders and looks boldly across the table at her sister. Her mouth feels dry but she manages to get the words out. "Christina, I've got myself another job."

Christina speaks at the same time, announcing, "I'm going to have the fillet of cod." Then she turns her full attention on her sister.

"It's in Sligo, lecturing in the college there."

Christina laughs nervously, her mouth forming the shape of an O. Then she asks, "Why?"

"Christina," Sophia reaches out her hand to touch it, "you've got to help me out here. I have to tell Mammy." She pauses, takes a breath and then says, "And I have still to tell Matt."

"Sophia," Christina says, her eyes filling up with tears, "what is going on?"

Chapter 4

"Damn it," Jim mutters, as he surveys the sirloin steaks in his fridge, now long past their sell-by date. "Another consignment for the waste-removal man. Jim, your self-catering modern-man plan is not working." He pulls a face. "Burger and chips again, then," he says resignedly, grabbing his battered leather jacket.

The shrill ringing of the telephone interrupts his march to the door.

"Yes," he says sharply. "Who is it?"

"Marianne," says a soft voice. "You must have had a bad day."

"I'm still having a bad day, and I was hoping to bring it to a close. What can I do for you?"

"Can you come over, Jim? I need to go over some

things with you," says Marianne, unfazed by his abrupt manner.

"Marianne, we agreed to meet tomorrow, I've finished for today. I'm just off to get something to eat –"

"Jim, I'm just beginning to cook something over here. I'll double up on the portions. That way you get fed, and you have one less client tomorrow."

"Oh, all right, if you put it that way. Beats spending the night awake, wondering what you'll want done next. See you in half an hour."

Marianne replaces the receiver and looks again at the business card she is holding: *Jim Crerand, Private Investigator.*

Marianne is back in her rented home in Dublin. It is a small, functional place, without frills. Its greatest attribute is that it gives her anonymity. She sees it as a temporary refuge and has negotiated renewable six-month leases with the owner.

She melts butter in the pan, adding garlic and onion. Then she adds both the fresh and smoked salmon. It has been quite a while since she has cooked a meal. She tests the fresh pasta and decides that it is cooked. *Al dente*, the sophisticates would say. Soft, but not sodden.

The doorbell rings, giving her a sudden start.

"Calm yourself, Marianne," she reproaches herself, softly. "Nobody knows you are here, other than Jim." Carefully, she turns the salmon on the pan and then turns down the heat. The doorbell rings again as she takes off her apron and slowly walks to the front door.

She can hear the voices of children still playing outside. The evening sun is shining like liquid gold, brightening up the neighbourhood.

Jim is at the door, wearing his trademark leather jacket and jeans. "For a moment there I thought you'd changed your mind," he says as he walks into the hall and hands her the bottle of wine. "I was going to bring a few cans of beer, but I thought better of it."

"Come through." She leads the way into her kitchen.

"Something smells good," he says and looks at the salmon on the pan.

"It's ages since I've cooked. We can talk while we eat."

"Great," Jim says and sits down at the kitchen table.

"What can I do to help?"

"Open the wine," Marianne says. "I hope you like salmon."

43

"Sure," he replies without much conviction. He is a tall well-toned man in his early forties.

"Good," Marianne says as she cuts slices of brown bread. "The recipe for this said to toast bread but I like brown bread with salmon."

"You're the boss," Jim says and gives her a bright smile.

Marianne tosses the cooked pasta in a creamy sauce with diced peppers. She then cuts the salmon into bite-sized pieces and mixes it in as a one-pot dish.

She catches Jim watching her with a bemused look. "What, you don't like it?"

"God no, it's not that. Less than an hour ago, I was en route to MacDonald's. My doctor would probably recommend your cooking any day above my usual diet. 'Planning for ulcers', that's what he calls it."

"Anyway," said Marianne, "here we are – salmon linguine with side salad and brown bread."

"Glasses," Jim says looking around the pristine kitchen.

"Over there." She points to a cupboard with glass doors.

"Right." He reaches for the glasses. "Have you lived here long?"

Marianne pauses to look at him. His dark eyes are direct and quite unnerving. She is aware that he already knows the answer. "Not long." She turns away again. "We're eating in the dining-room," she says with her back to him.

"Right, well, I'll bring the glasses and bottle in."

When they are seated, Jim pours wine into both their glasses. "I hope you like white," he says.

Marianne smiles to herself. He didn't bother to enquire what kind of wine to bring. She didn't bother to enquire if he liked salmon. It certainly was a please-yourself arrangement.

Marianne is fifty-two years old and there are some things she has never adapted to, like using metric. Nor can she adapt to trying out a new recipe without the customary compliments from Stephen and Liam. And now, she waits with bated breath for Jim to taste her food. She wonders if she has been too liberal with the lemon juice on the salmon.

Jim bites into it and chews it slowly. "Good," he says and nods his head.

Marianne tastes it and feels there is too much dill in it.

"So," Jim says as he clears his throat, "it's down to business."

Marianne looks across her dining-table at him.

"Don't you think there is just a little too much dill in it?"

"Dill?"

"It's a herb," she explains.

Jim smiles pleasantly. "I know it's a herb but I can't say if there is too much or not enough. It's good. I'm no expert when it comes to food."

"We used to eat out all the time. Stephen loved to read restaurant reviews."

"I see," Jim says with a voice that is bordering on boredom.

They eat for a while in silence.

"Would you like some more?" she asks when she notices he has cleared his plate.

Jim shakes his solid head. "No thanks." He pauses briefly and then continues, "It's not that I don't like it or anything it's just that I've had plenty already."

"Caught up in your work?" she enquires levelly.

"You could say that. Another unpleasant case that I am investigating, it's..." he lifts his large shoulders, "it's bad."

"I see," Marianne says, hoping he'll divulge some information but he doesn't develop it. She finds this reassuring in spite of her curiosity. He finishes his glass of wine. Marianne goes to pour him another.

"No, thanks," says Jim in a voice that brooks no argument. "Marianne, I'm not usually in the business of dining with clients. This work I'm doing for you seems aimless to me. I take photos of people that are connected to your past, keep you advised of their movements – you pay me. I can't get to the nub of what you're trying to do. There's usually an end product at the end of my client's dealings; it may be a divorce, fraud discovery, tracking down a debt defaulter ..."

Marianne fills her own glass and leans back in her chair. It's a while since she has drunk a glass of wine and she feels quite tipsy. Jim shuffles uncomfortably in his chair.

"This is my first time using this room. I've never had an occasion to before," she says.

"Personally I don't see the point in dining-rooms." Jim scans the room quickly like a thief doing a mental inventory of which pieces he will come back for.

She looks at him and tries to imagine him as a young boy and she can't. She guesses that he had an adult face even as a child

"Liam liked to eat in front of the TV." The words are laced with nostalgia.

Jim shifts in his chair.

"Do you find it uncomfortable – me talking about my dead son?" Marianne enquires.

He looks down at his empty plate and for a moment he seems lost in his own thoughts.

Marianne feels tears sting her eyes and she wants to lash out at him. "You men are all the same!"

Jim raises his head and meets her gaze. "I find it hard to understand why you're locked in this crazy world. There's no start, middle or end to this exercise. If you could tell me what you're getting out of it – it's aimless, futile."

Marianne snorts.

"I mean," he goes on to say, "you're not living."

"I need this done."

Jim opens his large hands in a gesture of defeat. "I know it's what you want to do and you're paying me handsomely to get some information for you; but you could do better things with your money."

Marianne sips some wine and then replaces the glass on the table, a sad smile almost parting her lips.

"You could get out there and start to live your life again," Jim breaks the silence to say. "You're a very intelligent, attractive woman. You are doing yourself no good doing this."

"Are you trying to suggest that I should get myself another man?"

Jim's lifts his broad shoulders and lets them fall again. "I don't know what I am saying. I just think you could do better things." He pauses and looks at a spot just above her head. "I just think life is too short and…" he waves a hand. "I'm tired," he yawns. He finishes his glass of water.

"Would you like a coffee?"

"Thanks. I could do with one."

Marianne gets up. "Would you care for some dessert?"

"No, thanks, just coffee," he says and picks up their dirty dishes to bring them into the kitchen.

"OK," says Jim. "Could we review where we're at right now? Out of the blue, you contact me regarding two people whose lives have overlapped yours at some point. Sophia Jordan, career woman, and Gavin Daly, general waster, whose latest venture is managing a gym. I spy on them, take photos and give them to you. Now I have more of them, so who first?"

"Gavin Daly," Marianne replies, stifling an angry retort to Jim's demeaning summary of her dalliance with these people's lives. Gavin and her son Liam

49

had gone to London together. He came over to Liam's funeral and had joined the mourners at Marianne's and Stephen's home. At the time his resume of Liam's last days was oddly comforting.

She looks fixatedly at the photos Jim puts before her and runs her fingers across Gavin's face. Her eyes moisten as the memories come flooding back: two little boys climbing trees at their leafy Kells home, Liam coming running into the house. "Mammy, Mammy, come quick, Gavin's cut his knee!"

Jim stands over her shoulder as she flicks through the photographs, his commentary alternately fading and resonating in unison with Marianne's flirtations between nostalgia and cold here and now: "Gavin, the public persona, married man with two children. Has a nice semi-detached in a good area in the city, drives a new car. Runs a gym in the inner city, and is under police surveillance. They suspect him of money laundering, but he covers his tracks well. Got a minor slap on the wrist when caught with unlicensed bodybuilding drugs at the gym. Frequently seen in the company of a northside gang who specialize in protection rackets and recruitment of doormen and security for the city's night spots. Those in the know predict that he will eventually fall foul of these same people. Some disapprove of the way he flaunts himself and would prefer him to be low profile."

Marianne pauses at some photos of a blonde girl. "Where does she fit in?"

"Mistress, not yet eighteen years old, smitten with Gavin, poor young fool." Jim returns the photos of Gavin to their wallet and hands them over to Marianne. "Any sign of that cup of coffee you promised me?"

"Oh, sorry, I almost forgot."

As Jim sips contentedly from a freshly brewed cup of coffee, he passes a second batch of photos to Marianne. "Here we go now," he says and pauses to observe her reactions.

Marianne picks up one of Sophia and looks at her face dispassionately. She feels her hate like bile rise from her stomach and leave a bad taste in her mouth. She hears Jim's voice in the background.

"All of this is about her, isn't it? Gavin is just a sideshow."

A photograph shows her leaving a building, wearing a well-tailored dark suit. "I wonder why she bothered doing something like science when she could have done modelling?" she suddenly says.

"Maybe modeling never appealed to her," Jim says and glances at his wristwatch.

It doesn't go unnoticed by Marianne. "Is my time up?"

Jim gives her an apologetic smile. "Sorry."

Marianne looks at the photographs again.

"She's very photogenic," Jim remarks when a silence starts to grow.

Marianne looks at another photograph. Sophia is walking hand in hand with her boyfriend Matt. "She is," she replies. "I'll go get you your money,"

She excuses herself and leaves the room. Jim leans back in his chair and looks around at the bland decor. The pale furniture would look better in a showroom window than in a room occupied by humans. A large abstract painting dominates one wall. Jim looks at the riot of colours thrown onto it. He doesn't hear Marianne coming back.

"You don't like the painting?" she asks with amusement, passing him an envelope.

Jim lifts his large shoulders up and lets them fall again.

It seems to Marianne that he carries a very large weight on those shoulders.

"No," he confesses honestly and this really takes him by surprise. He is not in the habit of revealing anything about himself to his clients.

"Are you not married?" she asks, as he isn't wearing a wedding ring.

Jim studies her for a moment, then gulps down the rest of his coffee. "Why do you ask?"

"No reason, just curious."

"You're not looking for a husband then?"

Marianne laughs. "Good gracious," she exclaims and finds herself blushing.

Jim smiles, pleased at her reaction. "I get asked all the time in my line of work," he says jokingly.

"I'm sure you do, but you can relax. I'm not husband-hunting."

After Jim has left, Marianne retreats to her sitting-room. The blinds are closed and the room looks gloomy in the muted light. Next door she can hear a door slam and loud voices. She closes her eyes, resting her head back in her armchair. Seeing those photographs of Sophia and Gavin raises simultaneous feeling of anger and sadness in her. They are alive. Her darling son's life had only begun when he was robbed of it.

She tries to picture her young son at the age of four. She's building a picture. Next door the TV is blaring. She smiles to herself, her eyes moist with nostalgic tears. He loved to dismantle things like old radios; he was fascinated to see how things worked. He was always sure he could put these things back together but this never happened. He was such a happy child, so easygoing. "Happy-go-lucky," was how her friend, Kathleen, described him. They were always trying to mould him, to shape him into the person they wanted him to be. The memory is too painful; she squeezes her eyes closed and invents a happier memory of Liam playing Snakes and Ladders with her.

Another memory comes unbidden to her. She always dreaded Saturday nights. Liam hated having a bath and Stephen was usually home and he took no nonsense. She can see a young Liam in the bathtub bawling his eyes out.

"I hate baths!" she can hear him scream.

She can hear Stephen shouting up at them, "You have that child spoiled!"

If someone had pulled back a curtain and said to her, "Look, Marianne, this is your future," and she saw herself alone on a Saturday night with no one, would she have done it all differently?

Sometimes memories come unbidden and rather than smother them she allows them to unfold. Right now she can picture a young Liam lying in the grass staring up at the clouds. She is lying beside him.

"Look, look, there's a bear!" he says.

"Yes, Liam, there's a bear sailing by," she whispers.

A wedge of evening sun beams in through a slit in the curtains. Momentarily it seems to brighten the room and then it suddenly fades.

"Oh, Liam," she cries, "my baby!"

Chapter 5

Matt has just phoned. "I'm on my way home," he says.

In the background Sophia can hear noise; she presumes he is leaving the pub. They always go for a drink on a Friday night. "Home," she mutters to herself. The word seems to echo. In her head she tries to hear the single piano note, but fails. Of course she forgot to ask her sister what the piece was.

She remembers how Christina had glared at her when she was unable to give a satisfactory answer as to why she was leaving Matt and going away. She had tried to explain in vague terms that she couldn't go on like this any more. That she had to get away.

"Get away from what?" Christina had asked, horrified.

"From everything. I just feel everything is getting to me."

"Then you should go and see a doctor. Running away is not the answer," she said sharply.

Christina had ordered coffee and fruit salad. She hardly touched them. She just clutched her napkin tightly as if it was a lifeline.

"I'm really sorry about all this," said Sophia.

"Sophia, Sligo is not the answer. You need help. Poor Mammy, she's going to be devastated! First Daddy and now you're going."

Sophia had nodded in agreement as she looked at her older sister with pleading eyes. "Will you tell Mammy for me?"

Christina smiled through her tears. "Of course I will – but Mammy is going to take this really bad." She paused and sat up straighter in her chair. "I thought that you and Matt would be getting engaged and all that ..." the words trailed off.

"I know, but I have got to leave Dublin. I just can't live here any more."

Christina shook her head solemnly. "You have everything and you are throwing it all away."

Sophia hears Matt's key in the door. She is sitting

erect and uncomfortably on the sofa. Normally, her legs would be curled under her, and a glass of wine would be at hand.

"Hi," he says. He is carrying a shopping bag. He plants a kiss on her forehead as he makes his way to the kitchen. "I'll cook tonight!" he calls.

"That's nice," she hears herself reply.

Her legs are shaking as she slowly gets up and walks into the kitchen. He has brought some pre-prepared vegetables from Marks & Spencer. He walks to the fridge and puts in a carton of orange juice. "We should go out more often," he says and turns to look at her. He grins, his dark eyes glinting with pride, "And you should wear that dress more often."

Sophia looks at a spot on the ground. She never really noticed the design on the tiles before. Now she is examining them as if they were the most complex things in the world.

"You look tired," he remarks and comes to give her a proper kiss. "How was your day?"

She can smell beer on his breath. "Fine," she says, unable to meet his eyes directly. Get it over with, tell him, she commands in her mind. Inside, she feels a little bit of her die. Part of her wants to leg it out of the place and let him discover the facts for himself.

She cannot bear to do what she has to do.

Matt is taking out the wok. He is going to make stir-fried vegetables, one of their favourite evening meals.

"Matt . . . before you start . . ." She forces herself to complete the sentence. "I need to talk to you."

"What do you want to talk about?" Matt asks lightly as he takes a can of beer from the fridge.

"About us," she replies gravely.

Matt knows by the tone that it is serious. He sits down on the sofa and she sits in front of him on the coffee table.

"I'm listening," he says as he opens his can of beer.

"Matt . . . I can't go on like this."

Matt eyes her cautiously. "Go on," he says and raises a questioning eyebrow.

"I have to leave," she says and finds the words that she has rehearsed are suddenly forgotten. She sees his pale anguished face. He is looking at her incredulously.

He attempts to say something but words fail him and he shakes his head in disbelief. "Leave?" he repeats.

"I'm leaving Dublin. I've got a job. Lecturing. Part-time. In Sligo."

"Jesus," he says and he is on his feet, pacing the floor over and back. "I don't understand," his voice is barely audible, "you never said anything about doing an interview for a job in Sligo."

"I'm so sorry," she hears herself say.

Matt looks at her, his eyes filled with tears. "There is someone else," he says. She sees him makes fists out of his hands. He falls down on the sofa, looking at her in horror. "You've met someone else," he repeats, this time accusingly.

She shakes her head furiously and then says, "No."

He is on his feet again, he paces and then stops, turns and comes to stand beside her, bends down and looks into her face. "Tell me, what's really going on here?"

Sophia squeezes back the tears. "I just can't," she replies.

"Explain it. No matter how weird it sounds, you've got to tell me what's going on."

Sophia straightens. "I don't think my father's death was an accident. I think it was deliberate and I was the intended victim. And I think the break-ins and the missing objects are somehow related to that." There she had said it all, put the thoughts into words.

His reaction is predictable: disbelief. She can see it in his face.

For a few moments the silence in the apartment is almost tangible, then the noise of traffic comes crashing back.

"Sophia," Matt says gently, "you cannot blame yourself for your father's death." He pauses and then, with great care, he continues, "It *was* an accident."

Sophia is unable to speak. It's like she is having an out-of-body experience. From some distant point she looking in at herself, lost to his persuasions, lost to the man that, until now, was her soul mate, the bedrock of her life.

He sits again and takes her two hands in his. He is still talking, slowly, softly. He takes great care as he selects each word, hoping for maximum effect.

"Look, I know there have been some strange events, but these things can't split us up – we can work it out together. We're stronger than all of these things. Please, Sophia …"

"No, Matt, please let me go. Don't make it so hard."

"Sophia . . . do you love me?"

She stares at the floor and doesn't answer.

Then he says, "Sophia darling, if you could look

me in the eye and say you no longer love me, I wouldn't fight you on this. But you can't do that. What you are doing is all for the wrong reasons. If there is a problem, it will follow you to Sligo."

She already knows he secretly feels she is overreacting. "Her reaction to the other stuff is off the wall," he had said to Claire.

Sophia squeezes his hands. "Please, Matt, let me go. Don't make this harder than it has to be."

"OK," he says and moves away from her. "Look, I'm sorry that I laughed when you thought someone in your office was out to get you. It was thoughtless of me. Maybe someone is. Maybe ..."

"Please Matt, I'm begging you, just let me go."

Sophia stands up. Her leather jacket is in the hall. Beside it is her bag with her mobile phone and her car keys. She sees herself walking towards the door.

"Sophia!"

She finds herself moving faster as she makes for the door.

Matt is beside her now, pulling her back, taking her into his arms.

"Stay tonight," she hears him sob into her ear.

"Please, Matt," she mutters but she knows he can't hear her because he is sobbing so hard.

Chapter 6

Marianne looks at the selection of bakery goods on offer. She stares, mesmerised by the selection. She came in with the intention of getting a scone and yet she fancies something different, but what?

"Marianne!"

She turns to see Carmel walking towards her. "Trying to decide what to have?"

Marianne is a little taken aback. She hadn't expected to see Carmel here this morning. Didn't she do art classes or something on Mondays?

"I was going to have a scone and then I thought I'd break out and have something different." Marianne pauses for a moment, weighing up the problem in her mind. "I just don't know what to have."

Carmel nods sympathetically. "I know the feeling."

"If you have time, we could go for a coffee?" Marianne says, surprising herself. She hadn't planned for this to happen, but, sometimes, opportunities arise and one has to go with them.

Carmel looks at her watch and frowns, then waves a dismissive hand. "Yes, I'd love a coffee," she says and turns to head towards the exit.

Just outside the supermarket is a café. Marianne follows Carmel inside and they order coffee and scones.

Carmel seems troubled. Immediately, she starts to talk.

"I'm so upset," she says and her bottom lips trembles slightly. "It's my daughter Sophia."

"What's the matter?" Marianne asks.

"She's moved to Sligo, totally out of the blue ..." The words fade and then she starts up again. "Oh, so much has happened! First my husband is killed in a car accident and now my daughter has left Dublin, gone to work in Sligo. I know it's selfish of me, but I had expected her to stay around, be here for me."

"I'm sorry to hear that," Marianne says.

"She's leaving her good job and her wonderful

boyfriend and going to Sligo to take up a part-time job as a lecturer."

"Maybe she wants a change . . . she may need to discover for herself whether her life here is right for her?"

Carmel shakes her head solemnly. "Something is wrong and she's not telling me."

"Oh, dear," Marianne says.

"I'm just worried about her. She looks awful – she's so pale and drawn-looking and she's got so thin. I can't say she's grieving over the death of her father because he was never close to the girls – or me for that matter." Carmel takes a sip of her coffee, pauses to look around the café, and smiles a greeting at a woman sitting two tables down. Her eyes come back to Marianne's. "She doesn't know a soul in Sligo. I think she's heading for a nervous breakdown."

Marianne sips her coffee. "Is there anything I can do to help?"

Carmel smiles. "You're so kind, Marianne. I just wish there was something I could do. I hate this having to stand back. I want to protect her. I know she's a grown woman but she's still my baby." Carmel wipes her tears away. "If her father was alive he'd tell me it's her life and if she wants to pack up and leave then I should accept it." She pulls her face together. "It's not as if she's emigrating. It's just I know something is going on, something that she's not telling me. She has always been secretive. Christina was always so different." Carmel shakes her head in resignation.

There is some resemblance between Carmel and her daughter Sophia, thinks Marianne. On Sophia, the proportions are just right. Marianne is studying Carmel's face, deliberating on what is wrong with it. Is it that her jaw is too big or her eyes too small? Is that what makes her look ordinary instead of beautiful? Or is it life? Has life reduced a lovely face to this haggard one?

"You know, once you have children, they consume so much of you. You forget about yourself," Carmel is saying.

Marianne nods in agreement.

"Do you regret never having children?" Carmel is asking her now.

Marianne is pleased with herself that she had the foresight to take off her wedding ring almost a year ago. For now it suits her to say that she is single, that she never had children. She has invented a life for herself. She has told Carmel that she lived in Perth for years and worked in a library there and, now, she had come back to Ireland to retire.

"You never miss what you never had," she responds quickly and hopes that Carmel won't keep going on about children. She considers Carmel to be quite tactless at times. Doesn't Carmel know that every woman wants to be a mother? Isn't that why God gave us wombs? Marianne looks around the café; it's mostly women, heads close together, talking. At the door, a man sits with the paper opened wide. She marvels at the space a man takes up in comparison to the women customers.

Carmel looks around to see who she is looking at. She narrows her eyes slightly. "He's married. I've often saw him in Superquinn shopping with his wife."

Marianne pulls the muscles on her face into a tight smile. "Carmel, I was just noticing how much space he is taking up. If they outlawed paper-reading here, they would have more seats available."

Carmel looks at her, baffled. She turns around again and looks at the man and then gives an indifferent shrug. "The things you notice," she says. She finishes her coffee. "Oh, I feel so much better now. You're a good listener." She pulls back her chair and then adds. "Thanks."

"Don't mention it," Marianne says and they get

up to leave.

"There's a really nice jacket in the boutique here, I just want to show it to you. See what you think?" Carmel says as they leave the café.

"I thought you said you weren't buying any more clothes until you lost a half a stone."

"Did I tell you that?" she says, obviously amazed at the fact that she can't recall it.

"Yes, you did, about two weeks ago."

"But it doesn't matter with a jacket," she says as she leads the way into the boutique.

Marianne looks at Carmel in admiration; here is the woman who can make the best of every possible situation.

"Here it is," Carmel announces, holding the red wool-mix jacket under her chin.

"It looks really nice – it suits your dark colour-ing," Marianne is saying and she knows this is true.

"I have a pair of black tailored trousers that would look great with this." Carmel takes off her rain jacket. "Of course I would really have to cut out the morning coffee and cream buns."

"Hi, Carmel," says the sales assistant as she sashays down to greet them.

"Hi, Susan. What do you think?" Carmel asks as she does a quick twirl for them.

"It's very flattering," says the sales assistant.

"It's lovely, I've already told you," says Marianne. "You should buy it."

"I will. But come on then, Marianne, you should treat yourself to something new! Nothing cheers me up more than something new."

Marianne smiles and feels the hypocrisy of all this. She doesn't want to be here in this boutique with Carmel, pretending to be her friend. Yet the thought of going back to her rented house and spending the day there doesn't appeal.

The sales assistant is looking at her expectantly.

Marianne quickly looks through the clothes rails. She pulls out a black jacket.

"What about this?" she asks a little frantically. For so long she has forgotten about fashion, for so long she has been wearing the same drab clothes, not noticing that they are no longer fashionable.

Carmel tilts her head and considers. "You always wear black," she remarks gently. "Why don't you try something different?"

"How about a nice chocolate brown?" the sales assistant is suggesting.

"Maybe," Carmel is saying cautiously. "Show us what you've got." She does another twirl. "I really like this jacket."

Marianne tries on a chocolate-brown jacket. "Nice!" She rubs her hand down the suede sleeve. "I love the feel of this."

"I like it," Carmel says.

"I've got some really nice cashmere jumpers that would look lovely under it. Care to try one?" the sales assistant suggests.

"Can you afford it?" Carmel asks, when the sales assistant is out of earshot. "I mean, you could put a deposit on the outfit. That's how I do it."

"No, I think you're right – time I treated myself to something new."

"Good, now I won't feel guilty about buying this."

Marianne leaves the boutique with a new outfit and for the first time in a very long time she has actually enjoyed herself and it's all thanks to Carmel.

Chapter 7

Dear Mammy,

I'm sorry for leaving Dublin abruptly without telling you. It was a cowardly thing to do. I just had to go and was terrified that you would talk me out of it. I know you will be hurt, since I told Christina and Matt. Please don't feel offended, I had to do this for myself. Some things just were not right in Dublin. I have found Daddy's death hard to deal with – it was my car after all. I continue to love you and always will. When I get settled in, I will come back to visit you. I don't want you to worry about me. Apart from needing to leave, I am fine.

Sligo is a great town . . .

Ten minutes later, Sophia reads over her letter. She surprises herself that she has written over six pages, filling it with nonsense about Sligo, as if she has been there for ages. It's only been two weeks. It's her way of assuring her mother that everything

71

is all right. She has to go out to buy envelopes. Emails are all the go but her mam doesn't approve, thinks it lacks privacy. Sophia squirms in embarrassment as she recalls the girls in the office giggling over raunchy messages she exchanged with Matt. She recalls feigning indignation, though secretly she was pleased – they probably weren't getting any. God, what she had to give up by leaving Dublin!

She posts the letter with a cheque enclosed, ordering her mother to buy herself something new. It doesn't really exorcise her of her guilt.

Going home to her empty apartment every evening is the hardest part. She misses Matt so much. Inside, her heart was breaking as she walked out on him, but she felt she had no choice. She was heading for a nervous breakdown and, apart from that, she feared that Matt or her family might suffer the same fate as her father. It was better if she went alone. Perhaps then Matt and her family could live in peace.

As he begged her to stay, she found herself concocting a story, there and then at their apartment door. It came to her easily while she looked into his frantic face.

"You're right, Matt, there *is* someone else. I met him months ago, at a sales conference. He lives in

Sligo and I'm going there to be with him."

She gripped her bag tightly and left without another word, Matt's pleas ringing in her ears. She was amazed at the ease of her deception.

That night going to bed he would have found the envelope where she had dealt with the business side of their relationship. She hadn't taken her solicitor's advice to seek her financial share of the apartment. She had made it bad enough for Matt and he would now be paying the mortgage on his own.

Sophia often has to suppress a feeling of panic when she thinks, "What if he finds someone else? Brings someone else into our home, our bed?" She has to remind herself it's not her business any more.

Has she acted too hastily? Should she have gone back to Matt at the weekends?

But she had felt the apartment was contaminated. Even thinking about it sends a shiver down her spine. And her relationship with Matt is now also contaminated, as she has lied about her reasons for leaving.

No, staying in Dublin would have been disastrous. She had been heading for a mental breakdown. And what if anything had happened to Matt, to her family? How could she have lived with that?

The days are long and uneventful. She buys some recipe books and learns to make some new dishes. Long walks along the beach help to relax her.

Instead of calling her apartment bare she considers it minimalist. The furnishings are simple. A single cream sofa dominates the tiny living-room, with a coffee table where her two unread novels rest. There is a desk with her laptop and printer and a study lamp that is usually the only light she bothers to switch on when she comes home. It all looks so temporary.

Winter is fast approaching, and she knows she should get her act together and do some classes. There are plenty to chose from: yoga, watercolours, car maintenance, scuba diving. Nothing appeals and it is easier to go back to her tiny apartment and attempt to read a novel or some magazines. She is thinking of buying herself a TV and some other furnishings. But doing that would make staying in Sligo a permanent arrangement and this is something she doesn't care to consider. Because in her heart there is still a faint hope that, perhaps, in time, things will sort themselves out. Perhaps, in a year or two she can consider going home.

As she lies in her bed each night she wonders what Matt is doing at that very moment. The temptation to phone him is immense and she has to keep reminding herself of how final she has made things between them. There is no going back. At least, in her new apartment she feels safer. She doesn't need to keep looking around her, wondering if someone is stalking her. Now, she is beginning to feel normal again.

The one thing that surprises her is that she is really enjoying teaching. In the laboratory, thirty second-year students are waiting on her. 100mls of tap water waiting to be tested to see how many solid particles are suspended in it. The class look hung over and detached. It is a Friday morning. She envies the simplicity of their lives. Not much matters to them except getting their grant aid, their parents' money, part-time jobs: anything that will fund all the things that they were told not to do. . Sophia's father was so proud of her when she went to university. Of course her mother was proud too but she didn't show it in quite the same way.

Looking out the laboratory window, she can see Ben Bulben. Tomorrow, she hopes to visit WB Yeats' grave in Drumcliffe Churchyard. This is truly a lovely place to live. Every morning she can look out at the strong solid shape of the mountains and lose herself for a few moments. Each morning the mountains look different; it seems to her that they are putting on a show while yet appearing indifferent to spectators. Sophia brings herself back to reality. The mountains won't worry whether she likes what they are doing or not.

Sophia turns her attention to the experiment they are about to do. The students have to follow a clear and precise procedure. Nothing is left to chance. This is what she likes most about science. It is factual down to the molecular structure. She watches the students pour the water through the dried filter paper. She wonders will they ever look at water in the same way again. To the human eye it is just water, but, after analysis, you can detect even the smallest trace of another element or substance in it.

"Doing anything nice for the weekend?" a cheeky twenty-year-old brimming with testosterone asks her.

Sophia smiles. Her mind drifts back to other occasions when young men have tried to chat her up. Once upon a time she loved all that, but not now. Suddenly, she is thinking about Matt and feels awful.

"Not much. Are you?" she replies and tries to suppress the horrible thoughts that pull at her, determined to bring her down. He grins and doesn't reply.

Chapter 8

Marianne lies back in her bathtub in the quiet of the late evening and thinks to herself that she remembers too much of the insignificant and not enough of the things that are really important. Her mind is spinning – she is going backwards. "Liam," she says and closes her eyes to conjure up a picture of her son from memory. She sees a seven-year-old boy. She remembers his small hands that were always so grubby. She remembers how she scolded him for marking his bedroom walls with crayons when he was about four. She'd forgotten about that. She squeezes her eyes tightly to stop herself from crying. Her mind is spinning again as she tries to remember happier times. These are much harder to recall. "Oh, Liam," she whispers. "My baby." She lets the tears fall freely down her cheeks. The crying stops of its own accord.

Her voice is nothing more than a whisper but she still starts to talk as if she is telling a story to some young child. "We loved Christmas, it was our favourite time of the year, we always had a tree. Stephen always took two weeks off at Christmas. Before Christmas I would spend ages shopping, cooking, decorating. I loved it and I loved to moan about it. Christmas brought out the child in all of us ..." Her voice fades but it's done the trick: she can see the three of them on Christmas morning, opening their presents. Stephen and Liam eagerly assembling a train set or building something out of Lego. She smiles to herself now as she thinks of the year they got Liam a puppy. "Ah," she thinks, pleased the reel in her head is still playing. She can see herself, Stephen and Liam taking Toby for a walk. Then the picture fades and her eyes spark with colour because she has squeezed them too tightly. She takes a few deep breaths to calm herself. Ah, she thinks, the moment, the minutes, the hours, the days, the years. All this bloody time I have, all this time on my own. She sits bolt upright in the bathtub when she hears the doorbell.

"Damn," she mutters crossly and gets out of the

bath. She quickly puts on her towelling robe, tiptoes into her bedroom and peers out the window. She can't tell who it is and she feels a little vulnerable to go downstairs in this state of undress. The doorbell goes again but she refuses to move. She hugs her bathrobe around her, hoping whoever it is will just go away.

Then she sees a man walk down her driveway. She recognises him instantly. It's Stephen's brother David. She is astounded. How has he found her? She's told no one about this house.

"David," she mutters and hears the longing in her own voice. A part of her wants to run down the stairs and open the front door and shout at him. "I'm here, David!" Yet she holds back like she has always done.

He stands for a moment and looks around him. She hasn't seen him since Stephen's funeral. David came when it was nearing the end for his brother. Stephen had asked for him. Marianne had taken all the furniture out of their dining-room and made it into a bedroom for Stephen and herself. For the first time in their lives, they had to sleep in single beds. "I want to see David," Stephen had said. They both knew he was nearing the end but they never actually spoke of it. Death was too terrifying a word to say. With David around, Marianne didn't feel so afraid of Stephen dying. She held Stephen's hand and he passed away peacefully in the end. David wept with her and she felt comforted by the fact that she was not doing this all on her own.

Now, David stands at his parked car for a moment as if he is considering his next move. Then, he takes a mobile phone from his pocket and after he dials a number he puts the phone to his ear. Her mobile phone starts to ring downstairs. She should have changed her number, is her first thought. He turns to look up at the windows. The bedroom is in darkness; she pulls back slightly from the window.

He opens the door of his car and gets inside.

Her heart starts to drum rapidly against her chest. The phone is ringing again. She is tempted to rush down and pick it up. What can he want? And why didn't he simply ring her? Why come here? The house is quiet again, the shrill ringing of the phone stopped. She turns and looks out the window again. He is starting up the car. He switches on the headlights and slowly moves away.

Marianne wonders if he has left a message. Why would he bother getting in touch? Stephen and David were never close, until Stephen was dying and, when it was all much too late, he turned to his brother for support. They really were chalk and cheese. Stephen was the successful businessman. David was the carefree one who never could hold on to anything.

Tentatively, she goes downstairs, careful not to switch on the lights. She is looking in on herself like she is playing a part. She doesn't really know this woman she has become. Certainly Stephen wouldn't recognise her. He wouldn't like the fact that she has stopped colouring her hair. It's silver now. "Marianne," he'd say, "why have you let yourself go?" If Stephen were alive, he would be sixty now. She tries to think of a healthy Stephen, but all she can picture is him lying on his deathbed, his face gaunt and haggard. She shakes her head and tries to think of happier times when they first got married but she can't. She pictures the small church, trying to recall the day. It was spring.

There is a message.

"Hi, Marianne. It's me, David." A slight pause. "I just called to your house but you're not home." He laughs. "I should have phoned to tell you I was coming to Dublin. I hope you don't mind me calling like this." Another slight pause. "Maybe you'd prefer to be alone, but I would like to see you."

Heavy-footed, she climbs the stairs again and

goes back to bed. Under the covers, she shivers. She glances at her watch and sees it's past twelve o'clock. It's too early for sleep. This is my life, she thinks with a tinge of sadness. It's empty. It's full of nothing. Her lip curls cynically when she thinks how her life could have been. There is no word to describe her status, unless widow, but now she's much more than a widow. There should be a better word for it, she thinks, like 'orphan' which so well describes a child that is left parentless.

Chapter 9

"Sophia, can you come in here?" comes the sharp request from the Head's office.

Sophia steps inside.

"Meet Ben Redmond," says Mary Leahy, in a stiff formal tone. "I need you to show Ben around the laboratories. Wear this." She presses a new pristine lab coat on Sophia.

Mary is a short lean woman who Sophia has never once seen smile. She always seems to hold her face in a neutral mode, never displaying any sort of emotion at all. If she gets satisfaction from her work, Sophia feels she conceals it well.

Mary is hoping that Ben Redmond's company will fund some new equipment for the chemistry laboratory. Sophia is indifferent. Ben is the managing director for an American pharmaceutical company. He is trying to recruit graduates. He is a tall man with an athletic build. Sophia guesses he is in his early fifties. He walks gracefully alongside Sophia, opening doors for her, while she tries to sound enthusiastic about the college. She is sipping water from a polystyrene cup. His suntan intensifies the colour of his grey eyes. She can tell by his body language that he likes her. She isn't interested; there is nothing to be gained by befriending him.

"*Sofffiaah!*" he says, as they walk down the corridor together. "That's a pretty name," he drawls. The words echo and she wonders why he has to talk so loud. "Mary tells me that you're new to Sligo."

"Yes, I am."

Students are loitering outside a lecture hall, laughing, talking and generally causing an obstruction. They are quite indifferent to Ben and Sophia as they try to make their way past. Ben is smiling to himself and she is growing curious as to what he finds so amusing.

"I've just moved here from the States myself," he drawls.

Sophia gives a polite nod to indicate that she has heard but doesn't add to the conversation.

They walk along and then Ben says. "I really

like your name."

She wonders if this is his way of chatting her up? Ben repeats her name very slowly like he is testing it out for strength. She finds herself smiling; she likes the way he says her name. He seems to add a depth to it that she has never felt before – *Soffiaah, Soffiaah.* Sophia smiles politely and continues with the tour. Her cool manner adds to the attraction.

After a tour of the laboratories he invites her to join him for lunch.

"I'd love to but I have to prepare for a practical after lunch," she replies.

"That is such a shame," he says with obvious amusement.

"Thank you, anyway," she says as she moves away from him.

She is walking back towards her office when she hears him say, "I seem to have lost my sense of direction."

Sophia turns around, her face pulled into a false smile.

His grey eyes are twinkling with amusement. "Would you mind directing me towards the main exit?"

"Of course, sorry," she says, slipping into her professional mode. "Very thoughtless of me."

"You're thinking about your afternoon class?"

Sophia looks directly at him. "No, to be honest I was thinking about," she pauses and then gives him a winning smile, "nothing much."

The corridors are full of young people going in every direction.

"Looking at all these young people makes me feel so old," Ben remarks as they make their way through them.

"I know what you mean," she replies.

"That offer for lunch is still on," he says when they reach the main exit.

"Thank you, but ..."

"How about dinner this evening?"

"I ..."

"Look, we're both new to the area, and I hate eating alone, don't you?"

"OK," she hears herself suddenly agreeing and wonders why she is doing this.

"Say seven?"

"Fine."

"Can I have your mobile number so I can call you when I'm leaving my office?"

Sophia regrets accepting his invitation so quickly. Instinctively, she knows that Ben has one motivation in inviting her to dinner, and she tells herself silently that he is in for a disappointment. Arrogant American bastard! She stops herself from saying it aloud, instead stating, "Ben, I don't want there to be any confusion about the evening."

He holds his hands up in mocking innocence. "I'm not confused. Haven't we agreed to eat together this evening?"

It is clear to Sophia that charming Ben doesn't know the meaning of the word no. This she finds amusing and has to admire his determination.

That morning, while driving to work, Sophia had heard a woman on the radio categorizing people into two groups. The first she called triangles and women mainly belonged to this group. They spent some time on their career and some time on their family and some on themselves. The other category was tubular: they spent time on one thing only. She would slot Ben into the tubular category. *Tubular Ben.* Ms Leahy would not approve.

Chapter 10

Marianne wakes early and drifts in and out of sleep, listening to the radio. News depresses her so she tends to turn off the radio when it comes on. Her stomach rumbles with hunger, reminding her that it has been quite a while since she last ate. She doesn't want to get out of bed. Another day, she thinks solemnly. She feels cursed by the fact that she is still alive.

Slowly she puts on her dressing-gown, shuffles her feet into her slippers and plods downstairs. Opening the fridge door she looks in and is amazed to see that the milk has not passed its sell-by date. This is a good sign, she thinks. She switches on the kettle, deciding to have coffee this morning instead of tea. She trims some blue mould off the bread and puts it in the toaster. The things you will do when you don't feel like going out! The doorbell rings, making her jump, and she glances at the kitchen clock: it's ten past nine. She tightens the belt of her dressing-gown and wades down the hall towards the front door. She opens the door, expecting to see the postman or someone trying to sell her something.

Her mouth drops open when she sees David standing on the step. She can't conceal her shock. She knows she looks dreadful.

"David, this is a surprise," she says and opens the door so he can enter. She glances at her reflection in the hall mirror and sees just how bad she really looks. Her hair reminds her of that of a troll doll.

"Marianne," he says and embraces her in a gentle hug.

She finds herself running her fingers through her hair as she tries to put some order on it. "I didn't sleep very well last night," she explains as she leads the way into the kitchen. "Would you like a coffee?"

"Thanks, that would be great," David says and looks around the bare kitchen.

For the first time Marianne sees the kitchen and herself as someone else might see them. They might see her empty cupboards, her greying hair as an indication that she wasn't coping very well. Indeed Marianne didn't care what people in general thought of her. But here was David, Stephen's younger brother, and she couldn't possibly let him know that she wasn't coping. The last thing she wanted was his sympathy.

"I called last night," he remarks casually as he sits and she places a mug of coffee in front of him.

"I was out," she says as she butters some toast. "Would you like some toast?" She offers him a piece. He takes it. She looks at the remaining piece that is left on the plate. Is it worth topping it with marmalade?

"I hope I'm not eating your breakfast?" David says as he munches happily.

She shakes her head. "How did you find me?"

David stiffens somewhat. "I called to your house in Kells. Remember you gave me a key? Well, when a neighbour told me she hadn't seen you for ages, I was worried and let myself in. I saw a newspaper on the kitchen table with this house circled in it and some notes and figures scribbled down about the lease. So I took a chance and here I am. I'm sorry, but I was worried about you. I didn't like prying but I had to."

Marianne stifles an angry response and smiles at him. Anybody but David would be on his way out the door, red-eared, by now. "But why didn't you just ring me?" she asks. But she knows the answer. He didn't want to alert her, didn't want to give her the chance of refusing to see him.

"Oh, it didn't seem appropriate," he says lightly.

David must be fifty-five or six, she guesses. Looking at him reminds her that she is getting old. His light-brown hair is now greying. His shoulders are slightly rounded and, when he smiles, tiny lines are etched around his mouth and eyes. He is still a handsome man and he is aging gracefully. He has a milder manner than Stephen and is known to be a habitual daydreamer. David hasn't been as successful as Stephen was. Their mother was always trying to make him into a duplicate of Stephen. She couldn't see that he was fine the way he was. It must have been a relief to David when all that stopped.

"How are you?" he asks softly.

Marianne feels the tears in her throat; she swallows past them. David has found her. This she finds amazing. David has come all this way to ask her how she is. She is overwhelmed by the simplicity of the question. There she was, thinking she had cried her quota last night for the next week; now she is ready to start all over again.

"I have good days and bad ones," she confesses.

David nods. "I'm in Dublin for a few days and I was wondering would you like to come out to lunch with me?"

His eyes are a lighter blue than Stephen's. There is something about him that always reminds her of her son Liam.

Marianne's mouth drops open; she can't possibly go out today. She looks and feels a mess.

"You're trying to think of an excuse, aren't you?" he says.

She is taken aback that he can read her mind so well. "No," she says and picks up her coffee cup and drinks from it.

"Look, Marianne. Stephen asked me to look out for you before he died. And, anyway, where's the harm in wanting to see you?" He coughs to clear his throat.

"Oh, David," Marianne says and impulsively gets up and walks around the kitchen table to him. She wraps her arms around his neck.

His arms are strong and protective as she finds herself being folded into them.

"I'm a mess," she says and pulls away from him.

David looks at this frail woman in front of him.

"So am I, but it has never stopped me from venturing forth to do the next stupid thing."

She shakes her head vigorously to disagree. Though Stephen always considered everything that David did was stupid. He followed his heart and not his head.

"I've got the newspaper in the car. There is nothing I would like more than to sit down and read it – and wait for you."

Marianne laughs. "It will take ages. I'll have to wash my hair, find something to wear. Call back tomorrow – I should be ready by then."

"Nonsense! Remember I'm the bad timekeeper in the family."

"That's right. Stephen was always giving out that you never were on time." She gives him an apologetic smile and then adds, "Sorry."

"Don't worry about it. I'm used to it."

"It must have been hard for you living in Stephen's shadow."

David gazes at Marianne and says candidly, "It must have been hard for you too."

"Yes," she admits and turns away from him. "I'll get dressed."

"Right," he says. "I'll make myself another cup of coffee, so take your time."

As she starts to walk up the stairs, she hears the kettle being filled with water, being switched on. She hears the sound of a cupboard door being opened and closed gently as he looks to see what is in it. He is probably looking for biscuits, as he has a sweet tooth. These simple little domestic things that people take for granted right at this minute sound comforting to her. She should have known he would find her. . David had given Stephen his word that he would "look out for her" and now he was fulfilling his end of the bargain. He lived at the other end of the country, in Leitrim. As far as she is aware, he never comes to the city. She finds her pace increasing as she hurries into the shower. She is looking forward to a day out. After blow-drying her hair she put on the pearl ear-rings that Stephen had bought her for her birthday. In a drawer is a new pink cashmere jumper – she pulls off the price tags and puts it on. She wonders is there another purpose behind his visit. Something tingles in the pit of her stomach, a strange sensation – something akin to excitement. Surely she couldn't be excited about seeing David? After all, he is Stephen's brother – a younger, not very successful brother who never got his act together. David's wife Sue and their two adorable children returned to her family in London when she could no longer put up with his crazy schemes. He had started out as a doctor but soon gave that up to study alternative medicine. David had let it all go; she wondered did he regret it? Sometimes she used to feel Stephen was unkind when he'd say: "David's done it again." Stephen couldn't understand why people didn't succeed like he could. He was successful and had the Midas touch in business. He was scornful when the people he loved most, like his brother David and his son Liam, just couldn't be like him.

As Marianne applies some foundation to her face, she has to admit there were times when Stephen's success had made him arrogant and blind to the other qualities that Liam and David had. She stands back from the mirror and looks at her aging body, feeling the stirrings of a young girl going out for the day. The pink jumper was an impulse buy from when Stephen was alive and had never been worn.

David stands up when she enters the kitchen. She is aware that he is impressed by the transformation.

"So, where would you like to go?" he asks.

Marianne smiles at him. This was so like him, always eager to please, and she could imagine the most ridiculous request not fazing him.

"We could go into town," she suggests.

"Sure," he says, picking his mug up from the table. He turns on the hot tap to wash it.

"There is no need to do that."

"I'm just doing it to show you that I'm house-trained."

She laughs at him and picks up her bag. "We could go to the Vermeer exhibition if you like? It's at the National Art Gallery."

"I'm not much into art exhibitions but I'm prepared to try anything once."

"Good, I've been meaning to go but ..." she pauses. "I've been busy."

David doesn't question what she has been busy doing, for it's not in his nature. Stephen on the other hand would have wanted to know why she hadn't gone if she really wanted to go. She shuffles into her coat in the hall and she wonders why she is doing it? Why is she continuing to compare the two brothers? Stephen is dead after all. She locks her door and follows David to his battered old car.

She is glad of his company. She loves being chauffeured around. This may be a terrible thing to admit in this age of independence. In her opinion there are some things that men do better, like driving. She knows Carmel would agree with her.

Carmel likes to talk to her about her husband. Carmel is angry with him; he died without ever telling her he loved her. "He never once said it to me in all the years we were together," she had said.

At least Stephen had told her on numerous occasions that he loved her. It was sad that she couldn't share with Carmel, couldn't tell her that she was grieving too.

People might look at her and David today and think they were a married couple. She wonders if he will enjoy the Vermeer exhibition. As far she knows, David has no interest in art. Stephen was the one that loved going to exhibitions and buying a painting when he fell in love with it. In David's simple country house, there were no paintings – only photographs of his children.

"I thought you hated Dublin. I never imagined that you would come here to live," David remarks as he stops at another red light.

Marianne isn't expecting this probing. "I just wanted to lose myself somewhere."

David nods. "That's understandable. You probably had to get away from all of us." She leans back in the car seat and closes her eyes, feeling that she will do her best to enjoy this day. Deep down she knows her loved ones would want her to.

"Marianne," David says quietly, "I worry about you." He is staring intently at the car in front of him. .

"David, there is no need for you to worry about me. I'm fine."

He turns to look at her, "Is there something going on, Marianne?

She laughs a little nervously. "Nothing is going on," she says impatiently.

"I'm lost," he suddenly announces, realizing he is not on the right road.

"When did you figure that one out?" she asks sarcastically.

"Right now," he says and waves with his hand. "I don't know which way to go to get to the city centre."

"Take a right here – it's pretty straight all the way after."

"Thanks." He keeps his eyes focused on the road ahead. After a few quiet moments he asks, "How do you stand this traffic?"

"It doesn't bother me." She's quite pleased with how in control she is with David, but then she always was with him. As she looks out the passenger window, she becomes aware that she is enjoying this. It's nice to sit back and not have to put in an effort. David is easy company.

"I don't know how you stand all this traffic," he says again.

Marianne doesn't reply; she doesn't feel the need to.

"I would hate to live here," he says and shakes his head dramatically.

"I just needed a change," she replies casually.

David sighs, a moment passes and then he says, "But you loved living in the country. You loved your garden and house."

Marianne looks across at him. She's pleased that he cares – it is nice but she knows it's not necessary. "I like where I live, I've made some new friends. I couldn't go back."

He turns his head to look at her and they smile at each other.

"So, tell me about these paintings we're going to see," he says.

"Wait until you see them – they'll speak for themselves."

He looks around him, bewildered. "Are we still going in the right direction?"

"Yes. If we weren't, I'd have told you."

"Yes, of course you would," he says and grips the

steering wheel even tighter.

At the Millennium gallery, Marianne manages to forget to worry about David's reaction as she soaks up the luminous Vermeer paintings.

Eventually, they make their way downstairs to the café.

"Those pictures were so lifelike," he remarks as they go.

"I love the way he manipulates the light. The soft sensual lines. It's like he had this magical paint-brush that captured the beauty of the domestic. They are just wonderful."

"I'm afraid I'm not much of an art critic so I can't go into a heavy discussion about it," he says in a deeper voice. "I don't know anything about tech-nique or light and shape and all that."

"But they touched you. You felt something when you looked at them."

For a moment David looks baffled and then he says, "I felt what a crazy world we live in. How lit-tle sense it makes. Though I must admit that's how I feel most of the time."

She nods in agreement and they turn to read what is on the menu.

"I didn't realise so many people liked art," David says, after they have collected their food and found a free table to sit at. "When I see large groups of people together it reminds me of ants. I think that's how God sees us. He looks down from his frothy clouds and sees us all running around and we look to him like ants do to us."

Marianne opens her chicken sandwich. She is starving and she starts to eat it straight away.

"Of course you might argue with me that He is not a He but a She," David continues to say.

Marianne swallows a mouthful of chicken and looks at him baffled.

"I'm talking about God," he explains.

"Oh, yes. Does he exist at all?"

"I'm sure he does. At least, he does for me," David says.

"Really, I didn't think you believed."

"Stephen was the one who didn't believe in anything."

"Yes."

"Funny, I'd never think of coming here," David remarks.

Marianne looks at him kindly. "David, you never come to the city so why should you think about coming here?"

"Good point," he replies and smiles at her.

"So what would you like to do next?" she asks.

He shrugs, a habit that Liam must have inherited from him.

For a time, they stroll around the galley. On leaving, they are greeted by the hustle and noise of the city.

"We could go and have a walk along Grafton Street and then have some coffee?" Marianne suggests. "There's any amount of cafes around there."

"Do you remember which carpark we docked in?" he asks.

She touches his coat sleeve. "Yes, I do."

He puts his hand on top of hers. "Good," he says.

Marianne is touched by this display of affection; it is opening up new

possibilities for her. Then she admonishes herself for being so stupid.

David makes a face. "I fancy a hot whiskey. Too much coffee is bad for me."

"But you're driving!"

"One whiskey!" he exclaims.

She is looking in on herself, seeing them as a middle-aged couple having a discussion about whether they will go for coffee or a drink.

"After this trip to Dublin, who knows when I'll be on the road again."

"Everything is OK with you?" she asks abruptly.

He doesn't meet her eyes when he replies that he's fine.

"I know a nice hotel where you can order your hot whiskey and I can get a decent coffee," she says.

David frowns. "Is it really posh and terribly expensive?"

"Oh, David, if you're worried about the money, I'll pay."

"It's not the money. I just don't feel comfortable in those places. They always have a hollow ring to them. I like a nice ordinary pub with ordinary people, not people aspiring to be something else."

Marianne laughs. "Pity I didn't bring the soap box."

"Sorry, look, let's go wherever you want to."

"I remember all those arguments you used to have with Stephen."

"I was terrible. I only did it to annoy him."

"I know," she says.

"Let's head to Grafton Street and then one of those cafés – I'll have tea and a bun instead," he says.

Chapter 11

They are sitting in an exclusive restaurant where everyone seems to talk in hushed tones.

"This is really expensive," Sophia remarks as she looks in horror at the menu prices.

"Don't worry about it, I can afford it," he replies reassuringly.

Sophia has worn black tailored trousers with a cream shirt. When Ben compliments her on how beautiful she looks, she looks at him warily. Ben is easy company. He simply talks about himself and all she has to do is listen. He is definitely tubular. Over dinner, he shows her a photograph of his wife Karen and their two teenage boys. His wife and sons have remained in Chicago, he says with a mischievous glint in his grey eyes. They smile out from the photograph, like their life depended on it. All those white molars and attitude make Sophia instantly want to dislike them.

"The happy family," she says, not caring about the sarcastic tone. She hands him back the photograph. The sarcasm is lost on him as he nods in agreement.

"My children are …" he stops himself, clearly lost for words, then rushes on with a host of adjectives, "amazing – talented – funny and, Jake, that's my youngest …"

Sophia is gliding away now, past Ben and his easy conversation. Her mother's shrill voice is ringing in her ears. They are in the kitchen of their home in Templogue. Matt and herself walk into the kitchen.

"This is a nice surprise," her mother starts to say and stops mid-sentence when she sees their faces. "What's the matter?" she asks, her voice a croaky whisper.

"Daddy is dead. It was a car crash. He was bringing my car to the garage."

"Oh my God, oh my God!"

Quite suddenly, her mother's voice is drowned out as Sophia's thoughts change direction. Does Mary Leahy expect me to sweet-talk Ben regarding funds for the college, she wonders. She dismisses this as an absurd thought: Mary would not know about their evening out. Nevertheless, it occurs to her, she could get the blame if things went wrong.

"So," she starts to say, as she smiles at Ben pleasantly. She feels she has a mission to accomplish.

He is smiling at her now, clearly amused by her. She can tell that he likes playing games. Goodness knows she has played enough of them in her time, but that was before Matt. Thinking of Matt makes her sad and she scrambles past the thought and reaches out for something else to talk about. In her mind's eye she can picture her hollow apartment; it is the only place she has to retreat to and it isn't very inviting.

Ben refills her wine glass.

"You know what I like about living here?" she hears herself say. "I don't have to keep looking over my shoulder. In Dublin it was a nightmare. Our apartment was broken into twice – nothing was stolen but someone was snooping through my stuff and ..." She pauses and sips some more wine.

Ben is smiling now, his eyes holding hers as she continues.

"In the office I'd leave down a file and I couldn't guarantee when I went back it would be there." She sighs deeply. She stops talking, takes a breath and realises she is confessing her fears to an absolute stranger. Tubular Ben can't help.

Ben refills her wine glass.

"I hated been first home in the evenings, I just dreaded going into the apartment." The words flow out now like she can't stop herself; she feels reckless.

"Sound like you were overworked," Ben says with obvious false sympathy. "Tell me, you mentioned '*our*' when you spoke of your apartment. Want to talk about it?"

"*No*." Sophia realises she should be having this conversation with Matt, or Claire for that matter. "I'm sorry, Ben. Wine has a bad effect on me, it makes me waffle on … and I …" She finds herself gripping the sides of the table. Her head is spinning. She focuses on Ben but he looks blurred. "I'm not feeling … very well."

He is by her side now. She hates this, this feeling that she is going to collapse. It reminds her of all those stupid stories of damsels in distress.

"Sophia," she hears him say from some far-off place.

She wishes Matt was here. She could trust him. He didn't carry a picture of her in his wallet. She knew he carried it in his heart. His face swims up in front of her now. He's looking at her, his eyes brimming with tears. Matt's face is pale and etched with sadness. Matt loved her, plain and simple. Sophia knows she will never know love like that again. A straightforward, simple, uncomplicated love. Ben helps her back into her chair.

"Sorry," she says apologetically.

"You're fine," Ben replies, relishing the role of able suitor.

"I'm okay," she says, standing up, determined not to let her knees buckle under the weight of her body.

"I'll take you home," Ben insists.

Sophia is too weak to protest. They leave the restaurant, she volunteers her car keys and she gives him directions to her apartment.

She is determined not to stagger as she makes her way up the stairs to the apartment, dazed. At the door, she composes herself long enough to get her keys back from Tubular Ben, and thank him.

She enters the apartment alone.

On her bedside locker is a picture of herself and Matt. It was the single joint possession that she took from their apartment. The photograph they had taken in Venice last year. Something about that photograph just sums them up. Tears well in her eyes, blurring her vision.

Her mobile rings suddenly. It is Ben. "Are you OK?" he asks.

Sophia nods. "Thanks," she mumbles.

Sophia awakens when she hears her mobile ringing. She lifts her head off the pillow and wonders where her phone is. She reaches out of the single bed and picks her bag up off the floor but the mobile stops ringing just as she is about to take it out. Her head falls back down on the pillow. "Damn," she mutters to herself. It starts to ring again. She rips her bag open and pulls her phone out. It's not Matt's number. She had lied too well: he believed her story about her coming to Sligo to be with someone else.

"Hi," Ben says when she answers. His greeting is very up-tempo and it isn't mixing well with her black mood.

Sophia sits up in her bed, and runs her fingers through her blonde hair. Glancing at her digital clock, she realises she could have slept in for her first class if he hadn't phoned her.

"Hi," she says as she throws the duvet back.

"How are you?" he roars into the phone, and she moves the mobile away from her ear.

"Fine – I'm just preparing for my first class this morning," she says in a bogus cheery voice.

"Good," he drawls.

"Sorry about last night."

"That's OK," he says smoothly. "Say, how about some breakfast?"

"Oh, I can't. I have a class at twelve but thanks anyway."

"I'm right outside your door with it," he says.

Sophia closes her eyes and wishes *Scotty* would beam her up.

"Aren't you going to let me in?" he asks.

"Well, I'm not very presentable at the moment. I'm a mess." She glances into her dressing-table mirror and is a little alarmed at her own reflection. She is quite shocked to see how pale and drawn she looks and her blonde hair is in bad need of a cut. "I really am a mess," she hears herself repeat and then laughs at herself.

"Can I suggest something?" Ben says smoothly.

"Sure."

"You just open the door. I promise I won't look at you. You go off and get showered and dressed and I'll have breakfast ready for you when you're ready."

"Ben –" she starts to object.

"Sophia, you can't leave me standing at the door with all this food," he says, his voice steady and determined. "You must be hungry."

With that, her stomach starts rumbling, betraying her.

"OK," she says.

Sophia walks into the kitchen, her hair swept up off her face. Her delicate features seem more clearly defined this morning. Ben notices the dark circles under her eyes. She's wearing no make-up and looks more like a student in faded jeans and a grey cashmere jumper.

Ben has just made coffee. "I hope you don't mind," he says as he pulls out a chair and sits opposite her.

She shakes her head and then says in a husky voice that her head hurts. She is hoping, despairingly, that he will lower the tone of his voice.

"Breakfast," he announces and spreads his hands out.

On the table are croissants, brown scones and a pot of coffee.

"Thanks," she says. Sophia straightens her face, composing herself to conceal the turmoil that is going on inside.

"I make really good pancakes. I'll make them some weekend if you like."

"Now, Mr. Redmond, you'll have us living together if you're not careful," she admonishes as she pours coffee.

"Soffiaah," Ben says as he butters a scone, "do you want to tell me more about the things you mentioned last night?"

She notices that he has even brought butter. He has shifted into counsellor mode and it clearly doesn't suit him.

"No," she replies and glances at her watch.

As he butters his scone he says, "I'm always here if you'd like to talk."

"Thanks," she says and she finds it an effort to look at him directly but when she does she finds an unexpected sincerity in his grey eyes.

He shuffles on the kitchen chair and then he announces unexpectedly. "You know, I really like you, and –"

"Look, Ben, I don't need to hear bullshit," she interrupts.

Ben smiles across the table at her. "I'm not going to bullshit you. I'm going to be honest with you." He looks at her levelly. "I'll never leave my wife and kids, so let's be practical here. We're both strangers in town and –"

Sophia doesn't let him finish. "You are so fucking arrogant!"

"I'm being honest." He gets up from the table. "I'd better go. Have a good day and call me if you get lonely."

"Bye," she mutters, as she hears him quietly close her front door. She opens her folder to read over the notes for her first class and tucks into a second croissant.

On her way to work, she finds her thoughts drifting. She is back in their apartment in Dublin. She is sitting on the sofa. Matt is moving about. He is walking towards the window. She is watching him. The slumped shape against the window. What possessed her to act so irrationally? For weeks, she secretly planned her departure from Dublin, convinced that if she got away then everything would be all right. She remembers their parting. She regrets telling him there was someone else. Why had she to lie so convincingly? Why couldn't he make contact if it was only to ask where he should forward her post to?

"I feel Sophia is holding back something," she recalls him saying to Claire while she listened silently in their bedroom.

She doesn't understand herself. Her mind is forever circling the same question. Why did she leave? Why did she split up with Matt? Was she simply suffering from paranoia?

Now she is playing out another scenario, seeing herself rushing across the floor and into Matt's open arms. Tears well in her eyes as she drives into the college grounds. She aches for Matt. She picks up her mobile and is tempted to dial his number. "Later," she tells herself as she gets out of the car.

As she makes her way down the corridor towards the laboratory, Ms Leahy steps out from her office.

"Sophia," she says and pulls the corners of her mouth back in an attempt to smile.

Sophia is tempted to tell her it causes less hardship on the facial muscles if you smile rather than frown. Ms Leahy is a real theory woman: she knows the facts but it is putting them into practice that causes her the difficulties.

"How are you getting on?" she enquires.

"Fine, thanks," Sophia replies.

"I just had Ben Redmond on the phone. We're going to get some funding. Not as much as we'd like, but it's better than nothing."

"That's great," she replies faking enthusiasm.

Sophia walks down to her laboratory and turns the key in the door. She is really glad that she has something complicated to do. She sits down at her desk. Her students saunter in, talking noisily. She wants to shout at them to shut up but refrains. She longs for Matt, she aches for him to enfold her in his strong arms, to whisper some comforting words, to tell her it is going to be all right. She can see herself back in their apartment again. In their bedroom, her wardrobe is already bare. Her packed cases are in her car. She realises she has little control over her life; she is like a puppet on some invisible string.

She puts on her lab coat and opens her notes. They are going to analyze soil samples for phosphorus.

Chapter 12

"I missed you from our yoga class, yesterday," Carmel says as they sit down with two frothy cappuccinos and Danish pastries.

"I met an old friend," Marianne says, immediately regretting her openess. *Got to be careful.* "Oh, I feel so guilty eating this!" she says, delighted that she can change the subject.

Carmel tuts. "You shouldn't – there isn't an ounce of flab on you." She pulls at her midriff. "Look at this. Isn't it disgusting? I'm getting so fat."

"Have you tried aerobics or keep-fit? They wouldn't be my preference, but maybe you would like them. We could go together."

"Yes, I suppose if I was going along with someone I wouldn't find them so bad. I'm useless when it comes to doing things on my own," Carmel admits.

"I know the feeling."

"It must get lonely having no family of your own. Now that Alan is gone, I have the girls – well, I have Christina, and Sophia until recently, but it's the grandchildren that I just adore. I dread to think what my life would be like if I hadn't my grand-children."

Marianne puts on a brave face and manages to reply. "You never miss what you never had."

"I suppose so," Carmel says, going into a reflec-tive mood.

"I like living in Dublin," Marianne says with con-viction. "I've made new friends and I have quite a good life."

Carmel breaks up her Danish pastry and puts a piece of it in her mouth. "These aren't as good as the ones we had last week."

"They look good," Marianne says and takes a bite. "Mmm, I think they're fine."

"Do you think so?" Carmel says and raises an eyebrow.

Marianne nods with conviction and thinks how easy conversation is with Carmel. Nothing is ever discussed but the simple things in life and it's wonderful.

"Fancy coming with me to that new restaurant that has just opened up beside you?" Marianne says as she sips some of her cappuccino.

"You mean the new Italian one? What's it called?"

"Goodness, I can't remember."

Carmel laughs. "Alan was always accusing me of forgetting stuff but he was no better."

"It's old age creeping up on us."

"Nonsense," says Carmel tilting her head up defiantly.

"So back to the main topic," Marianne says as she looks at her plate and realises that she has finished her Danish. "Will you come with me to that new restaurant? My treat."

"I'd be delighted. And if you don't feel like going home that night you can stay with me. I don't have a guest room as such. Sophia's old room is small and a bit of a mess, I'm afraid. I keep telling her that we should clear it out but she …" Carmel shakes her head, her voice thickens with emotion, "I don't know what has got into her, she's changed so much."

"Oh, dear, I'm sorry to hear that," Marianne says in a solicitous voice.

"She used to be so carefree and so happy. She didn't give a damn about anything. Now she's gone moody and she's so thin. I was sure she was on drugs but Christina tells me it's not that. She thinks she's having a nervous breakdown. Christina is promising to go every weekend to Sligo to see her but so far she hasn't managed it. Every weekend there is something on."

Marianne sips her cappuccino.

Carmel continues to talk. "She blames herself for her father's death. He was driving her car when the accident happened. I am praying for her, hoping that she will come to her senses and see that it was an accident, that she wasn't to blame." They sit in silence for a few minutes and then Carmel continues, "I was sure they were going to settle down and get married. Matt has a good job, working with computers in the financial services in town."

"I see," Marianne says.

Carmel takes another bite of her Danish pastry. "You know, it's great to talk to someone about it. Share it." Suddenly, Carmel seems to have lost her appetite. "I'm worried about her. I really think something is wrong."

"Maybe you should try and talk to her," Marianne says.

Carmel shakes her head resolutely. "I have tried to phone her but it's no use. She tells me she's quite happy and that it was the best thing she ever did to leave Dublin but I ..." Carmel stops and looks at Marianne.

Marianne feels herself holding her breath.

"There is something wrong, but I can't put my finger on it."

Marianne exhales. "I see."

"Don't pay any attention to me. What would I know?" Carmel looks into her empty coffee cup.

"Carmel, you're being too hard on yourself."

"Am I?"

"Yes."

"Maybe. She's a grown woman making her own way in the world. If she wants to pack up and head down the country to lecture in a college then why can't I be happy for her? Why do I get the feeling that something is wrong?" Carmel leans across the table. "She loved Matt. I was so sure they were going to buy a house together, get married and have children." Carmel's eyes fill up. "Oh, she never said anything to me but isn't that what couples do?"

"Not all. Some do break up."

Carmel pulls a face. "Yes, I guess they do."

"Shall we go?" Marianne asks.

"Yes, I suppose so. I'm just worried about her, Marianne."

"You could be worrying unnecessarily. You don't know for sure that anything is wrong. So stop worrying about it until you have proof."

Carmel stands up and puts on her brown tailored jacket.

"I really like your jacket," Marianne says as they leave the café.

"Oh, this thing. I got it in the sales last year."

"Carmel, you're amazing when it comes to getting bargains."

Carmel smiles in a self-satisfied way. "Yes, I suppose I am."

They walk across the carpark towards the main road. They wait for the lights to change, then cross and walk up Knocklyon Road towards Carmel's house.

"Come up to the house – I want to show you the photographs that Christina got taken of her children."

"I'd love to, Carmel, but I have to go into town – I have to start my Christmas shopping. I'll phone you to organize a night for us to go to the restaurant."

"That's fine, I hope I haven't delayed you,"

Carmel says with genuine concern.

It's bitterly cold and both their noses are reddening up.

"Look!" Carmel says pointing. "A bus."

"Great," Marianne says and walks as fast as she can towards the bus stop.

"Call me!" she hears Carmel shout after her.

As the bus pulls out from the stop, Marianne takes a seat window and waves out at Carmel.

Chapter 13

"It's post for you," Mary says.

"Thank you," Sophia says, a little surprised. She notices by the postmark that it has been posted in Dublin but she doesn't recognise the handwriting.

She is about to set off home. Soft rain is falling from the dark sky. She stands in the reception area and opens the envelope.

At once, her heart drums loudly in her ears: the first photograph is of her nieces. The same photograph that went missing from her desk. Her fingers flick the second photograph over. She stands motionless, students shuffling past her, eager to get away for the evening.

"Sorry," someone mutters.

"Excuse me," she hears another voice say.

She tries to move out of their way but is trapped in the main flow of student traffic.

"Ms, Ms," she hears some young male voices say jokingly. "Give me your hand, Ms."

She pushes forward and makes her way out the main door. She takes a few shallow breaths to steady herself. Quickly she races towards her car but isn't certain exactly where she parked it. Her stomach muscles start to heave and she has to stop. She bends over and starts to retch.

"Are you OK?" A young woman asks at her side.

Sophia looks up, her face wet with the dewy rain and nods. "Yes, thank you, I'm fine."

"Would you like me to stay with you for a while?"

"No, I'm fine," she says again in a firmer voice. She straightens herself up with her hands folded across her stomach.

She can't remember where she parked her car and she is beginning to panic. She starts to walk in one direction and then another, as she searches in vain.

"Please help me find my car?" she mutters to herself.

"Are you OK?" Mary Leahy asks, rushing towards her.

"Oh, yes, I just can't find my car," Sophia says

with an unconvincing nervous laugh. "I'm sure I parked it here … somewhere, around here."

"You did, right beside mine – come on, I'll lead the way."

"Thanks."

"There you are, see you tomorrow," Mary says and in a flash she is in her car and leaving before Sophia gets her keys out of her pocket.

Sophia collapses into her car and locks the door. With shaky fingers, she switches on the car light and examines the photograph of that man again.

"It can't be," she says. "It can't be happening again."

It's not a photograph of him as he was then, but as he might look now. It's a computer-enhanced image, something she has seen done on TV – on one of those crime shows.

Someone had got a photograph of him when he was eighteen or nineteen and then they had got the image doctored to show what he might look like now. All of her worst fears had followed her to a new location. 'Your problems will follow you to Sligo,' Christina had said.

Sophia picks up her mobile; she cannot go back to her apartment alone. She feels she has no choice but to call Ben.

"Hi, Ben, it's Sophia," she says. She leans back in her car seat and listens to his bright cheery voice.

"How are you, Soffiaah?"

"Fine, fine, a little tired, I had a long day." She wants to kick herself for saying that; she mustn't pretend, must tell him she needs support and company. Suddenly, tears are streaming down her cheeks.

"Are you OK?" Ben is asking her now.

"No, not really," she admits.

"Can I help in any way?"

"I just need to talk to someone."

"Sure, I'd be delighted to meet in . . . give me ten minutes to finish up here."

"OK, thanks." She hangs up without arranging a meeting-point.

Her phone rings before she gets a chance to call him back.

"Could we meet at the college?" he asks.

"Sure, no, I … I'm not sure, Ben."

"Soffiaah, you're in trouble, aren't you?"

Sophia confirms this for him by her sobs.

"I'll come and get you," he says with authority.

"I'm in the college carpark – could you come quickly, please?"

"I'm on my way."

"Good morning," Ben says, walking into the bedroom in his converted schoolhouse where they had spent the night together. He is light-footed and she never hears him until he is right there in front of her.

"Hi," she says sleepily.

"I've taken the day off to spend it with you."

"That's really nice," she says and she runs her fingers through her tossed hair to comb it. She figures he has already a day's work done, he being a tubular person and all that.

"I was thinking, we should go somewhere today."

"Yes, I guess we should," she says, a little alarmed that she is going to have to spend the day entertaining him.

Yesterday, she had decided not to tell Ben about the photographs. She deliberately left them behind her in the car. As her mother would say: out of sight, out of mind. So, she had told him that she had a hard day, that the students were very difficult.

He sits down on the antique bed that dominates the master bedroom. "Do you feel like talking this morning about why you sounded so upset on the phone last night when you called me?"

"But I told you, the students . . ." Her voice trailed off.

"Look, I know it was more than that. Just remember, if you ever need to talk, I'm here."

"Thank you, Ben."

Sophia is surprised at the fact she has slept soundly. She feels safe around Ben. Somehow, being here with him she was able to push everything else out of her mind. Now it all comes rushing back again. Why would someone steal a photograph of her two nieces? Was it a threat? Were they trying to tell her that the little girls would meet the same fate as the young man in the other photograph? Sophia feels physically sick at the thought. To survive the morning with Ben, she has to think tubular. Right now, he is her only protection and she cannot afford to lose him.

Ben breaks into her thoughts to ask. "You never talk about your family or your ex."

Sophia makes a face. "You don't talk about yours," she counters.

Ben smiles. "Well, I can hardly talk about my wife to you and I don't like talking about my children to people that aren't parents. They don't understand."

She wonders if she should feel offended.

He senses her change in mood. "Let me explain, honey. It's boring for people to listen to a parent going on about the wonders of their children."

"Ah, I see. Very considerate of you," Sophia says as she throws the covers back and gets out of bed.

"What happened between you and your ex?"

"Fear of commitment, it happens all the time," she says vaguely.

"Who didn't want to commit?"

"Oh," she says as she meets his steady gaze, "does it really matter?"

"I guess it does. I'm curious."

"I didn't want to, if you must know."

"I see. I know it's really selfish of me to say this, but I'm really glad. I didn't want to come to Ireland." He pulls off his T-shirt. "Now I'm so glad I did."

Last night making love to Ben was hazy, almost dreamlike because she had drunk too much wine. This morning she isn't sure if she can carry the whole thing off. Nevertheless she trails back to the bed, tossing back her hair. Ben makes slow passionate love to her, his masterly fingers stroking the right responses from her. She blocks everything out but the here and now with Ben.

The schoolhouse nestles under the hill of Knocknarea; it is a wonderful, tranquil place to live.

Days pass in a hazy way. It was built in 1890 but has been converted into a modern luxurious house. The only reminder of its humble beginnings is an engraving on the stone outside the front door. Sophia didn't plan to stay at the schoolhouse, it just happened that way. She continues to keep her apartment in town and most of her clothes are there.

She opens her eyes, and the room is filled with muted light. On her bedside locker is the book that she's currently reading. It's a novel by William Trevor and the bleak haunting writing suits her mood right now. Beside the novel she has placed her pearl earrings on a pottery dish that Christina's girls brought her from Spain. Next week it's Amy's birthday; she will be four. This will be the first birthday party Sophia has missed. Christina always turned their birthdays into real occasions and invited family and friends along.

Sophia sits up in her bed and slowly looks around the bedroom that she now shares with Ben. On the old chair at the foot of the bed are the clothes that she wore yesterday. The old pine wardrobe holds a change of clothes. The dressing-table has a vase with red roses in them that Ben surprised her with last night. "I thought you'd like them," he'd said, a little anxiously. Ben is eager to please her. She didn't like them, but acted like she was really pleased. She notices that she is doing that a lot lately. Not really thinking about anything, just going with the flow. Her eyes are taking in each detail of the bedroom. With a sigh of relief, she lies back down on the bed. Everything is in its place. Nothing had moved.

Somehow, she feels protected while she is around Ben. He may be using her, but Sophia needs someone right now and Ben has many positive things going for him. She wonders is it something in the survival gene, something primitive that makes her want to be here.

From Ben's bedroom window they have amazing views of the Atlantic.

It's Wednesday morning. She walks down the stairs and into the open-plan living-room. The walls are painted in burnt umber colour-wash giving the large space a comforting inviting ambience, the focal point of the room being the view of the distant ocean through the patio doors.

Ben is making pancakes. He is an expert. Of course, he would never have attempted them if he wasn't. He is showing off, trying to impress her. As she looks out the kitchen widow she notices the sky is grey and overcast.

"It's raining again," he remarks dryly.

He is constantly remarking on the weather as if it should be tailored to suit his needs. Sophia likes the rain; it seems to express what she is not capable of saying herself. The dark grey days, where not much is happening, only nature retreating, resting on the promise that spring will come again.

She sets the table and makes strong coffee, just the way Ben likes it. Ben's mobile rings and he gives her an apologetic smile as he answers it. Outside, she hears seagulls call. She admonishes herself for not getting up earlier and going for a walk. She is too far away from the ocean to hear the crashing of the waves against the rugged rocks. As she pours herself a mug of coffee, she can imagine the waves foaming and fuming with all that power against the rock face. Where is this all leading? Now, a tiny voice questions her actions but she dismisses it. There are always casualties, she reasons. She sees Matt's face. He's smiling, wearing that lopsided grin that always made her heart flip. She squeezes her eyes together so tightly that she sees stars. Then she opens them to look at golden crisp pancakes that are made to perfection. She starts to eat one and is delighted by the taste of it. She has never eaten anything so good. She feels detached from herself. Right now, she is in adjustment mode, swaying between the old life and the new one that is just beginning. Soon, she knows she'll be anchored down. Then, the nightmare will be over.

She glances up and sees herself reflected in a mirror on the wall, and it strikes her how much she looks like her mother. Carmel often comments that Sophia is too good-looking for her own good, aware that she herself falls far short of Sophia's beauty – her perfect proportions, her amazing blue eyes that you felt you were sinking into when she looked at you, and her wonderful cheekbones. Once, she was stopped on Grafton Street and asked if she had ever considered modelling. She laughed at the absurdity of it. She thought the guy was just chancing his arm; she took his business card but never called the number to make the appointment.

Sophia had never been without a man in her life. She never experienced true singledom. She had listened attentively to Claire and Christina moan when they had man trouble. Privately, she thought they were looking for too much. They were looking for the prince with the glass slipper. They had a fairytale notion of living happy ever after. No handsome prince was going to make their life better.

They could only do that for themselves. It was sad that women from the 21st century still believed in fairytales. Sophia wanted to share this knowledge with them but then she was all too aware that something was missing in her own life, something big. And if she turned and looked in at herself she might see a hazard sign.

Chapter 14

As Marianne walks up the path, she hears a car door open, and turns to see Jim getting out.

"Marianne," he says, somewhat formally and cold.

"Jim, you must have something for me," she says, in similar tone.

"Yes, I do, but I'm beginning not to like this. It's way over the top."

"Oh, that's a pity. Do you have another detective you might recommend? I'll get you your money."

"Marianne, listen to me. I am quite happy to continue providing you with photographs and information. But there are laws against stalking. I've seen some of my clients suffer for this."

She opens her door and switches on the hall light.

The place is chilly and uninviting. "I'm sure you have. Now let's see what you've got for me."

"OK, but I'll just say one more thing. You could be heading for trouble if you keep chasing down Gavin Daly. He won't take kindly to you snooping around him. He or, more likely his cronies, could cause you serious harm. You're going too far."

They walk into the kitchen. Marianne takes an envelope from the cupboard.

"Your money, Jim," she says, with outstretched hand.

Jim didn't understand. What would he know? He missed the point. However, her composure with Jim is feigned. It's too early to put up her feet up for the night. She is still wearing her coat. The house seems eerily quiet. It seems to her that the walls are closing in on her. Suddenly she finds herself grabbing her bag and leaving the house. She almost sprints towards the bus stop. She waves down the bus going back to the city.

She wonders if she should get something for David. He had come looking for her. Wouldn't it be nice for them to spend Christmas together? She should have asked him if he was in another relationship as she could save herself the trouble of playing gooseberry. There wasn't much point in buying David a pair of gloves. He'd lose them on their first outing. As for a watch, he didn't have much use for one; he lived on a farm and claimed the animals told him when it was time to get up and go to bed. She tried to think what kind of thing he would like.

He liked good food, so perhaps a hamper, and he loved to read. If she remembered correctly, it was travel books that he liked best. In fact, Stephen had once made the unkind remark that he loved to read about travelling but he'd done sweet damn all of it. Marianne sighs and feels the weight of her own sadness lying heavily on her shoulders. She leaves Arnott's with her shopping and trails up to Eason's to look at the travel books. Knowing David, even if she got it wrong, he'd still be delighted with it. Why had she closed her mind to him for so long? He had come to help her when Stephen was dying and yet since then she had treated him like some distant relative instead of close family. She was so obsessed with finding Sophia and Gavin that she had forgotten about him. "Poor David," she mutters. She knows that she can be cold and unkind. She has treated both Kathleen and David dreadfully in the past.

On the journey home, the bus is crowded with

weary-looking people. She wonders what stories these people have to tell. Was there one person on the bus who had a truly blessed life and, if they had, then why were they taking the bus? All these thoughts bob to the surface and she has no one to share them with. She indulges herself in the fantasy that there is someone waiting for her when she returns to her house. She imagines a fire crackling in the grate and perhaps a casserole in the oven. Wouldn't it be lovely to walk into a house that is lived in?

"Certainly not Jim, though," she shudders, remembering their earlier confrontation.

Misty rain is falling from the night sky and onto the dark pavement as she makes her way towards her house. She opens the gate and walks up the path. She turns the key in the door. She is back home and she sighs at the hollowness of it all. Her coat is wet and her feet are cold. As she dumps her shopping on the hall floor, she checks the answering machine for messages. It doesn't disappoint her that there are none – she wasn't really expecting any. And yet – she finds herself wondering about David. Did he get home OK? He could have phoned and said, "Hi, Marianne! It's me, David. I'm just phoning to say that I got home OK." She finds herself grinning as she listens to an imaginary conversation. David didn't do things like that. It would never occur to him to phone her. He didn't know she cared. Did she care? Really care? She doesn't know what has brought all these thoughts to the surface. She loves David of course – he is family – she has known him a long, long time.

She takes off her wet shoes and plods down the hall in her socks. She throws her wet coat on a chair and switches on the kettle. After she checks the radiators to see if they are on, she rubs her hands together for warmth. "Don't worry, I'll soon warm up," she announces. The kettle starts to boil.

She dreads the thought of Christmas. All that gift-wrapped good cheer is not for her. She feels no joy and, come to think of it, not much good will towards man or God. Come the New Year, everyone would be miserable because they would have overspent and over-indulged and she would have a head-start on them.

She has a lavender bath, hoping it will thaw her out. It is like the cold has seeped right into her bones. Nighttime is always the worst. Lying there staring into the darkness thinking about your loss. Thinking how different life could be if Stephen and Liam were here with her now. She'd never have met

Carmel or her arrogant husband Alan. She'd never have experienced living in the city. Even though Stephen's work took him all over Europe, they loved their Georgian house in Kells.

It then dawns on her that she never asked David about his children. She meant to, it just slipped her mind. Of course they aren't children any more, they are adults now. When David and Sue got divorced, Sue returned to her family in Kent. At the time, David's newest venture was farming and he remained on the farm in Leitrim. He claimed he was concerned about the environment and the way the world was treating it. He started his own organic farm. Stephen was disgusted with him, saying he had wasted all those years in college studying medicine. Even though his family were against his radical move, he stuck to it and surprised everyone by making it a profitable venture. David's children, Emma and Greg, spent their summer holidays with him. How easily families can disintegrate, she thought. She has a brother living in New York. They exchange Christmas cards but she doesn't like the idea of inviting herself over to spend the festive season with him. They were never that close.

In bed, her mind drifts back to David as she lies staring into the darkness. She wonders what is his house looks like now. It's years since she has seen it.

She gets restless and goes downstairs. After making herself a mug of hot chocolate, she tries to press some digits on the phone and hopes her memory hasn't failed her. She imagines that the phone is still on the hall table. Quite unexpectedly, the phone stops ringing and a woman says, "Hello?"

"I'm not sure if I have got the right number," Marianne says. "I'm looking for David Taylor."

"Who will I say is calling?"

Marianne hears the grown-up voice of a little girl. "Is that Emma?"

"Yes, who is this?"

"It's Marianne."

Emma squeals with delight. "Auntie, I can't believe it! We were just talking about you, weren't we, Dad? This is so weird! This is amazing."

Marianne is lost for words.

"I'm just home for a few days and I'm going back tomorrow. I wish I could see you again. It's been ages," Emma says. "We used to have such fun when you came to visit us with Liam."

"We had, hadn't we?"

"I hope to come home for Christmas. Perhaps we could meet up then?"

"Yes, yes, that would be lovely, dear."

"Dad would love it. Wouldn't you, Dad?"

In the background Marianne can hear David whisper, "What am I agreeing to?"

"Dad has told me that you're living in Dublin now."

"Yes, I needed a change."

"Did you sell your house in Kells?"

"Ah . . . no. It's empty at the moment."

"That is such a shame. It's a beautiful house. Remember the time you let me dress up like a princess, and I spent the whole day just walking up and down the stairs in one of your evening dress-es."

"Yes, I remember – the boys weren't impressed."

"We're both such romantics. I'll pass you on to Dad – he's making these very funny faces at me."

"Marianne, sorry about that – Emma gets carried away."

"That's OK. I forgot to ask about Emma and Greg when you came to visit."

"They're fine, but the sooner this girl learns some domestic duties the better," David says and chuck-les. "I'm not sure what she was saying on the phone but you're welcome to spend Christmas with us."

"I'd love to."

"Great. It will be nice to have some adult

142

company for a change."

Marianne hears a thud.

"I've just been hit with a cushion," David laughs. "So I'd better stop teasing. Why don't you take the train? Come anytime. Just phone me before you come and I'll collect you from the station."

"Thanks, David."

"We'll be really disappointed if you don't come," he says and then they say their goodbyes and hang up.

Chapter 15

"Gawd, Soffiaah, could we have a bit more order here? The bread-bin is empty again. I have things to do. I cannot spend my time continuously shopping for our breakfast. Give me a hand here!"

"Sorry, Ben, I'm just dressing. And would you stop calling my name like you're Pavarotti. My name is *Sophia*, not *SOFFIAAAH!*"

" Pavarotti? What do you mean? Tell me later – I can't wait now. I'll get something to eat on my way. Can we agree who's doing dinner this evening?"

"I'll do it. Talk later!"

Later, driving to college, Sophia suddenly pulls up and stops the car. *Our* breakfast. This was not meant to happen, she hadn't intended on getting tangled up with Ben. She still pays the rent of her apartment and most of her things are still there. Her fears surface again, and she drives on quickly to work.

Ben is leaning against the door jamb as he talks into the phone. She is sitting at the kitchen table, a cup of coffee cradled between her hands. Ben plays a pivotal role in his company. Listening to him on the phone issuing commands reminds her of her old self.

"That was Jason, in our Chicago office. They're just out of bed over there. I'll need to talk to Jason at his next review. Covering his ass from across the sea is a real ball-breaker. What are we eating?"

"Coming up," Sophia announces, bringing large bowls of spaghetti bolognese and garlic bread to the table. "Does the cook set the table as well?"

Ben looks silently at the food on the table. "We could go shopping once a week and buy some basic supplies," he suggests.

Sophia finds herself frowning at the thought. She hasn't considered doing things with Ben, doing the ordinary things like she used to with Matt. This is a different arrangement; she doesn't want it to remind her of her past. She just wants it to exist on a temporary sort of plane. With no fixed settings, no definite arrangements, just drifting along.

After the meal, she goes and sits in the living-room, with its wonderful view of the sea through the patio window. She curls her legs under her and stares out the window. Rain is beating against the pane, hitting off it and sliding down. Those simple notes come back again, slipping easily into her mind. In the local music shop, she has flicked through their selection but to no avail. It is teasing her now, like an unsolved puzzle, and she won't rest until she hears it properly. Walking to the patio window, she can see the Atlantic in the distance The notes surface again effortlessly. Each note is linked to another, until it becomes an exquisite strand of sound that she finds soothing. She could phone Christina and ask her – her mobile is in her bag.

She starts to rehearse what she'll say to her: 'Hi, Christina, it's me, Sophia.' She pauses and feels a tiny shudder run down her spine. Not a good idea. She knows Christina; she knows how she will react. She's not prepared to endure an ear-bashing for the way she has treated Matt. She has only made one phone call home to her mother, a brief exchange of pleasantries, nothing more. She is ashamed of her-self, ashamed that she could treat Matt and her own mother so badly.

"I love it here," she says to Ben as he comes to stand behind her.

He wraps his arms around her. "Good," he drawls in a self-satisfied way.

She can tell that he is preoccupied with other problems. She is just a plaything to him, someone to amuse him. Right now she can cope with it, she doesn't want anything from him. Being here in this renovated schoolhouse feels good to her. Ben is going back to Chicago for Christmas. She isn't looking forward to going home to Dublin. Too many problems to face.

Miraculously the rain has stopped. "We should go for a walk," she says.

Ben doesn't reply; he is wearing that concentrated expression that means 'do not disturb'.

"You look worried," she remarks.

"I'm missing my kids," he confesses.

"You'll see them soon."

Ben frowns. "That's the problem. I've been thinking about that." He pulls her closer to him. "I don't want to go home – I want to stay here with you."

Sophia is taken aback, yet she's pleased that he's putting her first. "Oh, Ben! You have to go home! Your boys will be so disappointed if you don't. I really don't want to be a home-breaker."

She sees the faint glimmer of something more in his grey eyes.

"Soffiaah!"

She hears the intensity in his voice that pulls it down, rids it of accent and makes it soft, almost desperate, yet tinged with a gentleness that she has never heard before. She feels a slight trembling in the pit of her stomach.

"I think I'm falling in love with you," he says.

She hears the self-mockery in his voice.

"Ben, you've got a family." She hears the resistance that is in hers. "This is . . ." She pauses, lost for words. She hasn't the courage to be honest and say: 'I don't love you. I'm not going to fall in love with you. This is only temporary.'

Ben plants a kiss on her lips. "Don't," he whispers. "Don't say anything."

Sophia smiles at him, relieved that for now they can go on as they are.

They walk hand in hand towards Strandhill. As they approach the ocean, they can hear it hissing with all its power and might. She imagines it to be a great symphony of passion. It is too beautiful to interrupt it with idle chatter.

A few brave surfers are gliding over the waves

with an ease that is enviable. A chilly breeze sweeps in from the Atlantic. As Sophia and Ben walk along the beach, the tide rolls in. Then it rolls back out again, washing their footprints away and leaving clumps of seaweed on the wet sand.

"I love it here too," Ben says breaking into her thoughts.

"Look over there, Ben," she says, pointing at a group of horse-riders ambling along the beach. "I think they come from the stables up the road. We should book in for a ride before the weather gets too bad."

"Yeah, OK," frowns Ben, eyeing the spirited horses somewhat nervously.

Chapter 16

Marianne takes up a discreet position near Gavin's house. She never approved of Gavin as a friend for Liam; she considered him to be a bad influence. Now he is married to Jill and they have two children. It's a sleepy Saturday morning and not much is happening.

Marianne likes to come and sit outside Gavin's house and watch. She is always very careful not to stay too long in case people become suspicious of her. She never immerses herself in thinking why she does this; reality is postponed. Usually, Gavin takes his children into town or to the swimming-pool. On one occasion, Marianne had unthinkingly followed him to Kells, where his parents lived. She had beaten a hasty retreat on that occasion when she woke up to the fact she was in the familiar neighbourhood.

Gavin hasn't changed so much. The tailored suits, the new car, struggle to give him an air of respectability.

"Give it a rest, Mum," she suddenly hears Liam say.

And she hears herself reply. "Liam, will you listen to me. Gavin Daly is no good. He is trouble and he makes trouble for everyone else. What is your father going to say when he finds out that you're still mixing with him?"

"Mum, I'm going to hang up now. Don't do this 'father' thing to me. Talk to you soon."

Liam had often told Marianne she was a nag. If she had only detached more, she thinks, perhaps he would have introduced them to Sophia. . He had told his parents that they wouldn't approve of her. What had he ever done that they had given their blessing to? Marianne was only trying to protect her precious son. Liam had become a stranger. She suspected that he was doing drugs when she discovered money had gone missing from her purse. Of course, he would never admit to it. What had happened to the little boy that used to ask was he allowed to go out to go to the shop? Had she been too strict? Had she not been strict enough? If they had a second child, perhaps Liam wouldn't have felt so burdened. How differently Marianne would have led her life if she knew the consequences of her decisions! For one thing, she wouldn't have tolerated Stephen being so strict on Liam. They never bonded, not like David had with his children. She remembers how she had never liked it when people remarked the similarity in personality between David and Liam. Now she feels they should have celebrated the fact that he was like David instead of playing it down like it was something to be ashamed of.

Stephen was almost ten years older than Marianne. They met when she started working in the same company as him. He had his footing well secured on a middle-management rung of the ladder. He easily climbed to the top position a few years after they were married.

They would have liked more children, but Liam's birth was difficult and the doctors advised them against having more. They didn't question it. At twenty-two, she was married with a son, and a husband who was seldom home. Marianne didn't complain; she felt she had nothing to complain about. She had a good husband and the most adorable son. Stephen had high expectations of Liam and he couldn't understand why his son couldn't fulfill them. Marianne felt torn between her son and husband. They were both stubborn and they both expected her to arbitrate between their constant feuding. Even when she did this, they remained at loggerheads, each seeking to get her back on their side. Of course, she knows now she should have taken a back seat and let them sort out their own problems but she didn't. She felt it was her *duty* to try and resolve every dispute that arose. It came to a point where she dreaded Stephen coming home, as she could predict there would be some kind of family dispute and she was generally piggy in the middle.

Stephen never learned the art of compromise and thanks to her over-indulgence, neither had Liam. It had taken her a long time to admit this. She had circled it for a long time, avoided looking into the vast wound of their lives together.

After the accident in London, Gavin came to see them. Only for him, they would never have learned the truth about what happened. He told them the awful story of Sophia's involvement in Liam's death.

Marianne finds herself thinking about her best friend Kathleen who has been such a support to her down through the years. Kathleen's own husband suffered poor health for years. Though there were times she complained and wept bitter tears, she never gave up. Marianne couldn't help but admire her courage.

At last, the front door opens and Gavin comes out. He is dressed in jeans and a track-suit jacket. He looks around him; Marianne holds the novel she is supposedly reading up to her face. He goes to his car. Marianne starts up hers, ready to follow him. His wife Jill comes out, holding their youngest. She puts the child in the baby seat in the back. The older child runs around the car. Gavin goes back into the house, appearing a few minutes later with a small coat. He chases the child around the car and then picks it up, screaming, and puts on the coat.

Stephen never did simple little things, like chase Liam around. Perhaps he did and I just can't remember, she thinks. She is determined not to let this day slide into one of her black days. In minutes, Gavin is reversing out of his drive; she is ready to follow him. There is always the possibility she will lose him; this has often happened before. She doesn't mind. There is always tomorrow or next weekend. Some people visit show houses on a Saturday, but Marianne has discovered a much better hobby.

Chapter 17

Sophia rushes to pick up her ringing mobile, as always running the flashing number through her head. It's Saturday evening and she is back in the schoolhouse. Ben will be back later.

"Hello," she says, feigning ignorance of where the call is coming from.

"Hello, Sophia, Claire here"

"Oh, right ... sorry, of course it is," she says, distractedly. *Compose yourself, Sophia!*

Sophia became friends with Claire when they met at university. It was Claire who suggested going to London to stay with her brother and earn some money to fund their second year at college. Sophia had a lot to be thankful to Claire for. And this is the sort of friend Sophia had turned out to be. She wasn't proud of herself but she just couldn't face Claire. She couldn't sit down and tell her what was going on. Talking to her would only open up old wounds. Some things were better off left in the past.

She finds herself interrupting an uncomfortable silence. "Look, Claire, I'm sorry I didn't get in contact with you but you know how it is ... things happen so fast."

"Really?"

"Claire, I just can't explain it."

"Try."

"I just had to leave Dublin, I felt the place was closing in on me."

"So you're better now?"

"I feel much better."

"I'm glad to hear it."

"So how are you?"

Claire laughs and Sophia knows that laugh of old: it's a hollow cynical laugh saved for people she has nothing but contempt for. "Have you seen Matt lately?"

"No, I haven't been back in Dublin since I left."

"Well, I'm delighted to hear you've settled in well. Look, gotta go, the noise is too much here, you know my number." The phone goes dead.

Sophia gulps down a large glass of wine she has poured for herself. Claire doesn't understand, she reasons. I'm keeping away from people who don't understand me from now on. Bolstered by alcohol, she decides to have a bath and put on something sexy for Tubular Ben. She has to keep in motion, she can't stop.

It's Sunday morning and they are having a lie-in. "Shh," she says to Ben, "listen to the ocean."

He turns smiling to her. "Sophia," he says.

Gosh, he *is* trying to please, she thinks.

There is a look of purpose on his face. They are about to make love and her mind is drifting. Mechanically, she moves with Ben, her body languid and complacent. She closes her eyes while Ben is kissing her lips, the top of her nose, her eyelids. Her mind is drifting, she can hear the chatter of children in a classroom. Ben's rhythm increases as he moves faster and faster inside her. She feels real tears slide down the side of her cheek and onto the pillow. She wonders what it was like to be taught at a school so close to the sea. Did the children stare out at the ocean and think that they were at the end of the world?

Ben stops suddenly. "Are you crying?"

"No, it's nothing, really. God, don't stop on me now."

Ben, reassured, starts moving again with urgency.

She continues to cry silently while she pictures herself walking on the beach at Strandhill. She marvels at the beauty of the place and how much pleasure it gives, without costing anything. The landscape has become familiar to Sophia since she has moved into the schoolhouse with Ben. Every morning when she opens the curtains she looks up at Knocknarea. On the summit of the hill there is supposed to be a monument to Maeve, the warrior Queen of Connacht. Perhaps next summer she will climb to the summit.

She turns to Ben, now smiling. "Sorry, I don't know what came over me."

"Mmm ... wanna do it again?"

They resume making love, with Sophia leading passionately. Tubular people cannot be fooled forever.

Later, they got dressed to go horse-riding. At the front door Ben stops and looks up at the leaden sky.

"It's raining," he says.

"It's only rain."

Sophia needs to get out, she longs for the feeling of exhaustion to sweep over her, so that she'll just crash out and have the pleasure of a full night's sleep. She leads the way towards his car, her head bent against the pelting rain.

"This is madness," Ben is shouting at her.

She laughs at him. "It makes me feel alive," she says.

"Soffiaah, you're crazy."

Later they return to the schoolhouse. Though it is Sunday he will still work this afternoon. Every day he communicates with his wife and children either through phone calls or email. His routine is predictable and orderly. The one thing that irritates Sophia about him is his habit of losing things. Usually, it is his car keys or mobile phone. Ben has, on occasions, called her Karen as he fumbled around looking in the oddest places for his car keys. "Sorry, sorry," he says in an apologetic voice. His attempts to be totally in control of his life seem futile; this she finds endearing and comforting. He too is bumbling around just like her. In two years' time Ben's contract will be up and he will be returning to the States. Sophia is aware that his wife and children will be coming to spend their summer vacation in Ireland with him. In the schoolhouse that she has fallen in love with. She isn't jealous that he has a wife and family, in fact she's pleased that he loves someone else. Her sister Christina would be horrified if she knew this. Christina is a romantic at heart and feels that it is every girl's right to get married and tie herself to a mortgage and children. Sophia envies her sister's simplistic view of the world. She reassures herself that what's right for someone else is not necessarily right for her. At least now she has peace of mind, which was something she didn't have in Dublin.

"Are you hungry?" Ben asks once they are safely inside. The wind howling wildly outside.

"Starving."

Ben's face creases up into a smile. He shakes his head in an exaggerated fashion. "We had a big breakfast."

"That was ages ago," she reminds him. "The sea air gives me an appetite."

Ben opens the locked door, which leads directly into the living-room. As they make their way in they are taking off their clothes. They mount the stairs two at a time, each trying to be first in the shower.

Ben pulls her sleeve. "Oh, no you don't!" He is shouting and laughing at the same time.

"That hurts," she says.

"Honey," he says, all serious and apologetic.

She makes a burst up the stairs, laughing all the way. "Gotcha!"

She is in the bathroom now, naked. She runs first into the shower. Ben is close behind. The hot water sprays her body.

Ben waits a moment and then gets into the shower with her.

"That's one of the things I love about you," he says. "Your sense of fun."

"OK, Granddad," she mocks. "Ever done anything naughty in a tight space?"

"Who's saying what's tight?"

"How about I treat you to lunch?" Sophia suggests as they stand staring in at the contents of the fridge.

"Sounds good. But we should have done some shopping." There is a slight edge to his voice.

"You mean *I* should have done some shopping," she replies calmly.

Ben's facial muscles twitch as he turns to look at Sophia. "I guess *we* should have done some shopping." She hears the apologetic sound in his voice and gives him a warm smile.

"Why don't you come to Dublin with me tomorrow, now that you're not working on Monday."

Sophia feels herself almost freeze at the thought of it. She doesn't want to go to Dublin; she doesn't feel capable of making that journey, not yet.

"I've got work to do."

Ben smiles, his grey eyes bright with amusement. "We could stay over." He pulls her towards him for one of his big bear-hugs. Sometimes, she wonders if she is acting as a substitute for his children. "I'll have you back in time for your lectures on Tuesday morning."

"Let's go to lunch, I'll drive," she says quickly, changing the subject.

"Is that your way of saying no??" he asks as he gets into the passenger side of her car.

She smiles to herself at his persistence. "You don't give up."

"Never."

"You are so used of getting your own way that you've forgotten how to compromise."

He reaches over and gives her a quick peck on the cheek. "So you're coming to Dublin with me?"

She has no intention of going to Dublin with him. She knows he will sulk. Wasn't that what children did when they didn't get their own way? Sophia didn't care.

Chapter 18

Marianne stares fixedly at the floor under the subdued lighting of her sitting-room. She has moved most of the furniture into the corners.

There they are, all set out on the floor. Some paid for, some stolen. Sophia, Gavin, Sophia's nieces, photos of houses, filofax . . .

Eleven forty-five. She rings Jim. She had not even argued when he added in an estimate for expenses on his assignation to Sligo. It was inflated, probably to dissuade her. Best she stick with him. Some of the seedier private dicks overlapped with the Gardai and at least Jim was honourable. She could cope with his unsolicited advice for a while longer.

"Marianne," Jim says, wearily.

"Have you got them?"

"Yes, I have, I'll be over that way in the morn –"

"Come over now."

"Could you hold on....?"

Marianne hears background music, doors opening, lavatory flushing . . .

"Marianne."

"Yes?"

"You're still there . . . and you're joking. I'm having a few drinks and you're just going to have to wait."

"Order a taxi, here and back. I'll pay you three hours on top, it won't take half that."

"Christ . . . OK, you win. But, Marianne, surely you're near the end of this project?"

"How much should I have ready for you in total?" she asks, ignoring his query.

Marianne tiptoes around the sitting-room, taking care not to disturb her neatly laid-out collection. Five after midnight. The phone rings. She fumbles to pick up the receiver to stop the shrill ringing.

"It's David," says a voice cheerily in her ear.

Damn! "David! Do you know the time?"

"No – I've been out on the farm – God, I see it now. I'm really sorry!"

"It's OK."

"I'll hang up."

"No, don't."

"OK," he says and clears his throat. "I was wondering how you're keeping?"

"I had a good day today."

There is a pause.

She runs her fingers through her tossed hair, listening for the doorbell. "Gosh, I've forgotten what I was going to say."

"Good," David says and she can hear him applaud. "That happens to me all the time and I'm glad that I'm in good company."

"Ah," she says, hitting back, "I just thought of it. What did you do today?"

"Well," he starts to say and pauses. "Well, it's winter time so it's easier for me on the farm."

"You've just told me you wrapped up after midnight. Have you thought of retiring?" she asks silkily.

"Often. There isn't much satisfaction left in farming."

"What will you do?"

She hears the heavy sigh and she wonders if he is sitting in his armchair in the kitchen beside the stove or if he's in bed? No, he'd never call from his bed, would he? She is pondering on this. No, no, definitely not. She can picture it. He's in the kitchen, his working boots off, his feet warming at the stove. A mug of tea beside him. This picture she finds less disturbing.

"There is so much I have wanted to do and I feel I have left it all a bit late."

"Like?"

"I have always wanted to travel."

"Yes, you did, didn't you? Remember when the children were small and you had that big map of the world and they were always pointing out places they wanted to visit."

"You wanted to go to Egypt and go for a cruise on the Nile," he says.

"Yes," she says, touched that he remembers. "I'd forgotten that." She hears herself laugh and realises how brittle it sounds. "And you wanted to visit South America – didn't you want to visit the Amazon?"

"Yes but I had to change it because Emma was afraid I'd get eaten by a native – she had this idea that they're all cannibals."

"You're joking – Emma is not that naïve. Where did she want to go?"

"Hollywood, of course. And our boys now – where did they want to go?"

"Oh, Liam and Greg, they wanted to be astronauts, go to the moon."

"You have such a memory," he says.

"Where are you now?"

"In my studio."

"I didn't know you had a studio."

David chuckles. "There is plenty you don't know about me."

Marianne doesn't know how to respond so she says nothing.

"Are you still there?" he asks.

"Yes," she replies.

"I took up photography as a hobby. It gets me away from this place one evening a week."

"I didn't know you were interested in photography."

"Ah, I'm not much good, I just enjoy it. I'm not much into standing back and analyzing it. Some days I look around me and I find things in the landscape or in town that I just want to capture. Some days, I see the way the sun comes down on the land, the way it is swathed in light and shade. Sometimes, I look at a tree and I see it just lazing there and I think to myself 'I'd love to capture that'." He stops mid-flow. "I'm waffling on."

"No, it's really lovely to talk to you. I'd

forgotten ..." She stops herself in mid-sentence, unsure of what to say next.

"Well," he says and pauses. "Emma is coming home from London for Christmas. It really pleases me that Emma and Greg still call this place home."

Marianne hears the pride in his voice.

"You were always a good father," she says. She realises that Stephen and herself accomplished very little for all their years of safe investments and guaranteed returns. In life nothing that really matters is guaranteed.

"She's always welcome to stay with me if she wants. I can even meet her at the airport," Marianne says, regretting it immediately

"She'd love that. I'll call her and tell her," David is saying with gratitude in his voice.

"Great."

There is a slight pause and then he says, "I had a really nice time with you in Dublin."

"Yes, it *was* nice." A car is pulling up outside, lights flashing. She almost trips across her collection on the floor, going to the curtains. There is nothing else for it: she will have to be abrupt. "David, I'd better go."

"So will you come for Christmas?" he asks.

"Yes, I will. I'd really like that. Bye!"

Twenty-five past midnight. Marianne opens her door as Jim walks through the gate.

"Problems with sleeping?" he asks, unsympathetically. He is bleary-eyed, but coherent, nonetheless. The taxi waits, lights flashing.

He passes over a small package. Marianne hands over her envelope.

"I'll call you."

"Don't I know it?"

Marianne goes back to her sitting-room, and begins to set out the new contents carefully on the floor. She cuts up some surplus photos methodically with a sharp scissors.

Sitting in the dim light, she finds herself wondering what kind of photographs David takes. It would be nice to see them. Knowing that David is quite shy, she feels that he will never show the photographs to her. She closes her eyes and tries to imagine what it would be like to take a trip up the Nile. She can see herself wearing a broad-brimmed straw hat, sunglasses and a cream shift dress. By her side she can see David, a large camera around his neck. He is smiling at her.

Six forty-five. Marianne gets up from her chair. Making a coffee for herself, she goes back to the floor for a further assessment.

Eventually, she goes to the phone. She dials. The phone rings.

"Yes," a voice says sleepily."

"Carmel?"

"Marianne, it's early – half-eight. Is something up?"

"No, no, how thoughtless of me. I'm such an early bird, I never thought that you might be different."

"I'm not actually. It's just the surprise."

"In a way, that's what I'm ringing about. Do you remember I promised to treat you to dinner in that new restaurant?"

"Yes. I remember. "

"I'm booking the table today, so tell me, what evening are you free?"

Chapter 19

Sophia is always exhausted after her day in college. Today they were in the chemical laboratory, attempting to find out the concentration of an unknown protein in a sample.

"This is what it's like in the real world," she told them. "Sometimes, experiments don't work out."

She enjoys working with the students.

"Gwen," she pauses beside a pretty, dark-haired girl, "two of your assignments are overdue. Have you any idea of when I might see them?"

Gwen is a tall girl, of athletic build. She is giggling nervously. Her name crops up whenever the student party circuit is spoken of. Everyone wants Gwen at their parties.

"I'll work on them over the weekend." Gwen

responds, shiftily.

"I want them next week, Gwen. You won't move forward to the next stage without them."

More giggles from Gwen.

Sophia stiffens but moves on. There is something familiar there, but it is not something she wants to confront. Stick to the teaching, she mouths silently to herself.

Back in her own apartment, Sophia stretches out on her sofa, her eyes closed. Her mobile rings and she picks it up, expecting it to be Ben, calling all apologetic. She hasn't seen him all week as he took her refusal to accompany him to Dublin badly. Too late, she recognizes the Dublin number as her mother.

"Hello, pet."

"Hi, Mammy." She hears how unnatural her own voice sounds. She is cringing inwardly with shame that she doesn't want to speak to her mother.

"How are you? I haven't heard from you in a while so I decided to call you." Nature hates a vacuum and so does Carmel. She laughs nervously and then rushes on. "I was just wondering how you're getting on? Are you settling in all right? What's the college like? Are you eating –"

"Mammy," Sophia breaks in to say, "I'm fine. Really, I'm fine. I've just been so busy. I really did mean to call you but, you know . . ." she lets the words fade out. "I'm really sorry . . ."

"Oh, that's all right, dear. I understand."

"How's Christina?"

"Oh, fussing over me in her usual way," replies Carmel, with false indignation. "Listen, a new friend of mine has just come back from a weekend break in the west. Says she loved it. I was thinking of venturing down that way for a day, maybe a night . . ."

"Oh, yeah, I never thought of asking you. Silly of me. I always thought you liked keeping close to home, and you've got Sarah and Amy to take care of while Christina is giving her music classes."

"They can manage for a few days without me. In fact it was Christina who suggested it. My nest will be still standing when I get back. I feel much stronger now . . ."

"Yeah, but listen, I'm sharing with someone right now, who's looking for her own place. You couldn't swing a cat here but decent accommodation is hard to find. Hopefully she'll have got her own place by the end of the month. You could come then. Would that suit?"

"Well, yes, I could wait until then. Have you talked to your nieces lately?"

Sophia feels her cheeks burning with shame. So many lies. She sits on the sofa, staring at the wall opposite. Her mother was very persistent, even saying that she heard that there was a Radisson Hotel near Sligo. Jesus, what if she ran into Tubular Ben, who takes his infidelity as routine? *'Soffiaah, are you not going to introduce me to your mum?'* Right now she needs a distraction. She had rarely heard her mother so forceful and positive.

She needs to settle down, maybe watch a good movie but there is no TV. Anyway, movies were Matt's department. He was the one who always could judge a good movie. Mammy, Christina, Claire. She could picture them all descending on her. Maybe even Matt! She left Dublin under a cloud, and she has added Tubular Ben to her secrets. Imagine telling Mammy someone had moved in with her, when the opposite was true! Well, at least until Ben got the hump at her refusal to go to Dublin with him. Sophia paces restlessly around her tiny floor space. She counts her footsteps. One, two, three, four, five, six, then back again. She feels caged in. Suddenly the place is claustrophobic; she feels the walls are closing in on her. It is Friday night. Most people were going out or crashing on their sofa ready to wind down for the weekend and here she is on her own in a small rainy town with no friends.

She peers through the blinds; the street lighting casts an orange glow on the gloomy street below. She leans her forehead against the window. "What will I do now?" She smiles to herself as she thinks of Ben. She allows the thought to settle in. She picks up her phone and calls him. Sitting down on the floor, she listens to the ringing tone. She doesn't consider whether this is right or wrong. She really doesn't care. This is no time to start debating the issue. She needs serious distraction and right now.

She listens to his mobile ring out. "Damn!" He wasn't going to answer it. Any minute now she would have to leave a message and she doesn't know what to say. She is starting to panic when he answers.

"Soffiaah," he drawls, his voice syrupy sweet, yet neutral, "nice to hear from you." He pauses, giving her an opening.

Nice one, Sophia thinks privately, and says, "Hi, Ben. What are you up to tonight?"

"Not much."

"I see. Are you at home?"

She hears the satisfied gurgle of laughter. "I'm here," a slight pause and then he adds, "in the schoolhouse."

"I see. I was wondering – fancy coming into town?"

"Sure," he drawls. "I'm just going to check my e-mails and then I'll get changed. Be with you in an hour."

"Great," Sophia says.

She throws the mobile on the sofa and feels herself deflate. It is like she has overdosed on chocolate. She knows he's bad for her but she's looking for a quick fix. Ah, Tubular Ben! He may proclaim his love, but what experience! Dublin seems forgotten. Why should he stir it up with her when there's an unspoken promise that she will be down on him in a short while? A thought crosses her mind. What does Mary Leahy, Head of School of Science, do on a Friday night? Sophia guesses she is probably reading some science journal and getting excited about some amazing discovery. Sophia knows that she is being unkind. Mary is a good person.

Later, Ben arrives wearing a Gant jacket and jeans.

"Nice oufit, and American too," she says. She is

slipping into a role that she has developed for him. He likes to be complimented, he likes a serious amount of attention. His wife must be having the time of her life not having to continually massage his ego.

From her minimalist wardrobe, she has taken her skimpiest black top and put it over black tailored trousers.

Ben glides into the living-room. His look is lecherous, full of lustful intent.

She stands a little distance away from him and gives him a bright smile. "So," she says and finds a nervous tension running down her spine, "what would you like to do?"

"Oh," he says as he shrugs his large shoulders, "I don't mind." He moves closer to her.

"Sorry about the other day," she says, immediately regretting that she is apologising to him.

"I'm sorry too. You're right — I am used to getting my own way."

His chin is just level with the top of her head.

"So, would you like to go out for something to eat?" he asks, a slight hint of amusement in his voice.

"You haven't eaten?"

Ben moves a little away from her. "I asked you a question, no?"

Sophia smiles at him, relieved that he is here, filling up the empty space in her living-room.

"We could get a takeaway," he suggests.

"No, I'd rather cook or something – I just don't fancy having a take-away."

"Ah," Ben says his face brightening with comprehension, "that's what you used to do with your last lover – order takeaways."

"Something like that," she admits. She feels she is dangling, waiting for the puppet master to pull her strings again.

"Let's go out then," Ben says.

Sophia smiles and picks up her coat.

At the door Ben hesitates. "Are we coming back here?"

Sophia looks around her characterless living-room. You could read nothing about the person that lives here – no photographs, no souvenir from holidays, nothing for the dead cells of her body to rest on.

"How is it out at the schoolhouse?" she says coyly.

Ben smirks. "Do you want to pack some things?"

Sophia turns around and sprints into her bedroom. "I'll just be a minute," she says as she hastily throws some clothes in her hold-all.

Chapter 20

Sophia is lying on the sofa in Ben's schoolhouse when she receives the call from her sister. Rain hurtles against the windowpane as if it is trying to break in.

Christina wants to confirm her visit.

"That's great," Sophia replies with faked enthusiasm.

"Since you're not coming to Dublin for Christmas, I'll go and see you and bring all your presents."

Ben has just arrived in the door; it is late, almost nine o'clock. He looks exhausted.

"Are you going to drive or take the train?" Sophia asks while she waves her greeting to Ben.

"I'm going to take the train."

"I'll collect you from the station."

She wants to crawl into a ball and hide. An echo of some past memory that she has tried long and hard to suppress over the years comes flooding back. She doesn't want to meet her sister tomorrow.

Ben is in the kitchen opening up their takeaway. Sophia tells him, as she picks at some chips, that her sister is coming to visit.

"I'm working tomorrow," he says, in a don't-involve-me-in-your-domestics sort of way.

"I'd better go back to my place tonight," she hits back, knowing this will upset his nighttime schedule.

Ben gives her a pleading look.

"OK, first thing tomorrow morning I'm out of here," she hears herself say.

"Likewise," he replies. "Now, let's eat."

Sophia doesn't sleep well; she keeps dreaming of Matt, seeing the hurt expression on his face. Tony and Matt are good friends, so she can only assume that he has spoken to Matt. Christina will have a first-hand account of how he is. Of course, she is curious. She does want to know.

But how can she explain to her sister that, while she was living in Dublin, she genuinely thought someone was out to kill her? The idea is outrageous, beyond belief. No wonder Matt was skeptical. That is why she kept it to herself, concealed the torment. She had no proof, no concrete facts, so the best thing she could do to save her sanity was to leave Dublin.

Christina disembarks at the train station. She looks around in exaspertaion.

"Gotcha," says a voice, tapping her from behind.

"Sophia, God, look at you," she says, grasping her sister tightly.

"Look at yourself, mother-of-two. How are they?"

Christina stiffens in her embrace, but an angry retort is suppressed, for now. "They're great. Mammy is minding them today."

"Look, there's a nice coffee shop up the road and we could –"

"Could we go to where you live instead, Sophia? I'd like to see it."

Sophia finds herself panicking. Her mother. The non-existent flat-mate. And a lot of her belongings are out at Ben's place. "OK. Let's do that. Have you been talking to Matt lately?" she suddenly blurts out. Well, might as well get it over with.

"Of course I've been talking to Matt. I told you

that last time. He's devastated and confused. Almost wants to come and see your new boyfriend for himself – he just can't believe it."

Immediately, Sophia decides to take her out to Ben's schoolhouse. She'll deal with the awkward questions as she goes along. The presence of Ben, confirmed by Christina, might dissuade Matt from coming. It's the lesser of two evils, she says silently to herself.

"This is nice," Christina says as Sophia opens the front door of the schoolhouse.

"Wait until you see the living-room – it's magnificent."

"Wow," Christina says, dropping her gift-wrapped presents on the cream sofa and walking towards the patio door. "Look at the view!" She turns and looks around her. "You've so much space here!"

Sophia takes off her jacket and goes into the kitchen to switch on the kettle. "Tea or coffee?" she calls.

"Coffee," Christina replies in an unfamiliar flat voice.

Sophia returns to the living-room to see Christina holding a photograph of Ben with his two sons.

"Who's this?" she asks, holding the photograph up to Sophia.

"Ben. This is his place."

Christina's mouth drops open. "I – I don't believe it." She shakes her head incredulously. "So you weren't lying to Matt! There *is* someone else! When did this all start?"

Sophia can't meet her sister's astonished look. "For heaven's sake," she waves a dismissive hand, "it's not serious. Basically, we're just – friends."

Christina laughs cynically and puts the photograph back on the mantelpiece. She turns her back on Sophia and stares out the patio window at the grey drizzle.

Sophia makes her way across the maple floor and hands her sister a mug of coffee. Fragments of a memory were piecing themselves together, it was there if she could just grasp it but she doesn't want to. She's severed her ties and for the moment that includes her family.

She feels she's made the right choice in bringing Christina here. It shows everyone, including herself, that she has no intention of returning home to Dublin.

Christina turns back from the patio door, a look of determination on her face.

"Sophia, this is crap, all crap. I can see now why you told Mammy about a flat-mate and the tiny apartment that you couldn't swing a cat in. Friends! Lies! All fucking lies!"

"No, it's true about the flat – I have a flat in town, you can see it if you want."

"Sophia, you are fucking a middle-aged man who has a wife and two children somewhere. All those lies about Daddy and your fears, and it's all because you sat on some middle-aged fucker's dick at a sales meeting! I should have known – all the scrapes we had to dig you out of before you met Matt! But I really thought you two were going to get married – and the funny thing is, he thought the same. And all along you were just using him. How could you?"

Sophia stands rigidly, gritting her teeth silently, half-expecting Christina to strike her. The two girls glare at each other and something about the haunted expression on Sophia's face tells Christina that everything isn't as it appears. "Sophia, what has happened to you?" she asks, the words tinged with panic.

"I …" Sophia moves away from the window and then sits down on the sofa. "I honestly don't know. I just know I like spending time here with Ben, right now. It's not permanent."

"Ah, so he has a name! Ben, Big Ben – what is it that he's got – the Tower of London in his pants? Matt, poor Matt!" She sits beside Sophia on the sofa and suddenly exclaims, "I'm getting you out of here, Sophia, now."

Sophia shakes her head. "No, you're not," she says, finding strength from somewhere. "I'm staying in Sligo. Ben is not the only reason why I'm here. Look – we'll talk about it later. Now, let's change the subject. Tell me how everyone is."

Christina quietly assesses the situation and then starts to talk. "Well, Mammy is just kinda sad at the moment. She's missing you and she's worried about you."

There is a slight pause. Sophia looks at her sister, bracing herself for the response to the next question. "And Matt?" she asks.

"Matt," Christina says and shakes her head in bewilderment, "he's heartbroken. I told you! Are you not even listening to me?"

Sophia covers her face with her hands. "I've caused so much pain."

"I told you – Matt came to see me, he doesn't understand it. Nor do I – that's why I had to come to see you. I had to come and tell you in person that you …" She takes a breath. "He loves you. He really does and you should come back to Dublin, fix this up between you. Don't leave it until it is too late." She sits back, red-faced with exasperation.

"It's already too late, Christina."

"Why? Why is it too late?" Christina takes her sister's hand in hers. She is waiting for an explanation; the minutes grow and nothing is said. In the distance, they can hear the quiet rush of the ocean as if it is hurrying off someplace else, somewhere more exciting.

"Can't you just try and explain it to me, please?" Christina says.

"I can't." Sophia shakes her head. "Things happened in my past that I never talked about to you or anyone and … lately things have happened and it's like my past is catching up with me."

Christina pats her sister's hand. She laughs but there are tears in her eyes. "I know what is wrong with you – you're scared of committing to Matt. You think every man is just like Dad, but that's not true. Matt is a wonderful man."

"I know." Sophia leans forward. She is glad her sister has missed the point.

Christina pauses for a moment before she gently makes her next suggestion. "Mammy is having a party on New Year's Eve. You are coming, aren't you?"

Sophia's nods and agrees that she will definitely be there.

"Sarah and Amy miss you. They keep asking when is Auntie Sophia coming to visit?"

"Christina, I just need some time to myself."

"Fine," she says and pulls her hand away. "You're impossible." She gets up and paces to and fro. She pauses at the patio window and stares out at the distant Atlantic. Sophia takes their unfinished coffee into the kitchen. "There is a really nice restaurant we could go to for lunch. It's a bit of a drive – would you be up to it?"

"Sure," Christina says.

For a while they engage in small talk about Christmas. What life-savers superficial topics like Christmas and the weather are, Sophia muses. "Sarah has written a card for Santy. Isn't that sweet?"

"Ah, that's so cute! I miss seeing her. You should have brought her with you."

Christina pulls a smile across her face. "It's such a long journey and I thought it would be nice for us to have some time on our own."

Sophia nods but doesn't reply.

Christina speaks again after a while. "Mammy is making such an effort for Christmas. She's trying to pretend everything is OK. It's going to be her first Christmas without you and Dad."

Sophia can't restrain herself. "Christina, I am thirty years old. I'm not a child. I can't go home just to please my mother – I have a life of my own, now. Things are just ... different. I just can't do it."

Christina sits rigidly in the passenger seat, her face turned to look out at the passing landscape.

The miles go by and then she says very gently, "You can't keep blaming yourself for Daddy's accident. No one blames you, Sophia, – not Mammy, not me, no one. If Daddy is up there looking down on us, I'm sure he isn't blaming blame you either."

Sophia bites her lip as tears start her eyes. "I'm sorry. I just can't go home right now. Please try and understand. Can we drop it now?"

Christina nods, grudgingly.

They have stopped at a crossroads. Sophia is looking all around. "I think I've taken the wrong turn. We're lost."

Christina laughs. "You mean I'm going to be trapped in this car for hours with you? Where exactly are we going?"

"To a little pub. I could have sworn it was

down this road . . ."

Sophia drives on and eventually they come to a tiny village with a church, a pub and a post office. After taking directions from a woman in the Post Office, they head off again.

"I mustn't miss my train," Christina reminds her as they drive slowly down a winding road.

"I know but we're nearly there," Sophia says with bogus confidence.

"Good. I'm starving."

Ben is on the phone talking to his children. He is having a pretty hard time explaining to them that he won't be home for Christmas. He is fabricating a story. "The project has gone pear-shaped," he says.

Sophia wonders, if she were the other end of that phone call, would she believe him? How would she feel if she knew her husband was cheating on her? She stands in the kitchen doorway. Ben is standing at the patio window, his back to her. His shoulders are slumped – the weight of guilt had to rest some-where. He is giving details, embellishing it with pointless politics that they are not interested in but which he feels will add to his case.

As soon as he is finished with his call, Sophia will call her mother. The Christmas-tree lights are reflected in the patio window. They are winking at her. "Happy now?" they seem to be saying. Ben insisted that they get a tree. "Come on," he said, "where is your festive spirit?" The taut line of his jaw swayed her against telling him that she hadn't got a festive spirit.

Ben and Sophia are making a lot of people unhappy for Christmas. She doesn't have to try too hard to imagine the disappointment that will be etched on her mother's face when she knows for certain that she is not going home. Tubular Ben sees nothing wrong with what they are doing. Under the Christmas tree are their gift-wrapped presents. I'm a coward, she admits to herself. Her mind is drifting back to other Christmases in the apartment with Matt. That feeling comes back to her, that eerie feeling that someone is stalking her. She feels a slight shudder run up her spine. Over the years she has become accomplished at blocking out unpleasant memories. So she turns her attention to something else.

That morning while she was driving into college she listened to a man on the radio telling his story. The year before he had spent Christmas Day sitting on a bench staring out to sea. He'd lost everything because of his drug addiction but this year he had his own place and he had made some new friends. His life was starting over. It brought tears to her eyes listening to him. There was a thread of despair and desperation running through his story that she could identify with. But she could not see the hope.

"I feel terrible," Ben says coming to sit by her side. He has finished his phone call. Now, he is looking for absolution for his sins or, at the very least, some comfort.

"You're lucky that they care enough to be mad at you."

He lies down on the sofa and rests his head on her lap. "Ain't that the truth?"

She runs her fingers through his hair, just the way he likes it and says, "You should have gone home."

"I just couldn't bear the thought of leaving you."

"Oh, Ben, I'd be here when you came back."

He turns to look at the Christmas tree. "Do you like it?" he asks.

"It's beautiful," she replies, knowing this is what he needs to hear as he has spent the past few hours decorating it.

"I wish my boys could see it," he says with pride.

"Yes," Sophia says vaguely. She kisses his forehead. "I have to ring my mother now."

"Oh, dear," he says and sits up. "I'll start dinner." He glances at his watch. "You have thirty-five minutes and no more."

Sophia laughs. "It won't take that long to talk to her."

"I know when Karen –" He stops himself and shakes his head. "Never mind."

She watches him walk into the kitchen, his shoulders still slumped, burdened with the weight of his decision.

Chapter 21

It is the day before Christmas Eve and Marianne is convinced that someone up above is helping her. Carmel loves to go out for meals, needing a sympathetic ear and occasional words of encouragement when she is moaning about her daughter or grieving about her late husband. But it has been disappointing that Carmel seems to know so little about her daughter's activities. Nevertheless, Marianne never gave up hope. And, now she is going to spend the night in Sophia's bedroom. She was tempted to phone Jim and tell him, let him know that she didn't need him to do all the dirty work. But she didn't. She is mindful that she has yet to get into Sophia's bedroom and, perhaps, all memory of her precious son might have been dumped in the bin years ago.

They are sitting in the restaurant, both of them wearing new outfits for the occasion.

"I'm so worried about Sophia. She never phones me nor comes to visit. She's cutting herself off from us."

Carmel is drinking really fast, her face is flushed and it is very clear that she is really upset. She has the perfect companion in Marianne who loves hearing about Sophia and isn't the least bit bored by the conversation.

"What was she like as a little girl?" Marianne asks, once Carmel has finished telling her the full story of the phone call.

Carmel's small eyes light up, she smiles her first smile of the evening. "Oh," she says with a heavy dollop of melancholy in her voice, "she was so adventurous, so demanding and strong-willed."

"I see."

Carmel is in nostalgic mood now. "It all goes by so quickly."

Marianne nods in agreement.

"I think motherhood is the hardest job in the world," Carmel says and looks down at her untouched starter of Caesar salad. "Children, they can hurt you so much and all you're trying to do is love them. I feel I have failed her. I feel I have done something wrong in the way I brought her up."

Marianne smiles beatifically. "But you brought her up the same way as you brought Christina up and look at her – she's a credit to you."

Carmel leans back and basks in her moment of glory. "Yes, Christina was a very different child," she says with authority. "She was never difficult, she was always so complacent, so agreeable but the funny thing is I have always loved Sophia that little bit more. Isn't that strange?"

"You're a mother. You saw in her something that needed more loving, I guess."

"I suppose you're right," she sighs. She looks around the plush restaurant. "This is lovely. You really didn't have to bring me here."

Marianne smiles and raises her wineglass. "That's what friends are for."

"So tell me more about these friends in Leitrim that you're going to see." Carmel starts to nibble at her food.

"There is nothing really to tell – they're just nice people and I'm very fond of them."

"I imagine it can be quite lonely going back to an empty house all the time."

Marianne doesn't respond. Instead she sips some wine.

"We always have a New Year's Eve party at our house," Carmel goes on. "You're more than welcome to come along."

"Are you sure?"

"Of course I'm sure. You haven't met Sophia, she'll be there. I wasn't going to have it so close to Alan's funeral but he'd have wanted it. He loved a good party, so I decided to go ahead with it."

A waiter interrupts to ask if everything is all right. They nod and he scurries away.

"I think Sophia has lost all interest in me," Carmel says as they wait for their main course to arrive. They'd both ordered duck.

"Oh, Carmel, stop that. It's all the wine you've had."

Carmel's eyes have filled up with tears. "Sometimes, children can say really hurtful things but they also can be true – if you care to listen to them. Sophia always complained about her father spending so much time away from us. When she was a teenager, she used to tell me that we'd be better off without him and we didn't need him. Every word she said was true but I hadn't the courage to put him out. And now, she's taken it into her head that she's to blame for his death. Did you ever hear anything so ridiculous?"

Eventually the waiter arrives with their duck. They stop talking until all the accompaniments are put on their plates. They exchange a look. The duck doesn't look very appetizing.

"I thought it would never arrive," Marianne says, picking up her knife and fork.

Carmel turns up her nose at the duck. "Christina went down to visit her in Sligo but she didn't say much about the trip when she returned. I wasn't even invited and when I did invite myself she told me I couldn't stay with her, that her apartment is tiny and she's sharing with another girl at the moment. I'd love to go down there and give her a good dressing down."

They tuck in.

"Mmm, tastes better than it looks – though it's a little overdone," Carmel says as she chews the meat slowly.

"It's not worth complaining about," Marianne says as they look around the overcrowded restaurant.

Carmel leans across the table and whispers. "We can have dessert back at my house."

Marianne nods agreeably.

Carmel has left a nightdress and dressing-gown on the single bed for Marianne. The bedroom is painted in blue with a dolphin bedspread. She has put a Christmas arrangement of artificial silver-painted cones and holly in the window, and a large blue candle swathed in blue tinsel on the bedside table. Quietly, Marianne begins to search. She is good at it now, professional. She opens the top drawer of the chest of drawers, lifts out the T-shirts, checks that there are no hidden treasures between their folds and returns them to the empty drawer. She does the same with the rest of the drawers. Then, she tiptoes across the carpeted floor to the wardrobe and opens the doors. Dark clothes hang from the hangers. Shoes and runners are stacked neatly at the bottom of the wardrobe. Just as she is about to begin to search through the clothes, she notices an old shoebox behind the shoes. She lifts it out, then kneels down and opens it. Inside are birthday and Christmas cards, some old letters and photographs. Marianne's hands are clammy with sweat as she pulls out the letters.

It's her son's handwriting. He wrote to Sophia.

At the bottom of the shoebox is a small photo album. Her hands are shaking as she takes it out. Her heart is beating fast, drumming in her ears. The wine is making her head feel fuzzy. Her eyes fill up with tears as she opens the photo album. On the inside cover is written: *To Sophia from your best friend*

Claire. Roughly, she wipes her tears away and there looking out at her is her son Liam. She feels her heart is going to burst. These are the last photographs of her son! Gavin had given her a few that were taken in a pub in London but they weren't very good. These are wonderful. She gasps for air and staggers backwards towards the bed. She attempts to sit on the bed but misses. She hits the floor with a very loud thud.

"Are you OK?" Carmel is calling.

"Yes! I'm fine!" Marianne pushes the shoebox under the bed and scrambles shakily to her feet as Carmel knocks and enters. "I was just going to hang my clothes and ..." Carmel is standing beside her now, helping her to sit on the bed, "I must have lost my balance."

Carmel laughs. "You're drunk!"

"Oh, no I'm not," Marianne says defensively.

Carmel laughs. "Go on, admit it, Marianne, you're drunk!"

Marianne gives a conciliatory nod. "Yes, I suppose I am."

"I'll get you a glass of water."

"Thanks," she says and grips the side of the bed with her hands.

Later, Marianne lies on Sophia's bed and stares at the ceiling. Under her pillow are pictures of her son and letters that he had written to Sophia. Marianne can't wait to leave this house and return to her own. She yearns for time and privacy to study these precious finds. Somehow, she cannot do it here, in this room.

And she must choose what items are needed for her trip to Sligo.

"Marianne, are you asleep?"

"Yeah – well, I was, sort of. I'm just getting up."

Marianne is sitting on the edge of the bed, the items removed from the shoebox safely transferred to her handbag. She has kept out a photograph of Liam and Sophia.

He is frozen in time, Sophia is moving on. She stifles her fury. Downstairs, she hears Carmel moving around. It's ten past ten. A new energy drives her. She cannot wait to get home and read the letters. She knows they are private but at the same time she has to read them. "Forgive me, Liam," she prays silently as she gets dressed.

"Good morning," Carmel says when she enters the kitchen. "How did you sleep?"

"Fine, thanks. In fact I overslept, I never sleep

in this late."

"I really enjoyed last night," Carmel says. "I'm putting on a fry for you."

"Oh, please don't. I couldn't face it this morning. A cup of black tea and some toast would be fine."

"Are you sure?"

"Yes, positive," Marianne says. "So, are you all set for Christmas?"

"Yes, though I'm really not looking forward to it. It's g-going to be h-hard..." she stumbles over the words, yet she keeps on going. "I miss Alan, the house is just so empty without him. Christina and her family are coming here on Christmas Day, which is great." She takes the toast out and passes the plate to Marianne.

"Oh, that's good."

"Christmas can be such a lonely time," Carmel remarks as she butters her toast.

Marianne finds the words stab at her heart; she can't look at Carmel. "Yes, it can."

"So," Carmel says and settles herself in her chair, "do you like Christmas?"

Marianne bites into her toast. She longs to tell Carmel about the wonderful times they used to have in Kells, but she refrains. "I don't really mind, one way or the other."

"I must show you the lovely outfits I bought for the girls."

Marianne glances at the kitchen clock. "I have a few last-minute things to get today myself."

"Oh, sorry, am I delaying you?"

Marianne shakes her head. "Goodness, not at all."

She is glad that Carmel doesn't expect her to linger, that she doesn't have to spend the morning making small talk.

Soon after, she is standing in the hall, clutching her bag close to her chest. "Happy Christmas, Carmel." She feels herself perspiring profusely and hopes Carmel won't want to give her a hug. She edges towards the door, smothering the shameful realisation that she is a total fraud. Carmel sees the good in everyone; she would be totally shocked if she found out that Marianne had ulterior motives for befriending her.

"Are you all right?" Carmel is asking.

Marianne feels jittery. "I'm fine." She hears herself laugh nervously. "I guess I'm suffering the effects of a hangover."

Carmel hugs Marianne at her front door. "Have a lovely Christmas and if you get back to Dublin before the New Year, call me."

Marianne is touched by her sincerity. "Thank you, Carmel, you're so kind."

"Don't be silly – can we just agree we have good times together?"

Marianne inches her way out the door, still clutching her bag close to her chest. She feels like she has just made a great escape.

The first thing she is going to do when she gets home is ring Jim. She has some more work for him. Then she will make herself a very strong cup of coffee to ease her pounding headache. She is too impatient to wait for a bus and flags down a taxi.

She is just walking up her drive and into her own safe house when she hears someone call her name. She turns to see Emma getting out of David's old car.

"Hi, Auntie!" Emma comes running up the path, her black curls bobbing around her, and throws her arms around Marianne. "It's so good to see you!" Her blue eyes are sparkling with excitement.

Marianne has to gasp for breath. "Emma!" she says. David meets her gaze and she sees the remnant of a smile still on his lips. "David," she says and smiles at him.

"I hope you don't mind us intruding like this," he is saying and all the while he is looking at her as if he is privately assessing the situation.

Her lips tremble as she pulls her face into a welcoming smile. "Of course not," she says automatically and then turns towards the front door, glad to have a diversion while she comes to terms with their sudden arrival. "I'm delighted to see you both." She leads the way into the house.

"Dad came to the airport to collect me and we decided to call to see you," Emma is explaining. David catches Marianne's eye and they smile at each other again as Emma continues. "I phoned you last night but you must have been out."

"Yes, dear, I was out with a friend." Marianne takes off her coat and hangs it up in the hall. She brings her bag into the kitchen, fearful to let it out of her sight. "Tea, coffee?"

"Tea, please," Emma says. She has gone from being an adorable little girl to a beautiful young woman.

"I'll make it," David says as he fills the kettle with water.

"Auntie, we're hoping you'll come home with us for Christmas."

"Now?" asks Marianne, startled.

Emma nods.

"Oh, dear, I have nothing packed. Like I said, I

was out last night with a friend and I just got back
. . ." She wrings her hands nervously together.

"We can wait for you to get ready, can't we,
Dad?"

"Yes, yes," David says in agreement.

"That's very kind. I was going to go to Kells to
see Kathleen, but . . . OK, then, I'll come."

"I can help you pack," Emma says. She hasn't lost
that eagerness to care that she had always shown as
a little girl.

"Yes, look, I will come with you, but I'd prefer to
bring my own car . . . I'll follow you."

"In the Micra?" asks David disbelievingly.
"You'll be all cramped up. Why not sit in with us
and relax?"

"Listen, David, my Micra has taken me further
afield than Leitrim. I might get there before you in
your old banger."

"Aye, if you remember the way. Emma, you
could travel with your aunt – you both have lots of
catching up to do."

"Done," said Marianne. "We might even stop on
the way! Are the sales in Sligo good after
Christmas?"

"Don't ask Dad," Emma says. "He's wearing
what he wore last time I saw him."

Chapter 22

Emma leans backwards in the car, as they continue on the road to Leitrim.

"No sign of Dad," she says, looking in the rear-view mirror. She suddenly leans across Marianne's view, peering at the dashboard. Marianne nudges her sideways gently.

"Fifty-three thousand miles in four years. You bought this new, didn't you? That's quite a few miles for someone who goes nowhere."

"You were always inquisitive," Marianne replies in admiration.

"Auntie, that's not fair. If you weren't so secretive, we'd be having a different conversation."

"Maybe. I was wondering about your dad. What's going on his life?"

"By the time you leave Leitrim, you'll have seen it all. Well, nearly all. He was into photography for a while, maybe still is. One woman kept appearing in his photos."

"Did you ask who she was?"

"God, no. It would be embarrassing – for him, not me. Poor Daddy thinks I wouldn't understand that people can have relationships at any age."

"Can I see them when we get there?"

"Only if you promise not to tell him. He would kill me."

"How is he getting on with your mum?"

"They speak. He hid his hurt quite well when Mum took us to London. So did we, come to think of it."

"It must have been awful."

"Yes, it was bloody awful."

"I'm sorry. I should have supported you more at the time."

"Oh, Auntie, it was hard for you too!" Emma patted Marianne's shoulder affectionately. "Did I tell you that Greg is gone to Australia for a year?"

"No, you didn't."

"Greg did engineering in university. I think he did it to please Mum. He keeps changing jobs and he can't seem to settle down at anything."

"Unlike you?"

"Perhaps. I had thought he'd have done art or at least architecture – he's a fine draughtsman. I did suggest to him that he should change direction but he said he didn't want to – he likes earning big money even though he gets no satisfaction from the work he does."

Marianne smiles and glances out the window, watching the mosaic of green fields whiz past. "And your mum?"

"She's remarried now, to a dentist. Greg doesn't like him."

"Greg was always very attached to his mother."

Emma frowns. "I wonder why it is like that?"

"It must be a mother and son thing. Liam was always attached to me."

When they arrive at the farm house, Emma insists that Marianne takes her bedroom. She herself will sleep in Greg's room.

"This is really nice," Marianne remarks when they walk into the bedroom. The walls are painted in dusky rose, the floorboards varnished and a love-ly embroidered quilt covers the double bed.

"Dad did all the decorating himself," Emma announces proudly. She flops on the bed, her black curly hair cascading down her back.

"It's lovely," Marianne says.

"I love it."

Marianne hugs her. "Thank you, darling," she mutters and feels tears of exhaustion welling up inside her.

"I'm so pleased you could come," Emma says. She looks so like her mother but her eyes are David's. "Dad gets lonely here."

"Yes, I suppose he does. You don't mind if I go out later for a while on my own? I just need some time alone."

"On Christmas Eve!" Emma's eyes open wide in disbelief. "Don't you want some company?"

"No. I – I just want to remember times past . . ."

"Dear Sophia . . ."

Marianne picks up another letter, crafted in Liam's erratic handwriting. She drifts towards bygone, happier days . . .

"Marianne," says Stephen, fixing his tie in the mirror, "I was looking at Liam's homework last night, couldn't read a word. Could you talk to his teacher?"

"Already done. She says it will either improve gradually or will remain his natural style."

Escaping her thoughts of the past, she cringes inwardly at some of her son's suggestive language. It is so difficult for a mother to read this. Her baby, putting on record all the feelings vibrant young men have but mothers don't want to acknowledge.

"Ahh, Liam, my Liam!"

It was a difficult time for all of them. Stephen was very disappointed that Liam had dropped out of university. He blamed Marianne, shifting the blame instead of taking a look at the role he'd played in it all. It still maddened her when she thought about it. They should have discussed it, but the years trawled in and out of each other and then Stephen got cancer and there wasn't much point any more. Liam always became her son when he did something wrong or didn't perform as he was expected to. "He's your son too," she should have said. Where do you begin when you have remained silent for so long?

The letters fuel her desire to make the trip she has planned. Earlier, in truth, in the company of David and Emma, her resolve had wavered. Now she is ashamed of that fact. She wants to spend this Christmas Eve with Liam, not here secure and comfortable in this warm welcoming house. She will go. She will go where her desire for revenge is keenest.

"I know what you're thinking," Emma says to Marianne. They are sitting in the living-room and David has just walked in. He has had a shower.

"Dad," Emma giggles, "if Mum could see you now! New shirt and trousers. Wowee! What do you think, Marianne?"

"David has had a lifetime of ribbing about his dress code, Emma. He doesn't need me to add to it."

"Ah, you're no sport! Congratulations, Dad. And cheers to us all!" Emma starts to laugh. "Last Christmas, when Dad came over to London to see us he bought a d –"

"Could we call a truce on the clothes stories?" David says. "You were not wearing too much when you came to the world and look at what you're wearing now!"

Marianne can't help but laugh. Emma is curled up on the sofa, her legs tucked under her. She is twirling her black curly hair in her finger. She looks so pretty – no, that isn't the right word. She is a very sexy-looking young woman.

"They were a bargain," Emma whispers, mischievously.

David nods in agreement. "She doesn't have to live on my income. Now, truce!"

"Poor Dad," she says mockingly. She jumps to her feet. "Anyone for a drink?"

"I'll have a hot brandy," David says.

"Nothing for me, thanks," Marianne replies.

"But it's Christmas!" says Emma.

"Go on!" David says.

She knows it is easier to agree than to argue with them. "Well, one so . . . I want to give the car a run later on. I don't want the battery to run down."

David nods silently. He is disappointed but had agreed with Emma that they would not intrude into Marianne's private space. He is also worried about Marianne but conceals that fact.

Emma leaves the room to go make their drinks.

The fire is radiating a soft orange glow. It is almost hypnotic to sit and watch it. David had sanded the wooden floors and stained them to give them a mellow look. The old sofa had been re-covered in rust check fabric. Tapestry cushions and a striking kilim rug gives colour and texture to the room. A scented tree stands at the bay window and makes the room look postcard-perfect.

Marianne is sitting on a restored armchair that once belonged to her. David was visiting them in Kells and they were getting their living-room redecorated. He was horrified to see that they were throwing out good furniture. He took an armchair and coffee table. That was as much as would fit in his car. He had restored the chair beautifully. She remembers Stephen and herself watching him drive away, the chair tied with rope on the top of his battered old car. Stephen shook his head despairingly. She remembers herself muttering something like "Poor David". Little did she know that one day she would sit on that old armchair, that was once a horrible shade of red, and feel strangely contented. She feels lucky to be included. Here in this shabby, yet wonderfully welcoming house, she gets respite, even if it's temporary.

David smiles and sits down on the sofa on the place that Emma has vacated.

"Do you mind that Sue has remarried . . . sorry, that came out before thinking."

"No, it's all right, I did for a while, but I'm OK with it now. Life moves on."

"And has yours moved on?"

"No, but for a while, I thought something was happening. With someone. But it turned out she belongs to somebody else. I never even knew that, at the start."

"Do you still meet?"

Emma pushes open the living room door.

"Drinks!"

"I hope you didn't put to much brandy in them,"
David says.

"Oh, Dad, lighten up, it's Christmas!"

Smiling, they clink their glasses.

Chapter 23

They head into town to get some last-minute supplies.

"Let's go for a drink," Ben says, breaking an awkward silence between them.

Everywhere they go, people are rushing to greet each other, embracing in loving hugs. The fragility of their relationship is exposed for them to see; even Ben appears incapable of false bravado tonight.

It takes ages for Ben to get back from the crowded counter with their drinks.

I hope there are no students here, thinks Sophia silently. She has been discreet in her relationship with Ben, as young male students can be cruel. Some of the stuff they throw at her is borderline, but it's part of being a teacher and female.

Christina's words echo in her ears: 'Look at all the scrapes we had to dig you out of before you met Matt!'

Perhaps a bit of religion would help, thinks Sophia suddenly. "Ben, I don't like it here. Let's go. Can we go to Mass?"

"Uh . . . OK, why not?"

"Stille nacht . . . Oiche Chiuin . . . Silent night . . ."
Sligo's answer to Charlotte Church sings sweetly in the crowded church. There are fewer drunks in the church than there used to be, "Midnight Mass" not being held at midnight any more. Sligo is becoming a multicultural town, and a small group of East Europeans join in smilingly on their verse. They obviously appreciate the gesture. The volume goes down when the Irish version is sung. Ironic, thinks Sophia, standing with Ben.

They disembark wearily from the car. Midnight Mass has not lifted them.

"Families, families," says Sophia aloud, wondering where in the world they might have escaped them tonight. Ben does not reply.

"Is that someone walking on the beach, Ben?" she asks, noticing a figure on the beach in the distance where a small car is parked.

"Looks like that."

"Stop a minute – it looks like a woman down there. You don't think she is going to do something stupid?"

"No, I don't, and I can't even make out if it's a she. Lots of people walk the beach at night."

"Christmas Eve, though . . ." Sophia feels unnerved by it.

"Let's get inside."

Sex is almost obligatory tonight, if only to relieve the silent tension. There is little fervour.

"OK?" Ben asks.

"Fine, it's nice," says Sophia. She reflects on a year filled with deceit, each of Ben's thrusts a dull thud of reality going directly to her brain.

Later she gets up to go to the bathroom.

"Ben!"

"Yeah?"

Sophia is at the window. A car in the distance is flashing its lights, directly facing their bedroom.

"Look! Couldn't that be the same car as earlier?"

"I really don't know . . . yeah, maybe, so what, anyway?"

"I don't like it, Ben, I feel something is wrong. Maybe it's a distress signal?"

"So what do you propose? That we get up and go down there? And get mugged? Soffiaah, it's one a.m. Let's get some sleep. It's probably some kids fooling about with a few cans and some dope. Or maybe even a hooker."

"Yeah – a hooker!" Sophia says in quiet dersion, surveying the silent winter gloom of the school-house's surroundings.

The familiar sensation of unease and tension falls over her like a pall.

Chapter 24

On Christmas morning Marianne is woken by bird-song outside her window. She lies as memories of her trip to Sligo race through her mind. It all seems unreal – the ghostly beach, the schoolhouse. Has she dreamed it? She switches on the bedside lamp, and her eyes fall on a pair of walking shoes covered in sand.

She takes the letters from under her pillow. She is weary of reading them; all she can do is stare at the photographs of Sophia and Liam standing together smiling into the camera. They are both clad in various shades of denim. Liam's arm is around her waist. They make a beautiful young couple. She looks at the letters, three in all, each one ripped open as if Sophia couldn't wait to read what he had written. She turns the envelopes over, once again reading his hasty scrawl as he wrote the address.

She drifts back to sleep and wakes sometime later when she hears voices downstairs. She looks at her wristwatch: it is only eight o'clock. Nevertheless she decides to get up. Then she notices the letters still beside her in the bed. She carefully tucks them away into her bag.

She has a shower and pays some attention to fixing her hair – she even glosses her lips. It is Christmas after all. Lurking in every corner of her mind are memories – some good, some not so good – but here she knows she can rest from them. It's like opening a door to another life. The house is a typical functional country house – she can even smell the turf fire and it's lovely – just what she needs. Here, at least she can get a reprieve; here she is with people she is very fond of. Perhaps she could even venture to say people that she loves.

She goes downstairs. "Good morning," she says as she walks into the warm kitchen. She feels herself being drawn to the stove like a magnet.

"Happy Christmas, Auntie!" Emma says as she pours her a cup of tea from the teapot.

"You're up early," says Marianne, smiling.

"I got up to help Dad," she explains as she

butters some toast.

"That was very thoughtful of you."

Just then the back door opens and she can hear David. "Is Marianne up yet?"

Emma laughs. "Yes, Dad. She's here in the kitchen with me."

"Good, good," he replies. He walks into the kitchen in his stocking-feet, carrying a small package wrapped in tinfoil. "Mrs Egan gave me some potato cakes," he says and leaves them proudly on the kitchen table. "How about some?"

"Dad, what about your cholesterol?" Emma says and eyes the package.

"But it's Christmas and it's ages since I've eaten any." He opens the tin-foil wrapping and shows them to her. "You used to love them as a child. When she heard you were coming home for Christmas, she made some especially for you."

"Oh, Dad, you didn't go down in those clothes, did you? At Christmas!" Emma says as she gets up from the kitchen table.

David is pulling off his old sweatshirt. He's wearing a plaid shirt similar to the one he wore yesterday. His faded jeans have seen better days. "Put on the potato-bread. Imagine the headlines: *Poorly Dressed Deserted Dad Dies From Starvation.*"

"You are going to have a shower and put on some clean clothes. Agreed?"

"I submit but, food first."

"I'll just have a small piece," Emma says, turning to look at Marianne. "How about you?"

"Yes, it's years for me too since I've eaten any," she replies.

David is smiling at her now, his eyes twinkling with delight. "You'll love it," he assures her.

"And so will my hips," says Marianne.

"Your hips are fine," says David. He takes some rashers from the fridge. "Can I have some of these please?" he is asking his daughter in a humble voice.

Emma and Marianne start to laugh. "Of course you can," Emma says.

"Is there anything I can do to help?" Marianne asks.

"Don't worry – relax," David says and grins at her almost boyishly.

Later, Emma keeps her promise and shows Marianne David's photos while he is tending to his cattle. They pore over them together.

"This is her, isn't it?" Marianne is looking coldly at the photograph, studying it closely.

"There may not be a 'her', they're only photos.

God, I shouldn't have shown them to you!"

"Don't worry. It's harmless fun. I'll say nothing."

A quick estimate by Marianne puts the lady in her forties, pretty, in a disorganized way. No make-up either. Marianne winces. It's probably nothing, she thinks. Wouldn't she be here, if there was something?

Chapter 25

Sophia is in the supermarket, looking at the grapes.

"Sophia!" she hears someone call. She looks up and sees a man a slight distance away, looking at her.

It can't be Liam, she thinks. It just can't be.

She stands frozen, a whirl of noise going on about her. He smiles at her while still keeping eye contact.

"Liam, is that you?" she asks. She becomes aware again that she's in the supermarket. Tentatively she puts one foot in front of the other and ventures to walk towards him. His face is expressionless and at a distance it is quite hard for her to make out if it's Liam or not.

A woman with a trolley pushes past her. "Sorry,"

she says.

Momentarily she breaks eye contact with him and when she looks for him again he's gone. She drops her basket and runs to find him. Her heart is thumping but she's got to see his face. She has got to know if the person was real or a figment of her imagination. At the top of the aisle she looks around her; she cannot figure out which way he has gone. She's lost him. Outside the shopping centre she collapses on the ground.

"Are you all right?" a woman asks in a motherly voice

"Yes, thanks," she replies, as the woman helps her to her feet.

"Would you like me to call your mother?" she asks.

Sophia looks into her gentle blue eyes. She shakes her head and then says, "No, thank you, I'll be fine. I just need a moment to get my breath."

"Happy Christmas," the woman says and walks away from her.

Sophia wants to follow her; she'd feel safe alongside her. But she can't, she can't possibly do that.

Then she hears a phone ringing. She opens her eyes and realises she is safe in her bed. She reaches out and picks the phone up. Her heart is thumping fast, the dream still vivid as she tries to pull herself together.

"Happy Christmas!" her mother's voice chimes into the phone, sounding alarmingly near.

Sophia's heart leaps to her mouth. She wouldn't put it past her mother if she had arrived in Sligo with the whole family and the turkey in the boot of the car. Then she hears the radio in the background. She breathes a sigh of relief. Carmel is in her kitchen in Templeogue, cooking no doubt and listening to the radio.

"How are you, sweetheart?"

"Mammy, are you okay?"

Her mother laughs. "Of course I'm okay, what would be wrong with me? Oh, darling, I hate to think of you spending Christmas on your own."

Sophia turns to look at Ben who is grinning at her. She turns her back to him. She's hoping Christina hasn't mentioned him.

"Mammy, you worry too much. Really, I'm fine," she says as she gets out of bed.

"Are you up yet?"

Sophia shrugs into her dressing-gown. "Now, I am," she says and walks out of the bedroom.

"I've been up all morning," her mother announces, with that air of martyrdom that she has perfected over the years. "Sophia, what is keeping you down there on this special day?"

"I just couldn't face going back to Dublin. I just couldn't face bumping into Matt."

"But you wouldn't bump into him out here. He's not likely to come out to Templeogue," her mother says and laughs at the absurdity of it.

"Mammy, please, what if Matt drove by the house and saw my car. I just couldn't risk it."

"Darling, it would have been lovely to have you here today. You can't keep running away from people. Christina is coming with Tony and the girls."

Sophia raises her eyes towards the ceiling. Her mother really can lay it on heavy. Why did she have to keep nagging? Couldn't she just take a break from it? It was the season of good will and all that. Events had pushed Sophia in this direction and now she was here and, for the moment, this is her choice.

"Look, Mammy, I'm really sorry that I won't be with you for Christmas," she says as she walks downstairs and into the living-room. She pulls the blinds to see what the ocean looks like on Christmas morning. No car. Ben was right. She smiles to herself: it looks no different than any other morning. "Remember the way Dad always dressed up as

Santa Claus for us??"

"Oh, indeed I do," her mother replies, her voice tinged with regret. "The years just fly by. You were babies and the next thing I know it you are going to college. And, now look at me, I'm a granny."

"You're a brilliant granny. The girls just love you, Mammy," Sophia reminds her.

She sighs loudly. "Sometimes I feel very old."

"Oh, Mammy, don't be silly – you're not old. Look, I promise I'll make it up to you. I'm not staying away deliberately to hurt you – it's just I need a little time on my own."

"Oh, sometimes I suppose I stick my nose in where it's not wanted."

Sophia laughs and her mother joins in.

"Would you listen to the pair of us?" her mother is saying.

Sophia walks into the kitchen, fills the kettle with water and switches it on.

"I hope you are coming to my New Year's Eve party," says Carmel.

"Oh, Mammy!" Sophia says and immediately regrets sounding so reluctant. "Goodness me!" Carmel says, taken aback.

Sophia is stabbed by the ghost of a memory. She recalls coming home from London after spending the summer there working. She remembers her mother opening her mouth and then closing it quickly as she saw how much weight Sophia had lost over the summer. "Goodness me," her mother had said, "you look awful!" This was her greeting. And then she took a second look and shook her head regretfully. "What's your father going to say?" Sophia had felt the jab. That was all she was worried about, what their father would say. Christina, eying Sophia furtively, had said: "Oh, Mammy, leave her alone!"

Sophia squeezes her eyes closed, shutting down the memory. It was so long ago she wonders what triggered that particular one.

Now, Sophia is finding the floor cold on her bare feet. She walks into the sitting-room and tucks her feet under her on the sofa. Her mother is still talking about the New Year's party, lamenting the fact that Sophia won't take the trouble to come. Sophia breathes a quiet sigh of resignation. "OK, Mammy, I'll be there, I promise."

"Sophia, you suit yourself. You always do."

Families, thinks Sophia, who the hell needs them? She just couldn't face her family this Christmas – her mother's fussing would drive her crazy.

"Will you go to the graveyard today, Mammy?"

she asks.

"We will go to the graveyard today, Sophia. Me, Christina, Tony and the grandchildren."

"Cut it out, that's not fair!"

"Maybe not, but it's how I feel."

Sophia opens her mother's present, predictably a bottle of perfume.

"Thanks for the present," she says.

"You're welcome, I hope you like it. And thank you for your present but gym membership for a year is really too much!"

"Enjoy it, it will do you good."

Sophia knows her mother doesn't want to say goodbye. She's prolonging the conversation for the sake of it. It was always the same: they would circle each other, endeavoring to say the right thing while never quite managing it. "OK, Mammy, I'll call you."

"Call this evening around six. We'll be finished our dinner by then and the girls can tell you what Santa Claus brought them."

Sophia tastes eggnog for the first time. "Not bad."

"Feel any better?" Ben says.

"Yeah, let's make the best of it." She snuggles up to him and feels the solid beat of his heart.

"I'd better phone my boys," he says eventually. She hears the pain in his voice.

"I'll make us some more Irish coffees."

Ben smiles and pulls her up off the sofa. "No, you won't. You'll start dinner."

Sophia makes a face. "You're much better at cooking than I am."

"I'll teach you," he says.

At last, Sophia has discovered the name of the piece of music: it is Debussy, *Claire de Lune*. Ben has a vast collection of CD's. On Christmas Day she searched through his classical collection and found it.

"I can't believe this," she said to Ben, as she waved the CD in front of his nose.

Claire de Lune was playing in the background. "At last I found it!"

For the past hour she had gone through his classical collection, putting them on, letting them play for a few moments and then moving on to the next one. She knew she was irritating Ben but she didn't care.

"Soffiaah," Ben interrupts suddenly. "Remember me? I'm here."

"Yeah, sorry... I was just about to call Mammy."

"You've already called her today on my phone,

you're doing my head in all day with that classical stuff, and I stayed over here because of you."

"Don't lay it all on me, Ben. You could have gone back to America and been back in a few days. You know you should have, you've got the hump, and now you're blaming me. I'm not taking it." Sophia sways to her feet.

"Where are you going to? You can't go back to your apartment and leave me alone. You're using me, Soffiaah!"

"Poor Ben. Alone, used. Tell me, how often do you volunteer for projects away from your family home? You're not going to say that I'm the first person you've stuck it to since you got married. C'mon, Ben, tell me, how many?"

"The others were nothing. You're special. I'm confused ... I didn't see this side to you before."

"There's lots of sides to me, Ben . . . you'd want to watch out. I'm taking this bottle back to my flat, and you can go to hell."

"No, I'm not letting you. You knew the score from the start. I've always been honest with you."

"Mmmm ... honest, now you wouldn't pass easily as anything other than a middle-aged married man, would you? Don't you call *me* a user!"

"All right, all right, I'm middle-aged, but what's

going on for you? What are you hiding from? There is something in your past – before what's-his-name you left behind in Dublin?"

"And what could you do about it if I told you? Take my knickers off again?" The tears come quite suddenly, increasing to despairing sobs. "I'm sorry, Ben, I'm really sorry!"

He reaches out and cradles her. "It's OK, it's OK . . . it's OK now."

"Liam . . . that was his name . . . we were students . . . there was a party. He just died on me, Ben, he just died on me."

"Wanna tell me more?"

"No. Hold me, just hold me."

In a drunken haze Sophia picks up the phone and dials her mother's number.

"Hi," she slurs. "Sophia here."

"Sophia, have you been drinking?" her mother asks.

Sophia laughs. "Why, Mammy, of course I have!"

"Sophia," she says and Sophia hears the disapproving tone in her voice. Carmel begins to talk.

Sophia isn't listening. She wants to say so much herself but can't. She feels a huge surge of affection for her mother. She remembers all the years her mother slogged away in the background, doing her best for them. It was her mother's shoulder she cried on when she broke her shoulder blade in secondary school. It was her mother that wore a path to her bedroom after that dreadful summer in London that had started out so well. It was in her mother's arms she had wept even though she couldn't confess, she couldn't tell her what had happened in London. She just knew her mother would never cope with the news. She longed to tell but couldn't and for years now she has kept her guilty secret to herself, the weight of it pulling her down.

"You should have come, you should have spent Christmas with us," says Carmel.

A thousand thoughts surface in Sophia's head but none of them are worth vocalising. Her mother wouldn't understand.

"Good night, Mammy," she mutters, and hangs up.

Chapter 26

Sophia awakens suddenly, hearing clothes hangers scrape across the metal bar of the wardrobe. Parched with thirst, she comes upright suddenly. Last night! What did she say to Ben?

He is getting dressed. He is going in to work today. The particular files he needs are in the office. He is picking a shirt to wear.

"Good morning, my dear," says Ben, cheerily.

"Uhh, yeah. Ben, what happened last night?"

"You were stressed out, Soffiaah, that's all. Said some wicked things, but it's done. Think nothing of it."

"You slept in the other room, Ben."

"I lay with you for a while. You were tossing and turning, so I moved out. No big deal, I'll be back tonight, if you want me, that is."

"Yes, of course. Did I talk about anything else?"

"Yep. Liam. That was his name, wasn't it? Tragic, poor bugger. We have to keep going, Soffiaah. Look, I'll see you this evening. We'll talk more."

Ben needs his work like she needs a walk by the sea. It will be a relief for her to have the place to herself and she wants to walk by the ocean regardless of what the weather is like. She loves the crash and thunder of the waves, hearing them makes her feel well and truly alive.

Sophia ponders over the last two days. She feels that their relationship has been exposed as a sham and she has become prostituted. In a few years' time, he'll be paying someone in cash and up front, she muses. She is both relieved and angry at his dismissiveness about Liam.

"Bye," she says and she hears his light footfall on the steps. She hears the heavy oak door slam. She listens to hear the car door opening, closing, then the engine starting. This is her cue to get out of bed. From the window she peers out and sees his sleek high-performance car zoom off down the road. Across the road she notices a man wearing an anorak who is staring up at her. She pulls back from the window, her heart racing. "Oh, no," she says aloud and hears the panic in her own voice. The newsagent's in Dublin. The man buying the paper! Tentatively she moves the curtains and looks out again but there is no one there. She sighs, relieved. "It wasn't him. I'm overreacting," she tells herself.

Downstairs she makes herself a strong coffee, sipping it as she paces through the house. It takes her a long time to muster up the courage to leave. Every time she attempts to open the door and go outside, something pulls her back. She is scared and, yet, she can't honestly say what she is scared of. It is doing her no good walking around in circles – turning over the same thoughts in her mind. She braces herself, and walks into the morning sunlight.

She takes a deep breath of cold sea air and wonders what craziness has come over her. After all, she is just an ordinary person leading a very ordinary life.

"This is all in my head," she tells herself. "Stop panicking."

She reaches the end of the road. She is now facing the sea. It feels like the wind is pushing her back and yet she feels determined to keep on going. She wants to see the ocean. Hear its fury. At last, she reaches the buildings that are huddled together. She pushes open the door of the coffee shop. Inside its warm air embraces her. Her eyes grow bigger as she looks out at some surfers who are riding the incredible waves. She buys a coffee and sits to drink it.

"Hi," a young man says, coming over to where she is sitting. His eyes twinkle when he asks her, "Are you surfing?"

"No, I just like to watch."

He has black curly hair and is wearing a dark jumper that his mother probably gave him for Christmas. He could be one of her students, for all she knows. She turns to leave. She is going to head back to the schoolhouse, play some music and continue reading her William Trevor novel. As a child, she loved walking in the rain, splashing in puddles and generally driving her mother crazy. She looks up at the leaden sky. "I like rain, but this is a deluge," she says to herself. Walking fast, she becomes breathless. She keeps her head down, as she attempts to avoid puddles.

She hears a car slow down. Dublin registration! "Would you like a lift?" the man in the car asks.

"No, leave me alone," she shouts, before realising she is speaking to an elderly man, gaping in astonishment at her.

"I didn't mean to alarm you."

He drives off and for a moment she hesitates and

wonders if she should go back to the café or keep going. While she is deliberating, she is getting wetter and her mind is quickly made up. She almost runs back to the schoolhouse. It is the most wonderful feeling to get inside and feel the safety of it, after battling through the heavy downpour that is going on outside. First she'll have a bath, then she'll make some soup and continue where she left off in her novel.

Chapter 27

"I really enjoyed this Christmas," David says as they walk down the narrow road.

"Yes, I enjoyed it too."

David slows his walk and turns to look at Marianne. "You're not just saying that to please me, are you?"

"No, no, honestly David, I'm not."

"Good," he says and they continue to walk on. The air is frosty and she can see her breath as she breathes out. Everywhere is touched by a light glaze of frost. She loves breathing in the clean frosty air. In the bare-limbed branches, birds are singing as if in thanks.

She watches her breath billow out as she says, "Emma spends a lot of time with Mrs Egan, doesn't she?"

"I'll have to take you up there and you'll see why. She has a son, Mark. Fine lad." There is a hint of satisfaction in David's voice.

"Well, I'll kill her. She never said anything."

"You could hardly justify killing anyone for being secretive, Marianne!" he smiled. "They are a little coy about their relationship, that's all. I know he went over to see her in London. Of course he didn't tell his mother where he was actually going – he gave her some story about going to an organic farmers' convention!"

Marianne laughed. "You don't seem to mind. I get the feeling you approve of him."

"I don't know if approve is the right word but yeah, why not?"

"And then you'd have your daughter close by. I'm beginning to think I misjudged you! You schemer!"

"It's in us all, Marianne, it's in every parent. Emma needs to want it herself though. I won't be giving her an opinion until she comes with hers, first."

So Emma might be coming back here to live,

muses Marianne. But he's putting no pressure on her.

David's intentions were always good. Look at his attitude to Sue, his lack of resentment. Another person, and she can quite honestly put herself in this category, might want to see an ex-spouse suffer. After all, Sue had taken his children to London and robbed him of daily contact. Not David. He was the one genuine good person she knew. Being around him was making her question her own behaviour. No wonder she hadn't contacted him to tell him she was moving to Dublin. Marianne felt he was the one person she knew that could truly let go.

"Don't you ever get angry?" she asks.

"Sure I do," he says as he looks out at the distant fields.

This is his home, where his heart is. He loves these fields that have yielded very little profit over the years. Stephen was always advising him to try farming in a better area where, at least, he could make a decent living. David couldn't get through to Stephen that he loved it here. He loved the simple beauty of the place.

"What makes you really angry?"

"The way we are treating the environment, the serious amount of waste we produce, the way the world is soon going to be controlled by a few multi-national companies ..." He pauses. "Need I go on?"

"No, that is plenty for now."

They have reached the top of the hill and David stops to look all around him. "There's the Egans' house," he says pointing.

Marianne looks around her at the patchwork of low-lying fields. The countryside seems quiet and still. Right at that very moment there are no birds singing or cattle lowing, no distant sound of cars or lorries on the main road, just the quiet. She looks around at the nondescript, unremarkable, barren fields (these were words that she remembers Stephen using to describe the place) and she sees how sometimes one has to look beyond that to see the magic.

In the end, Sue had got what she wanted. She had wanted David to continue his practice as a GP but he didn't want to. She had divorced David and found herself a professional man, a dentist. She had refused to accept anything but the best out of life and, bingo, she had got it! Or had she? It would be nice to meet up with Sue and talk to her. Conversation had never been strained between them as they always had the children to talk about. Now they could talk about growing old and draw from their treasure-chest of memories.

She looks at this unremarkable view and she feels she sees what David sees. The stillness is almost tangible. She wants to hold on to this, she wants to save this glorious moment for the rainy days. The sun is a benign orb of bright light. Clouds billow out and trail across the vast blueness. The landscape is lit up in fingers of light and shade. Nature is putting on a grand display, yet it remains indifferent to what mere humans think of it. Marianne feels well and truly humbled by it all. There is something here, in this place, that the Dow Jones could never measure or quantify. This she considers to be the best portfolio statement in the world. This is free. Until this very moment, she had never seen the beauty here before; she was blind to it and feels ashamed that all her trips here were more duty trips than a true desire to visit the farm.

Liam, Greg and Emma use to go fishing in the stream that flowed by the house. One fine summer's night they had even camped outside. For months afterwards, Liam had talked endlessly about it. Liam had adventures here.

She feels she has connected to something deeper. Here she feels she is breathing in the tranquil air of God. This thought is too crazy to share even with David.

David breaks the silence by saying, "You know, it was great having you here this Christmas." He bends down and pats his dog. "Good boy, Rover," he says, then continues, "And you're useful too – quick to make up a few sandwiches when you're put to it."

She hears the familiar tease in his voice.

"I enjoyed it."

"I'm glad," he says.

"I'm sorry about leaving for a while on Christmas Eve night," she says awkwardly. "You didn't mind?"

"God, no. This is your time away also. Sue might say you're a loner. I'd say, yes, and a sensible woman."

He sounds sincere. Is he though? How can he not even be curious as to where she went that night? Marianne stamps her feet: they are almost numb with the cold and she feels her nose is glowing. She rubs her gloved hands together furiously. "I need to warm up," she explains to David.

"Yes, of course. I don't feel the cold."

"I know," she says.

They have developed a habit of taking short walks every day. Marianne has noticed it is either the walks or the hot brandies or a combination of the two that is making her sleep better at night. She really is beginning to feel like a new woman.

"How quickly the time has gone," she remarks.

"Yes." He stops again and gives her a meaningful look. "You know, we should make the most of the time we have left."

A smile plays on her lips. "I was talking about Christmas and you are talking about life."

"Ah, yes, Christmas did fly by."

"You're right, David, we should make the most of each day. All we've really got is the day – none of us knows what tomorrow is going to bring."

"Agreed," he says, his voice trailing off as he looks around him at the patchwork of green fields. "And if there is anything we want to do then we should do it."

"You're so right, David."

David kicks some pebbles with his boot. "I know Stephen and myself never hit it off but he'd want you to be happy." He raises his head and makes eye contact.

Marianne looks at him, her face full of confusion. She is eager for him to stop beating about the bush and come right out and say it. She glances away and notices that the sky has lost its blueness and has darkened in colour. It's amazing how quickly things change. Now that the clouds are blocking out the sun, the countryside has taken on a sombre look.

"I think it's going to rain," she says, aware that she has ignored his last statement.

David looks up at the sky. "I think you could be right," he says and sighs.

They are standing close to each other. After a moment she says. "It's so peaceful here."

"It's a little bit of heaven," he says and she hears the genuine feeling in his voice. "I always found it hard when Greg and Emma went back to London after their summer holiday here. Some days I would just walk and then I'd stop to look around me, to look at God's creation . . . and I would feel ..." He stops. "I'm sorry – I –"

"No, go on, please, I'd like to hear it."

"I'd feel better."

"I didn't realise you missed your children so much."

"Men are so often written off."

"Yes, I suppose you are." She feels drops on her face. "Oh, the rain!"

"We'd better go."

Later, as they approach the house, she says,

"Thanks for this, David. You really don't know how much your having me here this Christmas has done for me."

David pats her hand affectionately. "It was a pleasure. I hope we can remain friends."

They smile at each other and she is almost tempted to hug him but the moment passes and they go into the house.

Marianne loves the smell of a turf fire. She watches David fill the stove with turf and then she asks to see some of the photographs that he has taken. David smiles boyishly. "I'd love to show you." At the sink, he washes his hands. "The ones for the next exhibition are not here – I'm getting those framed. But, come on, I'll show you some from last year."

"Great," Marianne says and thinks to herself how full her days have become.

"Dad loves having you here," Emma is saying to Marianne.

They are in the kitchen, stacking up the dishwasher. Emma has just told Marianne that she and Greg had bought the dishwasher the previous year. They hated doing dishes when they came home. "Dad says there is something very soothing about doing the dishes," she says sarcastically.

Marianne smiles at her sympathetically. "I guess we get stuck in our ways," she offers as a form of explanation to this modern woman who sees the world very differently. How did you explain that doing a simple task like washing your own dirty dishes can occupy your hands while your mind might turn a whole idea inside out and back again? You just couldn't. It was one of those things that one had to discover oneself.

"Are you happy living in London?"

"It's OK, but I'd really like to get my own place."

"Fed up living at home?"

Marianne is wiping down the kitchen table. Emma is standing with the brush in her hand. She is about to sweep the floor but she's in no great hurry to do so. Every so often she glances towards the window. Marianne pretends not to notice. Emma is waiting for Mark to drive up to the house.

"Mum and her new husband," says Emma.

"That's a shame."

Emma holds the brush tightly. "You don't mean that," she says with a certain edge to her voice.

Marianne pauses for a moment: "No, I guess not."

"She hated living here, hated it. She couldn't wait to get back to civilization." Emma laughs cynically.

"She called London 'civilization'." She starts to sweep under the table furiously. "Civilization, as she called it, didn't seem very civil to Greg and me. We were teased at school because of our accents, and called *paddies*. Some of the children calling us that were Irish themselves." She stops sweeping and holds the handle of the brush tightly. "It was dreadful. We couldn't wait for our summer holidays." She has a sad smile on her face. "You were always so kind to us. I remember the summer you came to meet us at the airport. Do you remember that? Poor Dad! It cost him so much – air fares were so expensive then."

Marianne realises that she has read the picture wrong. Emma still feels hurt by that whole episode in her life. They both turn to look out the window when they hear a car engine.

David walks into the kitchen.

"Not much work going on here," he comments.

Emma hands her father the brush. "We don't want to spoil you. I'm just going to go for a walk."

"It's raining," David says.

"Right then," she says and whirls around. "I guess I'd better see if there is anything on TV."

After she leaves the kitchen Marianne whispers, "I think she's expecting Mark to call."

"Thought as much. So, what are we going to do for the evening?"

Marianne is at a loss for words. An unexpected awkwardness is growing between them. It seems they are really excited to be left alone and, yet, when they are they don't know what to do with themselves. She looks around the tidy kitchen as if seeking out clues as to what she might reply. "I haven't thought about it."

"All we ever do is go for walks," David says.

"I like going for walks."

"I do too, but sometimes I like to do other things." He is looking at her now, waiting for her to say something. Marianne is eager for him to continue. "Would you like to go to the pub for a few drinks?" He lifts a questioning eyebrow.

"I'm not really a pub person. You go. I really don't mind staying here on my own."

Emma sticks her head into the kitchen. "See you later, I'm going out."

"Don't be late," David says and winks at Marianne.

"I won't!" Emma shouts from the hall. "See you sometime tomorrow."

"As you see, my daughter always takes my advice. Come on down to the pub with me. You might enjoy yourself."

"No, honestly, I'd rather stay here."

She finds herself eventually agreeing to go with him. Upstairs, in Emma's bedroom, she applies some make-up and spends some time fixing her hair. She is pleased now that she brought along the new outfit that Carmel suggested she buy. "Ready or not, here I come" – she recalls that was what their children used to say when they played hide and seek in these very rooms with their sloping ceilings and varnished floors. A treasured memory that only seems a breath away. Right now her pain is with her but somehow it doesn't jab at her like it usually does. Somehow it has eased a little.

On the way home from the pub, as they sit in David's old car, he starts to tell her about the northern lights. She is amazed at his knowledge. They occur in the circular band around the geomagnetic North Pole. Rays of auroral light dance across the night sky. Marianne is fascinated; she has never heard of them before.

"I'd love to see them."

"Folklore has it that Eskimos used to think the aurora was their dead relatives trying to get in contact with them."

"That's a wonderful story," she hears herself say. Sometimes folklore and the realm of the imagination can make so much more sense than fact. Out there somewhere are the spirits of Liam and Stephen, dancing on some mystical light. She can imagine them telling her that they are OK. She rests her head back against the comfortable old seat of David's car as they journey home after listening to traditional music and drinking a few too many hot whiskeys. She couldn't ask for more. David had just told her the perfect story to end the best day she had in a long, long time.

Chapter 28

Sophia had the best intentions of going home for New Year's Eve but she cannot bring herself to face the disapproval of her family. And, there, lurking in every crevice of their semi-detached in Tempogue is the fact that she has lost Matt. "I am a coward," she says as she dials her mother's number.

"Darling," Carmel says, her voice high-pitched with excitement, "how are you? When are you coming home?"

Sophia wants to hide, she wants a great big gaping hole to appear in the centre of the living-room floor and for her to fall into it.

"Oh, Mammy, I'm really sorry," she confesses and then she coughs – it's the most pathetic cough that she has ever heard. "I'm really not feeling very well. I was at a party last night and I must have eaten something bad and I don't feel great today."

"You poor thing! Tell you what, we'll come to visit, immediately after the party –"

"That won't be necessary," she cuts across her mother's suggestion.

"Oh. Why not, dear?"

"I'm just not up to visitors."

"I'm your mother, not a bloody visitor!" Carmel says and slams down the phone.

Sophia doesn't phone her back. Instead she covers her head with a cushion. She longs to reach out for her mobile; she aches to dial Matt's number. Just to hear his voice again. Right now, she is imagining the comfort of being held by Matt. She curls up on the sofa with her eyes tightly closed. All she can do is conjure up a picture of him.

Her mobile rings, bringing her back to the present. It's Christina using her older-sister voice. "Sophia, you promised Mammy you'd come to her party. She is so disappointed. You were the reason for the party and, now, you're not coming."

"Oh for God's sake, Christina, get a life!"

"I have a very good life, thank you very much!"

"Yes, sorry, I know you have."

"In fact, I'm pregnant again."

"Congratulations," Sophia says. "That's great."

"Yes, we're really pleased." There is a pause and neither girl speaks.

"Any other news?" Sophia asks, regretting it immediately

"Let me see now . . ."

Sophia knows her sister is enjoying this. She may be angry with Sophia, but she's in chat mode. She needs to unload the titbits of information she has picked up over Christmas. What good is news if you cannot pass it on? She can spend hours making small talk. Usually, Sophia tunes out, occasionally saying "Really?" or "Is that so?" Having a conversation with Christina can be very predictable; she just goes on and on about nothing. All she is really looking for is someone to listen to her.

She has now stopped talking about her daughters and what Santy brought them, and moves on to talk about a shopping trip. Sophia is trying hard to catch up. She is telling Sophia about having to visit SuperQuinn to buy a chicken – only for that she'd have used her local supermarket. Luckily she had put on her new jacket because it was so cold. "I met some of the neighbours. Thankfully I looked respectable," she is saying now.

Sophia wants to yawn with boredom. She is

wondering where this conversation is going. But she dare not ask, as Christina gets annoyed if you interrupt her. She goes on to tell her that she met Donna with a very tanned good-looking man in SuperQuinn. Sophia doesn't know anyone called Donna. Before she can say this, Christina reminds her that Donna was in her year at school. Sophia can't place her but pretends that she can.

"Well, anyway," Christina says, "guess what she said about you?"

"How would I know, I wasn't there," Sophia replies in exasperation.

"Donna says she is delighted to hear that you won't be around as she wants to marry this one. You should see him, he's gorgeous..." she stops and shouts at her husband who she calls 'Daddy'. "Daddy, can you get Sarah a drink?" Then she continues, "Imagine she still remembers how you always were such a hit with the boys!" Christina laughs.

"I wasn't," Sophia protests but she can't be heard over Sarah whining. She is just about to hang up when the place goes quiet.

"I'm in the bathroom, it's the only place I get any peace," Christina whispers.

There is another pause and Sophia says, "OK,

look, I'm just going to –"

"Hold on a minute. Oh, let me see. Remember Rachel?"

Sophia wants to scream but manages to say. "No, I don't remember her."

"Of course you do, she was at our wedding. We went to college together."

"Yes," Sophia says, wishing she had the courage to speak his name. To take the proverbial bull by the horns and say, 'How is Matt?'

"Well," Christina says and again she goes into a long-winded conversation about all that happened to her while Rachel lived in New York. At this stage Sophia has moved from the sofa to stand and stare out the patio window. Dusk is slowly creeping in from the sea. Soon, Ben will be back from work. She is willing her sister just to speak Matt's name and, eventually, she does.

"Oh, yes, I almost forgot to tell you: Matt is seeing someone."

Sophia leans against the patio door and finds herself slowly sliding down it. "Really?"

"Yes, he's much better – it's great to see him looking so well. He called around with presents for the children for Christmas. He didn't forget the children just because you two split up. He is just so kind."

Sophia is aching to ask who is he seeing but finds the words stick in her throat. She wants Christina to tell her. "He had us over for dinner … oh, let me see … what night was it," she sighs, "let me see, Christmas Day was on —"

"Oh, for heaven's sake, what does it matter what night he had you over!" Sophia snaps.

"If that's they way you're going to talk to me I'm going to hang up. Goodbye," says Christina and then the phone goes dead.

Slowly Sophia raises herself off the ground. She replaces the phone on the coffee table. She really wants to break something. Her eyes are smarting with tears as she looks around her but there is nothing that will give a satisfying crash – only Ben's photographs of his children. In the kitchen are a lot of expensive crystal glasses that would break with a very gratifying musical chime to them. She imagines herself storming in there in true Hollywood dramatic style, breaking all that glass. But who would clean it up?

She picks a cushion up off the sofa and thumps it while she wails with self-pity and confusion. "What am I doing?" she says, her voice muffled by the cushion.

"Are you OK?" Ben calls. He is taking off his

coat, his briefcase beside him on the floor.

She feels the blood rush to her face. She didn't hear him coming in.

"Sure," she whispers in reply. She is well and truly pleased to see him. With Ben here she will be occupied and she won't have to think.

"What was that all about?" he asks.

"My family. Need I say more?"

"Oh, dear," he says as he pulls her into his arms.

Later, while Ben is sleeping, she phones Christina. "Sorry, I know it's late." "That's OK," she replies in her good-natured voice, which makes Sophia feel even worse.

"So did you have a nice time?"

"When?"

"At Matt's place. Dinner," she says, steeling herself not to lose it.

"We had a wonderful time – so tell me, how was your Christmas??"

Sophia takes a breath. There is nothing for it: she is going to have to ask Christina more about Matt. It is quite clear that she is not going to volunteer the information. "I had a nice Christmas." She takes a breath and then plunges on. "So," she hears herself say, "about Matt."

"Ah, Matt," says Christina. Sophia can tell that her sister is taking great pleasure in making her suffer.

"Who is he seeing?"

"Claire."

"Oh," she says. She wants to say that she is happy for Matt and Claire. She wants to say she doesn't care but she finds she can't speak. "Claire," she mumbles incoherently.

Christina sighs sympathetically. "You did know that she always fancied him?"

Sophia is lost for words but manages to say, "I guess."

"Well, she went to your apartment one night to see you as you hadn't returned her calls and Matt invited her in ... and I guess the rest is history."

"They'll make a nice couple."

"He deserves someone good, Sophia."

"Yes," she says – she has lost the drift of the conversation. "Bye," she says, steeling herself not to break down and cry.

"Bye, oh, and Happy New Year."

"Same to you and hubby and kids."

"Take care, Sophia, and please come home and visit Mammy before she drives me insane."

"Yes, of course."

Sophia is downstairs wrapped up in Ben's dress-ing-gown. She is playing the piano notes in her head now. She just feels so sad. Right now, she wants to retreat to her own bare empty apartment and play that music and just be on her own. She trudges upstairs to Ben's bedroom. He is sleeping. She picks up her clothes off the floor.

He turns in the bed, "Sophia," he whispers, "what are you doing?"

She wipes the tears away and comes to sit on his bed. "Ben, would you mind if I went back to my place tonight?"

"No, if that's what you want."

"Yes, I just need some space," she says lightly, though inside she feels the dead weight of each word as she says it.

Ben looks at her curiously. "Of course, go ahead. Call me, though," he says with calculated ease. "Are you mad with me about something?"

Sophia shakes her head. "No."

"There isn't something I'm missing?"

"No, no, honestly, Ben."

"Care to tell me what's the matter?"

Sophia looks over his shoulder; she's unable to meet his gaze.

"It's a dreadful night out there," he remarks,

tilting his head towards the window.

"It's not so bad."

"OK, honey," he says as he lies back in his bed. "I'll call you tomorrow."

Stars are twinkling down on her. She wonders if there is anyone else in the universe feeling as miserable as she is right now? In her car, she feels the tears build in her eyes. *"Matt and Claire!"* she screams and grips the steering wheel tightly. Jealously is raging within her and it feels so strong that she thinks she could kill her best friend.

Chapter 29

Marianne closes the door of her rented house in Dublin, inserting the house key in the keyhole inside. A dreadful feeling of nausea creeps over her and she steadies herself by placing her back against the door. A musty odour assails her nostrils, the inevitable result of an unoccupied house being bolted and airless for a significant few days. The feel-good factor, brought on by her escape to Leitrim, evaporates instantly. The drive back to Dublin had not forewarned her of this inevitable sensation – there is enough happening on Irish roads that demands your full attention.

"Reality, my reality," she muses.

She slides to the floor and reflects on her time-out with David and Emma in Leitrim. While there, she had felt somewhat restored and less affected by her life's experiences and tragedies. Living in this moment is dreadful, too dreadful to take. Survival right now is imperative and she lends her mind and soul to fantasy for temporary protection.

"David, I really have enjoyed the last few days and I was thinking about moving on, properly and permanently."

"Yeah, it might be good for you. I'd struggle to live where you live right now. Any ideas on what you might do?"

"Well, Leitrim is not such a bad place, is it?"

"It's a lovely place, Marianne. Go for it, if that's what you want. Look, there are endless properties around here on the market right now. Do you want me to make enquiries for you?

"Eh, yeah."

Reality and the present bolt back immediately.

The unfinished conversation regarding David's mystery woman in the photographs . . . "She belongs to someone else," he had replied. Aye, but so many people " belong " in situations where the heart lies elsewhere. Behaviours in such relationships manifest themselves in many ways. "What would the likely characteristics be where David is involved?" she asks. Letting go? Yeah, probably. But he is a man, Marianne reminds herself, buoyant and virile. The word "trysts" comes to mind. Secretive and risk-laden. Occasional idyllic nights at David's farmhouse or urgent fumblings in cold, foggy cars.

"Get a grasp, Marianne, get a grasp," she says aloud as she trudges wearily towards the living-room.

Marianne is waiting in the reception area of the hotel for Jim. She is early as she wasn't quite sure how long it would take her to get here. She picks up her bag and strolls out to the conservatory to stare out at the sea. The waves glide in and out and it is almost hypnotic. She glances at her watch and feels there is nothing for it but to sit down and order some tea and a scone and just wait for Jim.

But he soon arrives. "You're early," she says, quite pleased with him.

"Marianne, I did her apartment in town on my last visit. Now lover-boy's hideaway. The detail! I don't get it!"

"C'mon, Jim. You know I'm after more, and I hope you've got it. I've paid you up front for this. It's important."

"I've got some photographs," he says as he takes a padded envelope from his pocket. "I also got his wife's address. He has two teenage sons." He places it on the coffee table.

Marianne feels the excitement of it running through her. "Great," she says and looks eagerly at the envelope. "May I?"

"By all means," he says and lolls back in his chair. "Would you like tea or coffee?"

"Coffee, please." She opens the envelope, eager to see the photographs.

"I've picked out the best ones," he says.

A waiter hovers. "Coffee," Jim says.

"Would you like something to eat?" the waiter asks.

"No, thanks," he says.

Marianne takes out the photographs of Sophia and Ben. The first four show them walking along the beach holding hands. Already, she had got herself another man. How dare she? Marianne is furious.

Life is so unfair. Marianne's heart misses a beat as she sees a close-up of them kissing. She flicks through them quickly. She sees Sophia at the patio window, wearing a man's shirt. In the background, she can see Ben.

Marianne is impressed with Jim's efforts. No need to tell him, though. Keep him on his toes.

"Sophia has still got her apartment in town but she spends a lot of her time there in his. He works incredible hours and Sophia stays in the schoolhouse, going for walks or lazing around. His wife's name is Karen. Like I said, I got his wife's address while I was in the schoolhouse. It's on the envelope."

Marianne picks up her bag and passes him an envelope. "The balance."

"Sophia may have seen me," he says as he is putting the envelope away. "I'll have to use someone else next time."

"Are you saying that it would cost me more and I mightn't be able to afford it?"

Jim looks agitated; his ulcers are troubling him, again. With that he takes a tablet out of a packet and starts to suck it. "It's not that. She's a smart woman. You can't keep snooping around like this."

"Thanks for the advice," she says crisply.

"What is this all about?" he asks, his curiosity getting the better of him.

Marianne doesn't reply.

Jim holds up his hands. "OK, I won't pry."

"You look exhausted."

Jim nods in agreement. "I'm off on holidays for a few weeks," he says as he stands up.

"Good for you."

"I should be back in a month if you need me, you have my number."

"Thanks but I think you've done enough for me."

"Are you going to post that off to his wife?"

Marianne's eyes lighten up with mischief. "What do you think?"

Jim buttons his coat. "I hope you know when to stop," he says wearily. "I've been in this business a long time and people get carried away, lose the head." He pauses and looks down at the photographs. "Good luck," he says and turns to leave.

"Enjoy your holiday," she says.

Jim nods. He turns to walk away, then pauses and turns to look back at her. His voice is softer than usual when he speaks. "I'd really like to enjoy this holiday. No calls, please. Watch out for Gavin, but I've told you that before, haven't I?"

Marianne waves a dismissive hand. "Thanks for the advice, Jim."

All she has to do is take it to the post office and send it off. She can imagine his wife, coming down for breakfast some morning and seeing this padded envelope on the hall floor. She'll look at the postmark and see Ireland. "Boys, we've got a package from Dad!" she'll shout up the stairs. She'll go into the kitchen and start to prepare breakfast. Marianne can picture the scene. She can see all the heartbreak and sorrow that is about to unfold. At night, Karen will lie in her bed alone, staring into the gloom. Perhaps she will wonder what possessed her husband to act so recklessly. Her mind will be working overtime. Perhaps she'll see a therapist and talk about it. Perhaps not. She will question her every decision. She will feel like she is walking around carrying a great big question-mark on her back. Why? Why? Why? Why did he do it? Why me? Why now? Why didn't we all go to Ireland and stay together as a family? Why us? All these questions that have no real answers.

Chapter 30

January is almost over and Sophia is glad. She has all her exams papers corrected and the dreaded results given back. Now her students know what they have to work on for their summer assessments. Sophia is back in Ben's schoolhouse. Her temporary retreat back to her own apartment only lasted a few days. She is sitting curled up on the sofa, a cup of coffee cradled in her hands. Her eyes are closed and the volume is very high on the stereo. She jumps suddenly when it stops playing.

"Ben," she says. "You gave me a fright."

He stands beside his state of the art music system with his back to her. His shoulders are slumped.

A nervous smile flickers across her face. She is standing now looking at him. "Ben, what is it?

He turns to face her. He raises his eyes ever so slowly to meet hers across the room.

"Soffiah," he says.

She hears the panic in his voice. She sees the desperate pleading in his grey eyes.

"What is it?" she asks. Her legs are shaking; but she knows she should walk towards him. The very least she could do is hold him. Something terrible has happened.

He is looking at the floor now. And for the first time she notices the brown padded envelope in his hand.

"Ben," she says.

He is looking at her in cold astonished shock. He remains standing beside his stereo, where his collection of CDs line the wall. He shakes his head as if he is still trying to come to terms with something awful.

She walks those few final steps to where he is standing.

He hands her the envelope. "Have a look."

Her hands tremble as she takes the envelope from him.

With a few quick strides, he is standing at the patio widow, his hand leaning against it.

Slowly, she sits back down on the sofa and in

slow motion she takes out the photographs. The first shows them kissing on the beach, the waves crashing in behind them. She flicks to the next photographs: they are holding hands as they make their way into a restaurant. She sees herself wearing one of his blue shirts at the patio doors; Ben is in the background. Someone has been spying on them all over Christmas.

"These were on my desk when I got into work this morning," Ben is saying. His voice is low and ominous. "From my wife's solicitor. She's looking for a divorce." He thumps the glass. "Fuck! fuck!"

Of course, he doesn't want a divorce. This was just some fun. Time out of his real life. Poor Tubular Ben.

"I don't understand," he says and shakes his head. "I don't understand." With a few quick movements he is sitting beside her. "Who would do this?" He is looking at Sophia, waiting for her to say something.

"Ben, I'm sorry."

"Sorry," he says and snorts. He is standing again now. "I've got to get back to Chicago to see Karen, try and explain."

Sophia puts the photographs back in the envelope.

"Not going home at Christmas was a bad idea, alerted her, made her suspicious. These agencies have networks word-wide, you know. God, what am I going to do? She'll go to the head of the corporation, no doubt."

"Maybe," she says. She recognizes the photo type. The feelings of terror return to her stomach. She remembers the man she saw from the bedroom window. He was carrying something . . . a camera. Yes! God! It is starting all over again.

"Your ex could have done this?"

"Matt?" she says and shakes her head. "No, never, he'd never do something like this. And how would he have got your wife's address?"

Ben shakes his head in confusion. "Perhaps he broke in here while we were out."

"Yes, maybe you're right."

Ben grips her by the arms. "You need to find out for me. I need to know who the hell has done this!"

"OK," she says as her mind scrabbles to come to terms with these new and horrific events.

"Perhaps it's someone in your office."

"No, no," he says with conviction. "I'm sure it isn't."

Sophia folds her arms across her chest, protectively.

"You need to go to Dublin and find out if it's your guy that's been involved," he says.

"I can't. I have a lecture tomorrow. What does it matter, anyway? You've been found out."

"Gawd, woman, it does matter. It might not be just my wife, it could also mean my job."

"I'm sorry, Ben, I really am."

He looks at her coldly. "I'm taking time off work. I need to go back home and try to talk to Karen."

Sophia nods. "Yes, of course." She picks up her coffee cup and takes it to the kitchen. Slowly, she pours the contents down the sink. If only she could turn back the clock half an hour. In slow motion, she goes up stairs and packs her few belongings. She knows she will never be here again.

Ben is still standing by the patio window. The sky is leaden with rain clouds. He turns when he hears her footsteps on the wooden floor. He pulls the corners of his mouth into a tight smile when he notices that she has packed her bag. She wants to cry, not for Ben or his family, but for herself. As she leaves her key on the coffee table, she feels truly alone. He can't wait to get rid of her and, yet, it hurts. It hurts like hell and she doesn't know why because she doesn't love him. She doesn't even like him. Tubular Ben is looking out for number one. He was contented to have a little fun with her while his wife didn't know about it. Now that she'd discovered it, he didn't want to play any more. Bastard, she thought.

"Call me if you find out who's been doing this."

She nods and then says, "Sure."

Chapter 31

Marianne's hate for Sophia is so strong she can almost taste it. Her hate has given her direction, dictated the pace. Sometimes she has thought she would suffocate, it has burned inside her with such force. She recalls her telephone conversation with Jim before Christmas.

"Marianne, why, in the name of God, do you want me to give you the location of this love-nest over the phone? What are you going to do with it? Is it your way of satisfying yourself that I am not fiddling you? I am down in Sligo, goddamnit, and I'd really like to be somewhere else!"

Marianne holds her breath; she can feel her lungs expand with the excess air, her heart beat increase, she's back in that place again.

A few seconds pass and then Jim says, "Here it is then, if it makes you feel better. No extra charge. Think of it as a Christmas present!"

She feels divided, more like her own self, that mild-mannered woman that she once was beginning to emerge again. Over the past few days, she has grown used to recalling pleasant moments on the farm with David and Emma at Christmas. She particularly likes to recall her walks with David. There were times on the farm when she felt her hate diminish, become almost miniscule. On the farm, it didn't matter any more. She could forget about Sophia and Gavin. Now that she is back in Dublin in her rented house, she is questioning her motives. Doubts have started to settle in, erode her earlier convictions. Perhaps a trip to the graveyard in Kells would help. This is not normal, she admits. What am I doing? I don't want to entertain normal, I don't want to forgive. The need for hatred and vengeance is so strong, how would she fill her days if she let go?

She banishes for now the thought of visiting Kathleen in Kells. Too much forgiveness and preachiness there. While she still lived in Kells, she had confided her story to Kathleen and told her how she felt about Sophia. She told Kathleen the full story about her darling son finding his so-called girlfriend in bed with another man. She can recall with such clarity Gavin coming to their house in Kells before the funeral and telling them the full story. She could smell the stale odour of beer and cigarette smoke off his clothes; her stomach had started to heave. Yet she remained, sitting on the living-room sofa with Stephen by her side and they listened to what Gavin had to say. Tentatively, Kathleen had suggested that Gavin might have been lying, but Marianne insisted on clinging to what he said.

"I mean, wouldn't this Sophia have come herself, if she wasn't such a self-centred harlot?" she said.

Kathleen's life can continue, she can tend her garden and her grandchildren can visit at any time. Kathleen has reasons to live, she has a purpose. Marianne is in limbo, hovering in a place between this life and no life. Right now, she feels her mission is to make life as unpleasant as possible for Ms Sophia Jordan. To sit down at Kathleen's table and try to make simple conversation about mutual acquaintances is impossible for her right now.

Now, Marianne stands at her kitchen sink. Guilt tugs at her elbow. "You really should phone Kathleen," it whispers in her ear, using that same coaxing voice that she often used with Liam. She lashes out with her tea-towel, belting it against the sink.

"Damn you, Stephen, you were never here for me!" she hears herself speak a truth that she has harboured for a very long time but never dared to voice. She leans against the sink for, inside, she is crumbling. A great anger surges inside her, and she swipes her teacup and plate with her hand off the sink. She hears them smash against the floor. Never before has she broken anything intentionally, never before has she voiced her truth. Tears of self-pity spill down her face. "Help me," she mutters to herself, craving the tender folds of someone's loving arms. She straightens up and looks out her kitchen window at the clear blue sky. She looks down at her feet.

"Sorry, cup, sorry, plate, I didn't mean to destroy you," she says and laughs to herself. She stoops down and starts to collect the pieces of broken crockery. Her mother had a china teapot that they had stuck back together with glue. Perhaps she'd do the same, glue the pieces back. It would act as a reminder, she thought, of just how damn angry she could get. She's discovered that she has a temper. In the end, it didn't matter, nothing mattered. This was a day that could be chalked off as a very black day. She wanted to crawl under her duvet and hide away from the world.

And yet, the sky is blue. "Stop this, Marianne," she says briskly as she wipes her nose and feels a sudden lightness about her, as if some great weight had suddenly been lifted from her shoulders.

She imagines her son is standing at the kitchen doorway, like he did on the morning before he left for London. Marianne had wanted to suggest for him to get a haircut before his trip but felt there was enough tension without adding to it. His rucksack was already waiting in the hall. Marianne was holding back the tears as she pretended to clear away the breakfast dishes. Of course, Stephen was away on another business trip.

"I'm off now," Liam said.

Marianne couldn't help it. She had tried desperately hard not to cry but she couldn't help the tears submerging in her eyes and her lips quivering, stopping her from speaking in a clear voice like she had hoped to.

"Are you sure you don't want me to drive you to the station?" she had asked again.

"Mum," he had replied the words laced with irritation, "Gavin's mother is driving us."

Then he turned and left without a final farewell.

Her son had grown into a stranger. She heard the front door slam, she watched from the living-room window as he walked down the drive. He waited at the gate for Gavin's mother. A few minutes passed and then Gavin's mother appeared. Marianne watched her son get into the back of the car. That was the last time she saw him alive.

Liam had wanted to go to London to be with his girlfriend, a girl they had never met. Marianne had suggested to Liam to bring her to visit but he had refused.

The memory is as fresh and as raw as ever.

Kathleen once told Marianne that, each day, she thanked God for all the good things that were in her life. Marianne wears a troubled expression as she tries with all her might to think of something good in her life.

As she is picking up the pieces of broken crockery, she thinks of her limbs. "Yes, I am thankful for my limbs," she says sarcastically. "I'm thankful for the cup and plate to break." She sweeps up all the tiny pieces. "I'm thankful for this day, I guess." Listening to her own voice makes her feel uneasy. "I must be going mad, I'm starting to talk to myself."

Marianne looks around her kitchen. It's like the

kitchen feels cheated because it is never used properly. She remembers that she has yoga this morning and she clings to this like a lifeline.

Carmel is determined to lose some weight. Shed that spare tire that falls out over her waistband. They have that in common, a tendency to put on weight. All those years of watching her darling husband and precious son tuck into dessert while she herself looked on enviously. She remembers kissing her son's chocolate lips and longing to have some of the bar he offered her.

At the yoga class, Marianne feels a tinge of disappointment when Carmel doesn't turn up. Marianne is curious. She can't possibly leave the class to call her. Play it cool, she tells herself. Maybe she'd call around later to Carmel's house. Marianne tries to relax and warm up for her yoga postures. Her body is tense and she cannot concentrate.

"Focus on the breath," Zoë their teacher says.

Marianne inhales and imagines all the air going into her lungs. Yet, her mind drifts. She's in David's kitchen again. She can actually smell the turf fire. She imagines that she has made scones and she is taking them out of the oven. David is outside tending to his cattle. In a few minutes he will arrive in, she will make a pot of tea. Marianne finds herself smiling. The room is filled with a Zen-like calm and Marianne can feel it. What is happening to me, she wonders? She closes her eyes and sees the blue sky that Zoë has prompted them to imagine. She exhales as she hears other people exhale.

"Raise your arms," Zoe says and Marianne turns to look at the woman next to her. Zoë continues to speak softly and slowly.

But for Marianne, the benefits of yoga remain sporadic; it seems nothing can exorcise her fully.

While she was around David and Emma she felt almost normal. She felt alive. Even needed.

Reluctantly, Emma had packed to go back to London. It was written all over her pretty face that she was in love with Mark and hated leaving.

"She looks pretty gloomy today," David remarked as they watched her walk up the path towards the house. From the kitchen window, David and Marianne watched Mark's car drive away.

Marianne knew exactly how Emma felt. She hated leaving too. "Maybe Mark will follow her to London," she said.

"Maybe," David replied.

It's useless. Her mind won't listen to her body and she just can't hold the postures this morning.

She is thinking about David again. She imagines herself walking down the path towards the road. The trees are arched like naked limbs towards the sky, she can hear birdsong. The class is over and she cannot remember one thing they did. She is indecisive. She doesn't know what to do. Go and see Carmel or go back home?

"See you next week," a woman says, smiling at Marianne.

She is so lost in thought that she forgets to answer. She has got to get back on track, she tells herself. She braces herself and walks up the road towards Caramel's house. The door is answered on the first ring of the bell.

"I've been trying to phone you," Carmel says holding her phone up to Marianne. It looks like she had been crying. Marianne takes a breath and walks into the warm hallway.

"I was at yoga."

"Come on into the kitchen and have a cup of coffee with me – I completely forgot about the yoga class." Carmel leads the way down the hall.

"I'd rather a cup of tea this time, if you don't mind," Marianne says apologetically.

"Yes, of course. I keep forgetting you would rather have tea. I'm just all over the place this morning."

"Would you like me to make the tea?" Marianne says, getting up from her chair.

Carmel attempts to smile but her lip wobble and she starts to cry. "I'm just so worried about Sophia. She never came to see us at all. She promised she'd come for the New Year and she didn't."

Marianne pours boiling water into the two mugs, dunking the tea bags up and down. She looks over at Carmel, sobbing at the kitchen table. Shafts of buttery light beam in the window. If Vermeer happened to walk in on this scene, would he want to capture it? Would the ordinariness of this scene appeal to him? Would he want to freeze this moment in time for other generations to ponder on? Would people observe this simple domestic scene in another hundred years and want to step into that world for a moment? Why was the woman at the table crying? Why did the woman making the tea have a faraway look in her eyes?

"You'll get the milk in the fridge," Carmel interrupts her train of thought to say.

Marianne places the cup of tea in front of Carmel. She wants to reach out and touch her but she dares not. She cannot afford to get involved. Carmel blows her nose quite forcefully and then straightens up in her chair.

"Children," she says and dunks a chocolate biscuit in her tea. "You are so lucky not to have any. They cause nothing but heartache."

Marianne sips her black tea. She has been drinking it for years now. She started to drink it after Liam's funeral. Shopping became such a chore she couldn't be bothered going out to buy milk. Meeting other mothers in the supermarket was almost unbearable. A trouble shared is a trouble halved has no application in her case.

Why me? Why my son? Why? Why? Why? The number of times she has asked herself that question. She wondered how God doled it out? Did he look down from his billowy clouds and see Marianne looking too happy with herself? Did he smile gleefully and say, "Here you are, Mrs, a little something for you!" Her son was dead. Was that how he had done it? And if that wasn't enough he returned again. "Stephen, your time on earth is up," the wise old man with the beard said and all the while she had begged him to take her. Life wasn't fair. If God really did exist, he had a lot of explaining to do.

Chapter 32

"One euro and ninety cents, please. Don't take the lid off the coffee, it's not allowed.

Health and Safety Regulations," the man says officiously.

"Uh, sorry." Sophia counts out the change on the train's tiny bar counter.

"Let me buy you a drink, instead," says a man who is drinking from a bottle of Budweiser at the bar. "No rules, either."

"No, thanks," she says, aware of his lecherous gaze.

Sophia returns to her cramped position on the train.

The train will take less than three hours to reach Dublin and she is too exhausted and fearful to

288

drive. At least in the train she doesn't have to concentrate on anything, her mind can drift. A cream Formica table separates her from the woman and child opposite. The woman looks Asian and it's hard to make out the sex of the child. The child is huddled up close to its mother with black hair sticking out from under the beige hood of its coat. Sophia wonders where are they going? The train chugs along giving the impression that it might just stop altogether if it took the notion. It must be hell for a child to be stuck on a train for such a long journey. Sophia is curious but she is reluctant to strike up a conversation with the mother. Just then the mother turns from staring out the window and looks at Sophia. The woman is grim-faced with dark circles etched under her eyes. It unnerves Sophia; it's like the woman is a reflection of her own inner turmoil.

Sophia smiles at her warmly. "Hi," she says.

The woman smiles back and shyly looks away as if she is embarrassed to be caught staring.

Maybe they are going to visit relatives. There must be a purpose for the trip. For hours now they have sat on the train and watched the dreary countryside unfold as they make their way towards Dublin.

Sophia reflects on her own reasons for going back to Dublin. She recalls the man on Grafton Street passing her the details of his modelling agency. Photogenic.

"Yes, that's it, I'm going back to Dublin because I'm photogenic. No matter where I go in the world, some unknown person or people will take photos of me," she reflects with bitter wryness. There is no safe place and she is almost past caring. She will expunge part of her guilt by visiting her mother. And Christina. Maybe Matt and Claire. She hopes Claire will be doing the guilt thing. Bitch! How could she?

I'll look for Matt first, she decides suddenly. Talk to him, explain to him. Without the Ben part. Fuck him and his instructions to her. Sophia already knows that Matt is not involved in Ben's woes. Matt suffered enough when she left him, she reasons. I'm sparing him by not telling him. Hopefully, he does not already know. She and Matt had a loving rela-tionship and a vibrant sexual chemistry existed between them. She blushes as she remembers some of their escapades. Occasionally, she made efforts to tell Matt of her past.

She recalls one right now. "Sssh," Matt had said, placing a lip upon her fingers. She was spread-eagled, naked on their king-sized bed. He surveyed her intensely and said: "All of this is mine from here on; nothing else matters."

She leans her head against the cool window pane as if seeking consolation. There is none to be found as the window vibrates, adding to her tension. She sits up straighter, her eyes closed, as she visualises Matt's handsome face. The way he'd smile wryly at her when she did something that amused him.

Sophia contemplates ringing Christina to enquire if she told Matt about Ben. Maybe she told someone else who passed it on. She thinks of Claire, taking her place in the bed she had shared with Matt. Her anger rises. Her so-called best friend!

"Tickets, please."

Sophia sits up, startled to see a uniformed man looking at her impassively. She rummages in her bag, her pockets, but cannot find her ticket.

"God, I don't know where it is, I got it at the dispenser in Sligo ..."

"I'm afraid you'll have to buy another one, ma'am," he says coldly.

"Hold on a minute, do you mind if I check the bar? I was there earlier – I may have left it there."

"OK, but come back to me. I'm not going to chase you. There is a fine for this type of thing, you know."

The man behind the bar recognises her instantly. "You're looking for this, I presume?" he says, holding up her ticket.

"You can thank himself there, he noticed you drop it."

Budweiser Boy is still standing in the bar carriage, leering stupidly at her. "You should have had that drink. You dropped it when paying for your coffee. Barman, give the lady a drink on me."

Sophia waves a dismissive hand at the barman and mouths a silent curse at his sole customer. The ticket man is now standing beside the bar carriage, and dutifully passes it through his recording device.

"You must love your job," she says, with heavy sarcasm.

Eventually the train arrives at Connolly station, the last stop. She watches the Asian mother gently wake her child. It tugs at Sophia heartstrings just watching them. There is so much love and tenderness in the mother's touch. The child stretches itself and yawns. Its tiny hands peep out from under the large beige coat and stretch out towards its mother. The movement is so lovely it almost brings tears to Sophia's eyes. This is love in action, Sophia thinks to herself. This is something I may never experience, a fact she reflects on with sadness. The mother is speaking to the child in some foreign language. She points out the window. The child sits up and wipes its eyes. Then it looks sleepily out the window. The child then looks at Sophia. She smiles back, then takes ten euros out of her wallet and attempts to give it to her.

"For you," she says to the child.

"No, thank you," the mother says, smiling politely.

"Please, it would make me happy," Sophia says touching her chest.

The child reaches out a hand for the money.

"No, thank you," the mother says again.

"Please," Sophia says and gives the money to the child.

The Asian woman looks at Sophia and quickly looks away, then bends her head and says, "Thank you."

"You're welcome," Sophia says and leaves her seat quickly.

People rush past her as she makes her way towards the exit. No matter what tragedy hits you it doesn't stop the world from revolving. City life is pulsating around her but she feels strangely detached from it. She feels conspicuous as she looks around her to see if any one is following her. She walks briskly on, keeping pace with her fellow commuters. On leaving the station, she turns left and left again into the Financial Services Centre. The drum of her heartbeat against her chest seems to get louder with each step she takes. She is dreading this. Yet, she is eager to see his handsome face again.

She intends to drop in unexpectedly on Matt. She glances at her watch. It's only eleven fifteen. The Harbourmaster Bar. I'll go in there for a while and compose myself, she thinks. This is where Matt went most Friday evenings to wind down with his work colleagues. How often she had dropped by to collect him! Matt liked a few pints, but he was strictly second division compared to what some of his mates might put away.

She enters the bar, which has also established a reputation for good food. Come one o'clock, it will be thronged with young men and women who epitomize the era of the Celtic Tiger. She will ring Matt before then; she does not want him walking in upon her. Sophia is by no means alone in the place; several people have dropped in for their mid-morning break and the place is buzzing nicely.

How would someone fit in here? she ponders.

You'd have to be young, have your own apartment, drive a brand new car and wear the latest expensive clothes. BT for the ladies, Louis Copeland or FX Kelly for the lads. She smiles to herself as she recalls the unfortunate Born Again Christian who had taken up a position outside the bar one Christmas past with his loudspeaker and leaflets. *"I was cash-rich but soul-poor!"* he boomed. *"Haven't you done well for yourself, they'd say to me, when I knew I had no self. I was at the bottom and in despair until God came into my life."* He remained serene when a few belligerent lads and ladies taunted him. "We need more of this, man! We'd take you into the bar, only you wouldn't get served. Where are you sleeping tonight? We'll go down later and get you!"

"Sophia, what in the name of all saints are you doing here?"

"Fiona," she replies, turning to face Matt's secretary. This was not how she planned it but, then again, she had no plan. Fiona tilts her dark head sideways, her eyes bright with curiosity. Anything that Sophia says to her will spread like bush-fire through the office.

"Gosh, you still look great, always did, you lucky bitch! Where have you been? You were there, and suddenly you were gone without explanation.

Wait 'til I tell you –"

"Fiona, shut up for a minute. I hope Matt's not coming down, is he? I don't want to meet him like this."

"No, no, he's not in today. I've news about him – I'll tell you in a minute. What would you be doing around here if you didn't want to meet him?"

"Impulse. I was planning how I'd contact him … I just came in for a coffee."

"You went straight to the end of the plan, and I see you have no coffee. It's almost noon. They'll be starting the menu shortly. Fancy lunch?"

Sophia, relaxing a little, peruses the menu. Fiona is on the phone, asking a colleague to cover for her. She chooses a fresh crab salad from the menu and Fiona points out a tandoori chicken salad, while continuing to talk into her mobile phone.

"I'm paying, no arguments," says Sophia as Fiona puts down the phone. "You were going to say something about Matt?"

"Yeah – he's been promoted. Assistant Director of Information Systems. He deserves it. He's a whiz with computers. He's kept me as his secretary, and that means I get promoted too! Well, I had to do an interview with Matt, a formality, but company procedure."

"That's great, I – "

Fiona interrupts her again, mimicking Matt: "'Come in, Ms Shaffrey, close the door, I need to see your credentials. Show me your credentials!' We were nearly on the floor laughing."

"Hands off . . ." says Sophia, her voice suddenly trailing away.

"You're joking. I would be too if I were to say anything like that is going on. It was, though, the first time I've seen him laugh, really laugh, since you left. Why did you go, Sophia?"

"Just had to. Can we put that on hold – you still haven't told me where he is today."

"I don't know, other than he took a day off. Working big hours lately, probably crashed out at the apartment."

"Is he seeing anyone?"

"I don't know that either, I wouldn't think so. You'd hardly expect him to be celibate though. In another situation, I'd volunteer to warm his sheets for him."

"Harlot! Now, eat your food."

Sophia finds she is enjoying herself immensely. Fiona is easy company and helps her to banish her woes for now. The food is to its usual high standards and they clear their plates. Fiona is reminiscing about the rugby internationals when Matt would try, in vain, to match his buddies, drink for drink. He'd be plastered, and Sophia would have to take him home. It would only be about three times a year, but it was enough at the time – it would take Matt days to recover. Funny, she thought, I am almost basking in the glow of it right now, almost like being a part of Matt again. Her thoughts are interrupted.

"What are you going to do now? I'll be going back shortly."

"I'm going out to see him, Fiona. I'm going to face it, for good or bad."

"Do you want him back?"

"Yes."

Sophia always worked late, back when she was ambitious and had her sights set on a higher position in the company. There was always a meeting or a presentation to prepare. She realises now that she had taken Matt for granted. I really didn't treasure what I had, she thinks as she zigzags her way through the thronged pavements. Her feet are taking her towards Matt's apartment. It has to be done. She can't go back to Sligo this evening without doing it. With every tentative step she takes, she thinks that Claire might be there, she might have moved into the apartment with Matt. They were both hurting from bad experiences with other people. They were both on the rebound. Christina had also said … her mind goes blank. What exactly did Christina say? She tries to think. Oh, yes. Matt had come to visit and brought Christmas presents to the children. Sophia could kick herself for not being more attentive but it had always been a problem with her. When her mother or Christina started to talk, she would automatically switch off. Claire had always maintained that Sophia had changed after that summer in London. "It must be me," she admits to herself. While this crazy chatter is going on in her head, she is still putting one foot in front of the other and making her way towards Matt's apartment. She isn't thinking about what she is about to do, she is just following the footpath.

"It's Sophia," she replies when he answers the intercom button.

"Come on up," she hears, his level tone betraying nothing.

Two minutes later they are looking into each other's eyes.

"Sophia," he mutters. She can see that he is visibly shocked by her appearance. "Are you okay?"

He is still holding the door ajar, she standing on the threshold.

"Hi, Matt," she hears herself whisper.

"This is a surprise," he says and opens the door fully. "Come on in."

Chapter 33

Marianne sits silently in her armchair, nursing a cup of coffee. The euphoric feeling of Leitrim is gone and is replaced by a depression that is rampant. She goes hurtling into the past . . .

"Mrs Taylor, can we come in?" two police officers on her Kells doorstep are enquiring.

"Yes, yes. What's the problem? Has Liam got into trouble?" Marianne said anxiously, thoughts of Gavin Daly flashing across her brain.

"Could you sit down, Mrs Taylor? It's more serious. I'm afraid there's been an accident. Is your husband contactable?"

Marianne hears the words; it does not register with her that the female officer is leading. She looks at each of them, sitting uncomfortably in their chairs. An accident, the roof of an apartment block, Liam falling. She feels she is falling with him . . .

She blocks out what they are saying to her.

"Mrs Taylor? Mrs Taylor ? Your husband . . . he really needs to know."

"Yes, yes. Of course. I'll ring him."

Marianne comes back in to the room. "He's coming right out."

"Do you want us to stay with you?"

"No, I mean, yes. Can we go to the kitchen? I'll make tea."

For Marianne, it didn't matter about the luxury of a living-room; it was the kitchen that women always gravitated towards in times of trouble and indeed celebration. It was comforting and familiar and it was her domain. At least in her kitchen she felt in control. Was she the only woman that reacted this way? Maybe there were different types of women who found consolation in different places like their bedroom or their garden.

The door of the house opens. Stephen is coming into the kitchen. Marianne is on her feet. The emotion inside her combusts and then explodes.

"It's Liam! We've lost him, we've lost him forever." She staggers and darkness descends.

Stephen was on the next flight out. Her doctor insisted that she was not going. It was a long wait. After phoning her friend Kathleen, she sat down at her kitchen table and waited. Kathleen came immediately and over unfinished cups of tea, they organised her son's funeral. Even after the funeral Kathleen called every day. Marianne feels guilty that she has forgotten about Kathleen. Is her husband Geoffrey still alive? She hadn't intended to forget her but she couldn't reconcile her two worlds. Here living in Dublin and her real life in Kells.

She walks out to the hall table and picks up her phone. She hesitates; she can't do it. 'It's only me,' Kathleen would announce in her bright cheery voice as she came in the back door.

"Only me," Marianne says out loud as she walks into her living-room. The TV is on but she has it on mute. It's a re-run of *The Rockford Files* – she wonders if the actor is dead now? What's his name again? Lately her memory has been slipping, she can't remember things like she used to. She sits down and looks at the TV screen. Kathleen never forgot to call her even when she went on holidays. 'I'm just phoning to say hello,' she'd say. 'See how you are.' It's been over a year now since she last saw Kathleen. She is a few years older than Marianne. Her sons are all grown up now and have moved away. The least she could do is phone her.

She has been so preoccupied with Sophia and Gavin. Finding them has taken up so much of her time. Last October, after the death of her husband, Marianne decided she was going to find them. She had got her solicitor to find her a decent detective. He came up with Jim. She was curious. She wanted to find out what had happened to the girl who had survived while her son had died. And Gavin, such a delinquent, she was quite surprised to find that he was married with children. There really was no predicting how things would turn out. Marianne went to Jim's tiny office in Drumcondra and told him she was looking for a girl called Sophia Jordan. She really had very little to go on, except that she knew she lived in Dublin and had studied in UCD. Marianne had never met her but she knew that Sophia had been in their house in Kells one weekend while they were away. She also knew that her son was in love with her. That dreadful summer Sophia had gone to London to work. She had got a job as a chambermaid in a hotel on Russell Square. Liam had followed her there. Only for Gavin, she would never have known the truth. It was against her wishes that Liam had gone to London with Gavin. Marianne had never liked him; she insisted that he was a bad influence on Liam. But her son wouldn't hear a bad word said against him.

Finding Sophia and snooping into her life became her total preoccupation – together with a little snooping into Gavin's life. She wanted to see how those lives had unfolded. As far as she could see, they were doing fine. Life was treating them better than she had expected.

When Jim gave her Sophia's home address, Marianne just couldn't help it: she had to go to Templeogue and see the family. She wondered if they knew what their daughter had done to her precious son.

Marianne had parked her car on the opposite side of the road. She watched Sophia's parents come and go. Before the fatal accident Alan left for work every morning around eight o'clock, and usually Carmel left about ten to do some shopping or else to a class. Then, later in the day, she went to visit Christina. She was quite the doting grandmother. An ache of loss and regret grew inside Marianne as she watched Carmel. These were things that she had been robbed of.

Chapter 34

Standing in their old apartment, at first Sophia feels disorientated. She scans the place quickly and smiles, relieved. Amazingly, it looks the same. Any moment now, she'll be her old self. Matt hasn't changed a thing. Her novels are still on the shelf beside his and the watercolour she bought last year still hangs on the wall. She feels a slight trickle of hope run through her. She is bracing herself as she waits for him to hurl accusations her way. She is aware of Matt staring at her and she feels herself blush under his steady gaze. She is waiting for him to say something. Nothing. He heads for the kitchen. The kettle switches off. The smell of toast is scenting the air, making her stomach gurgle. She feels unsure of what to do. Should she go into the kitchen or should she stay in the living-room and wait for him?

"Are you hungry?" he shouts from the kitchen. The apartment is on the second floor. She walks towards the window and looks down at the opaque dusk, people passing by on the footpath. Cars form a long sluggish line as they attempt to make their way home. They decided to buy an apartment in the city centre rather than face commuting into the city each day. Everyone is homeward bound, she thinks, and turns to look at Matt who is standing at the kitchen door staring at her.

"You've cut your hair," he remarks. He's the first person to comment on it.

She meets his steady honest gaze. "Yes, just a trim," she replies.

He gestures for her to sit down and she does. Matt comes into the living-room carrying a tray with coffee and toasted bagels topped with his favourite cream cheese. She notices the pottery mugs on the tray. When they first started dating, they had gone to Kerry for a weekend. It was on that weekend that they had decided to move in together. They were passing a pottery shop and Sophia had noticed some lovely pottery mugs in the window. They went into the shop to have a look.

"Let's buy six," Matt had suggested.

"Let's buy two," she had said. Matt had looked disappointed and she had gone on to explain that they weren't going to share these mugs. These were their own special mugs, a symbol of their love for each other.

The mugs were used on special occasions only. When they first moved into the apartment together, they had coffee in them. When Sophia had got promoted, it was from these mugs that they drank champagne. If the roles were reversed, she would have dumped them in the bin without giving it a second thought. Is he trying to make some kind of silent statement?

"Help yourself," he says.

Sophia takes half a bagel with cheese. "Mmm," she says as she bites into it. "This is good."

They are facing each other: Sophia sitting on the sofa, Matt on the recliner opposite, the coffee table dividing them.

"How is work?" she asks.

Matt shakes his head, his lips a thin unforgiving line. "You hardly came all the way from Sligo to ask me that."

Sophia ventures to look at him. She notices his dark curly hair has grown since she last saw him but, apart from that, he looks the same.

"No, I guess not." She sips some coffee and puts her unfinished bagel back on her plate.

"You used to love bagels and cheese," he says.

"I'm not hungry."

"I'll have it so. Waste not, want not."

Sophia can feel the minutes ticking past. It's like she has been rigged up to the biggest clock ever and it is ticking away inside her. *Tick, tock, tick, tock,* it's going. There is an unnatural calmness in the apartment. Then she realises the TV isn't blaring. "Did you have a nice Christmas?"

"It was OK," he says and puts the last of his bagel in his mouth. "As you well know, I'm not mad about it. Too commercial."

"Yes," she says nodding her head in agreement. "It is too commercial." She wants to kick herself. It sounds so pathetic and she feels so inadequate. Mentally, she is telling herself to get on with it and talk, but she just can't do it.

"Had you?" he asks after a beat.

It takes Sophia a minute to comprehend. "Yes, it was OK. I stayed in Sligo."

"I know," he replies, staring at her coldly.

She deduces from this response that he knows about Ben. So, Christina told him. There was a possibility that he might have visited Sligo over Christmas. He might have taken those photographs and sent them to Ben's wife.

'Nothing ventured, nothing gained,' was a favourite quote of her father's. She squares back her shoulders and plunges ahead. "Were you in Sligo over Christmas?"

Matt glares at her. "No. Why are you asking me such a ridiculous question? What would have been in Sligo for me?"

She knows it is causing him a lot of effort to stop himself from hitting her or at the very least throwing her out of his apartment. "I don't know. Christina had suggested you might –"

"Might what? Humiliate myself further? Sophia, I get your title to the deeds of this place in the post. Get real. I went to my parents for Christmas – remember, we were supposed to go together this year, because last year we went to yours. And for the New Year, I went skiing with Tony and Brian from work," he says, a little loudly. He is on his feet now.

"I'm sorry, Matt," she says, her voice no more than a humble whisper.

Matt snorts. "You're sorry?" He swings round to face her, his breathing heavy on her face. "What the fuck are you sorry for?"

"For hurting you so much," she says.

"Oh, well, I'll recover," he says and laughs manically.

"I'd better go," she says.

"Yes!" he shouts. Those lovely blue eyes that had always looked at her with such tenderness are now looking at her with hate and fury. "Do that!"

He picks up the pottery mug that she was drinking from and throws it at the wall. It shatters and black coffee spills down the white wall.

"Matt!" she hears herself say.

He takes the second mug, sending it to a similar fate. "There," he says. "Now, do you know any decent decorators?"

She moves forward instinctively and bends to pick up a pottery fragment.

"No – leave it as it is." He is standing with his hands on his hips admiring his handiwork.

She feels something is slipping away from her. Gasping for breath, she manages to say, "I'd better go."

Outside the apartment door, she leans against the wall, her body shaking uncontrollably. She squeezes her eyes closed and tries to suppress the scream that is building up inside her.

Chapter 35

The inquest had recorded Liam's death as misadventure, with no evidence of foul play. Marianne had tried to implicate Sophia Jordan in his death and, at her insistence, the police interviewed Sophia in London.

"I'm sorry, Mrs Taylor," the policewoman afterwards advised her, for the umpteenth time, "there is no evidence Sophia Jordan had anything to do with your son's death. In fact, she was – eh, with another man when Liam fell to his death. I really don't see what more we can do."

"What about Gavin?" The post-mortem had revealed traces of alcohol, cannabis and ecstasy in Liam's body.

"We've made exhaustive enquiries. It seems he

doesn't even do drugs. He submitted to voluntary tests in connection with a separate matter. Sophisticated tests back up his story: he is not a user."

Stephen put on a stoic public face at the time of his son's death. At home, he became morose and brooding. They both were in terrible pain and, for a short while, had acted out the role of newly-weds to help each other cope. Newly-weds indeed! Sex with Stephen was always perfunctory. For him, focus and performance was confined to the sexual organs, and increasing the frequency in mid-life was merely a reaffirmation of what always had been. It was not that it was unpleasant in any way.

Intimacy, yeah, that is what was missing, intimacy of mind and body, Marianne muses to herself. That phase did not last that long in any event, Stephen refocusing on work quite quickly.

"Where did I read it," she mumbles to herself. "A man who is good in the boardroom is less likely to translate well to the bedroom." She is angry with herself for tarnishing her husband's memory with these thoughts. Wasn't she nicknamed 'Miss Prude' at school by groping suitors with smacked faces?

Anyway, Stephen's cancer put paid to all of it ... She puts her coat on, but reverses at the hall door.

Suddenly, she is dialling David's number. The phone lifts at the other end. Marianne takes her coat off and lets it fall on the hall floor. She walks back into her living-room and sits down on the sofa.

"So," he says and she hears the softness of his voice, "how are you keeping?"

"I'm fine," she says. A strange warm sensation runs through her. This feels intimate. Her insides quiver ever so slightly. "How are you, David?"

David groans. "I'm fine but I find the place really quiet without you and Emma," he says.

"You do?" she says and this pleases her.

"Call it February blues," he says and chuckles to himself. "Emma phoned yesterday to tell me that Mark is going over to see her next weekend."

"That's great. She still thinks you don't know about the first visit?"

"Yes."

"Aren't you pleased?"

"I suppose so, but what happens if she comes back here to live and she hates it. What happens if history repeats itself?"

"Oh, David, Emma is different to Sue," Marianne says solicitously.

"Is she?"

"Well, yes. Sue was born and raised in London,

her parents were well off and she had no skills to prepare her for living in the countryside. She found it lonely and she just couldn't stand not having a Marks & Spencer on the high street."

"I guess you are right."

"Of course I'm right," she says boldly in the hope that it will stop him from worrying unnecessary. "Maybe Mark would like to go to London to live."

"I doubt it."

"I see. Well, we can only hope for the best."

"Yes, indeed," David says.

All too soon, Marianne feels that the conversation is going to come to an end. She is searching desperately for another topic, anything to prolong it. "Well, then," she says, "I'd better go."

"We should do this more often."

"Yes," she says eagerly.

"Great, great."

"Bye, David," she says and closes her eyes to block out the awful longing that is building up inside her.

She regrets that the conversation ended so soon. She has to do something on this day. She is the Mistress of Misery for Sophia, but she is running short of money and ideas in prolonging it.

There is nothing for it: she will ring Kathleen and

talk to her. Kathleen answers on the third ring. She sounds the same. Last time Marianne saw her she had been complaining of stomach cramps. She knows she shouldn't have left without leaving a forwarding address or, at the very least, an explanation. She could have told her that she was going to spend some time with her brother in New York.

"I understand," Kathleen replies after a lengthy explanation from Marianne as to why she left Kells without saying goodbye to her.

"How is Geoffrey?"

"Thank God, he is well," she replies.

"I have to go back to check on the house – perhaps we could go for lunch if you like?" Marianne suggests tentatively.

"That would be lovely, I'm looking forward to it already," Kathleen says without a hint of sarcasm.

Kathleen has four adult sons. She married young to Geoffrey, eighteen years her senior. He is now living in a nursing home and does not recognise his family. Kathleen visits him daily. Yet she keeps going with a dignity and courage that is enviable. These are qualities that Marianne knows she doesn't possess. She was not prepared to let go. That old anger just needed a little encouragement and she'd be back on track again.

Chapter 36

"Sophia Jordan!" Carmel stands at the door of her house staring at her daughter. She looks at her watch. Seven thirty in the evening, no car in the driveway.

"Aren't you going to let me in, Mammy? It's cold out here."

"Of course. I can't believe it, after all that's happened. Sit down, I'll put on the kettle."

Sophia had taken a taxi home. She had stood outside the house while she calmed herself before ringing her mother's doorbell. She had missed the train back to Sligo. And "Matt, can I go to bed while you wreck the apartment?" was hardly an option.

Sophia awakens the following morning, glad that her mother had limited her interrogation. It was as if Carmel had sensed she needed both home and space at the same time. Carmel has already phoned the college to tell them that Sophia is sick and won't be in for the rest of the week, and she has promised to organise a sick note from the doctor for her. She really did think of everything. Sophia just couldn't face phoning Mary Leahy herself.

She opens her sister's wardrobe and looks at the various tops that are hanging there. Christina uses her mother's house like a second home; she is always here with her two girls. Carmel and Christina seem happy with the arrangement but it would drive Sophia mad; she just couldn't cope with having her mother around on a daily basis. She knows she's being unkind. Downstairs she can hear her mother talking on the phone. She pulls out an old sweatshirt and pulls it on over her pyjama top.

Carmel is mopping up the kitchen floor when Sophia comes in.

"Sorry, Mammy," she says.

Carmel smiles at her beautiful daughter and at that moment she feels she can do no wrong. She aches to throw her arms around her and hug her tightly to her and tell her that she loves her.

"Come on in," she says as she briskly dries up the

floor. "I don't know what I was thinking about, washing the floor!" She puts the mop away.

Sophia is glad to be home; she feels safe here in her mother's kitchen. She can use this week to rest and come to terms with all that has happened.

Her mother is filling the kettle at the sink. "Tea or coffee?"

"A very strong coffee," Sophia says.

Carmel is popping bread into the toaster. "I'm making you a good breakfast of scrambled eggs and toast," she announces.

Sophia feels terrible; she doesn't deserve this much loving. She watches her mother busy preparing breakfast for her. It seems so normal, so commonplace, yet she feels totally disconnected from it. The thought of having to eat scrambled egg is making her feel sick. She knows she's not up to eating it.

"Is Christina coming around this morning?" she manages to ask, feeling she has got to put in an effort – pretend for her mother's sake that she is all right.

"No, not today."

Carmel deposits a plate of the most perfect scrambled eggs in front of Sophia.

"How come your scrambled eggs always look so good?"

Carmel smiles and sits down at the kitchen table beside her daughter. "It was the only thing you would eat as a child and I learned to be really careful making them. I didn't want to turn you off them too."

Sophia picks up a forkful of egg and puts it in her mouth. "Delicious," she says. Eating here in the kitchen with her mother makes her relax and, for a while at least, she feels normal. She surprises herself by eating all her breakfast.

Carmel helps herself to a slice of toast and puts some butter and marmalade on it. "I shouldn't," she says. "I just love toast, it's my comfort food."

"So, what do you do on a Tuesday morning when you're not baby-sitting?"

"This morning I was going into town with Marianne. I was going to buy some new gear for the gym."

"We can still do that if you like. Tell me about this Marianne," Sophia says.

Carmel shrugs indifferently. "I can do that tomorrow or at the weekend, I'm in no hurry. As for Marianne, I met her before your father died. She wasn't at the funeral. Knew nothing of it until afterwards."

Sophia does not want to go down this road.

"Have you gone to the gym at all?"

"Yes, of course I have," Carmel says and quickly looks away from her daughter. Sophia knows that she is lying. Her dear mother couldn't tell a lie to save her life.

"What would you like to do today?" Carmel is asking as she takes their dirty dishes off the kitchen table.

"Oh, I don't mind – we could go out for lunch?"

Carmel beams with motherly pride at her daughter.

Sophia has been dreading a good telling-off from her mother, but it hasn't come. Such motherly instinct, knowing when the time is not right to pry. The guilt resurfaces.

"Oh, Mammy," she sobs, "I have made such a mess of everything."

"No, you haven't," Carmel says while they hug fiercely. "You're just going through a bad patch, you'll see. Take a few days off work and stay here with me and we'll sort it all out."

Sophia is too exhausted and beaten to disagree. "I'm so sorry that I've been such a lousy daughter."

"You haven't, my darling, you've always made me so proud," Carmel says with such conviction that Sophia feels truly loved.

Sophia looks down at her sister's sweatshirt and her old pyjamas. "I'll probably get something upstairs in my case. Just as well that I didn't bring all my stuff to Sligo."

Chapter 37

Carmel is all apologies to Marianne on the phone. "I'm really sorry about it," she is saying. "Sophia is here," she whispers, "She's upstairs having a shower – I don't want to leave her on her own."

"Is something the matter?" Marianne asks innocently.

"I'm not sure."

Marianne can hear the motherly concern in her voice.

"I'm hoping she might talk to me today and tell me what's going on. Something must be, she looks awful. She came here late last night. She wasn't making much sense."

"Oh, dear, I'm so sorry to hear that," Marianne

says and she has to stop herself from asking more questions.

"I'm hoping she'll stay with me for a few days."

"Yes, that would be lovely. Perhaps that's what she needs – a rest. Is there anything I can do to help?"

"Ah, no, I mean thanks for the offer, but I don't think so. I think the best thing I can do is just be here for her."

"Yes, you are so right. Try and give her some space and maybe she'll talk of her own accord rather than you asking her what is wrong."

Carmel laughs. "You mean rather than me interrogating her."

"Whatever."

Carmel sighs. "I will. Look, I think I hear her coming downstairs, I'll phone you tomorrow."

Marianne places the phone back on the hall table. The house seems hollow and airless. She has nothing to do here today. "Sophia is recuperating at home," she hears herself say aloud. Poor Sophia, what a miserable ten years she has had climbing the career ladder, she thinks sardonically. She is young and vibrant and all she needs to do is click her fingers for some willing male to come panting. A new surge of rage and energy surfaces. She feels excited.

Sophia is beginning to feel the pressure and this is nothing more than she deserves. She had caused her son's death and she had walked away without any feelings of remorse or regret. Marianne wonders, if she said Liam's name to her would she even remember him? They were getting closer and closer and soon they would meet. What then, Marianne wonders? She didn't know. Liam would tell her what to do when the time was right.

Chapter 38

"OK, thanks, we'll be there by one thirty."

"What's that, Sophia?" her mother asks.

"We're going to Thornton's, at the Fitzwilliam Hotel. It's a Michelin two-star. I only got us in on a cancellation."

"We can't go there. It'll cost a fortune."

"No, it won't, Mammy. That's a myth. For a few euro more than your average, I get to treat my mother in style."

"I'm going back upstairs to change. Style, as you say it, demands style. Come up yourself, you may need to reconsider what you're wearing."

"Cheek!"

Thornton's dining-room had a feel of old world elegance about it and Sophia is glad she has borrowed a suede jacket from Christina. Her mother looks fabulous in her light blue *Escanda* suit. If she saw the right man, would she go again, Sophia wonders. She stifles a giggle.

"I'll have the chicken," Sophia tells the waiter.

"I'll go for the lamb," says Carmel

"Drinks?" he asks.

"The house white will be fine for me," says Carmel quickly.

"OK. Two glasses of house white, please."

Carmel's eyes are darting around the place. She leans forwards. "Are you sure you can afford this?"

"Relax," Sophia says. She forces herself to smile. Why does her mother always have to fuss? Why can't she just enjoy it without asking such stupid questions? Matt would always laugh at her and tell her to just ignore Carmel. Absence certainly was not making her heart grow fonder.

"Wait until I tell Marianne!"

Carmel is too busy looking around her, taking in every detail of the soothing interior. "We could bump into someone famous here," she says and giggles girlishly.

It is a long time since Sophia has seen her mother so excited.

The food arrives. The waiter pours two glasses of

house wine and Carmel takes a sip, relaxing into her seat. They eat quietly for a while, pausing between mouthfuls to exchange tit-bits of news. This is real food, comforting and restorative, Sophia thinks to herself. The service is faultless.

"I'm having an espresso coffee to finish," Carmel says, wiping her mouth and hands with a white linen napkin.

"Oh, have a dessert, Mammy!"

"No, no, just the coffee."

"OK, I'll go for that, too."

As they sip their coffee, Carmel says, "Sophia, I've held back until now, but Matt, he –"

"Aw, Mammy, I was wondering when you'd get around to it."

"OK, Sophia, I won't be labouring it, but you and Matt were meant for each other. You also lived together for four years and you had bliss, don't deny it. In my day, there were no trial marriages. I went straight from my parents' house to the marital bed with Alan."

"You're not going to start discussing your sex life with me?" says Sophia, glad of an opportunity to blot the raw pain she feels.

"No, and will you lower your voice" said Carmel, red-faced and exasperated. "Be serious, and get serious. Matt's your man."

"Wish it was that simple as you say, Mammy, I really do."

Chapter 39

Marianne is standing outside Sophia's apartment in Sligo. The landlord that rents the apartment to Sophia is on his way to let her in. She's told him over the phone that she is Sophia's mother. "My daughter is in hospital," she said with counterfeit concern. "I need to get into her apartment to collect some clothes and medication for her. I'm after coming from Dublin and I forgot to bring the keys with me."

"I'm on my way," he said.

Marianne couldn't believe her luck. She watches a small fat man getting out of a very big flashy car. His enormous stomach seems to lead the way and his short legs have a hard time following him. He smiles as he makes his way towards her. She guesses that he is the landlord.

"Mrs Jordan," he says, as he gets closer to her. Keys are jangling from his belt. "Sorry I took so long." He reaches out his wide short hand to shakes hers. He is slightly breathless. "Traffic."

"Thank you for coming,"

"How is she?"

"She's comfortable," Marianne says.

He takes some keys off a ring. "I always keep a copy," he jangles them in front of Marianne. "The number of times tenants have rung me when they've lost their keys!" he shakes his head in exasperation.

"This is very good of you, Mr . . ." She pauses as she tries to remember his name.

"Call me Pat," he says and chuckles. "Or Paddy if you like." He opens the door and ushers her into the building. Pig-blue eyes glint out from thick black eyebrows.

Marianne feels almost exhilarated by what she is doing. She is hardly listening to him as he leads the way upstairs to the second floor.

"Here we are," he says with a flourish. Never before in her mundane life has she dared to do something like this.

On those previous occasions, in Dublin, she had

talked Jim into lending her his master-keys. Initially he had point-blank refused of course, until she made him an offer he couldn't refuse. Yes, she had paid heavily for that – and almost lost his services. For a few mornings she cased the joint – an expression she had heard used on TV. Matt and Sophia left for work each morning at the same time. Once they were gone she would use her set of keys to get in. She looked through Sophia's photo albums, but there were no photos of her son. "Naturally," she had whispered to herself, sardonically. No need to inform Matt of her past. Nice and cosy, if not demure. She went through Sophia's wardrobe to see what kind of clothes she wore. She scanned through her diary, just checking dates and events so she could come back sometime in the future. Marianne was also looking for some clue as to how Sophia felt about Liam. Did she love her son, that was the burning question? Was his death for nothing? She found nothing to satisfy her curiosity. Their bathroom was well stocked with luxury bubble bath, scented candles and bath salts. Once, while in their apartment, Marianne lit the candles and filled the bath with water and poured almost a full bottle of bubble bath into it.

"Do you need any help?" Pat is saying, bringing

her back to the present. He has opened the door to Sophia's apartment for her.

Marianne gives him a sincere smile even though she thinks he is a very creepy individual. "I'm so grateful, Pat," she says. "I really am." She can't wait to get rid of him.

"I hope Sophia will be OK, Mrs Jordan," he says as he stands on the threshold.

Marianne blesses him with a sweet smile. "Thanks, I'll just collect some stuff and then I will head straight back to Dublin."

"You have my number," he says.

Marianne is tempted to close the door in his face. He is the last man on earth she would phone. He leaves at last.

Marianne shivers; the apartment is cold and eerily quiet. She is surprised at how empty the place is. There isn't even a TV. Marianne sits on the sofa and looks around her. She notices the hold-all inside the door. She must have dropped it there when she returned from the schoolhouse. Marianne picks up her bag and takes it over to the sofa. She opens it and feels no guilt or shame for what she is about to do. Noticing the William Trevor novel, she moves the bookmark back halfway. She notices the sexy underwear and wonders if they were a present from Ben for Christmas. Sophia seems to favour black. Two black T-shirts. Tailored black trousers. She fingers the black cashmere top and knows that it is expensive. A pair of faded jeans. At the bottom of the bag is a little purse. Marianne shakes it and hears coins jingle. She opens the purse there is nothing inside but spare coins and, goodness, what looks like a spare key!

In the kitchen, Marianne decides to make herself a cup of tea. She switches on the kettle and it starts to boil. She walks into the bedroom and notices that the bed has been made up. A few tops and casual trousers are hung in the wardrobe. Marianne opens a tub of Body Shop coca butter and rubs some on her dry hands. She sees some juicy lip gloss and wonders what it must be like to wear it. She tries some on and looks at herself critically in the mirror. She really is being mischievous. She feels like she's a young girl again, let loose in some rich aunt's bedroom. Back in the kitchen, she puts a tea bag in a white cup.

Then her heart leaps in her chest when she hears a knock on the door.

"It's me, Pat!" he shouts from outside the door.

Marianne almost drops the teacup in fright.

"Do you need any help bringing stuff down?" he asks.

Marianne rushes to the door and opens it, a bright smile firmly fixed on her face. "I'm fine, thank you," she says.

He is looking at her closely; he must be on to her, she thinks.

"What is wrong with your daughter?" he asks.

Marianne's eyes grow bigger in her head; she wasn't expecting him to have any interest in the details.

"They're not sure yet, they're just doing tests."

"Uh, OK. Will you be long more?"

"Ten minutes, please. I am looking for some herbal remedies she was taking and I need to use the bathroom."

"Ten minutes, then."

Marianne rushes back to the bedroom and goes to work. She is frenzied, manic, and is panting heavily as she stands back to admire her fancywork. She grabs a small hold-all and shoves a few items of clothing in. Composing herself, she shuts the door as Pat comes up the stairs again.

"Got them."

"What?"

"The herbal remedies," she says waving a small blue box at Pat's nose. "Thanks again."

Chapter 40

"Mammy!"

"Yes, dear, what is it?" replies Carmel, going to the bottom of the stairs.

"Have you moved any of my stuff, I mean, when you were tidying up, or whatever."

"No, not that I recall, but you know me. Sarah goes in there occasionally – she had all your clothes out from the wardrobe one day. I think she had ideas of wearing one of your white blouses as her communion outfit. Anything wrong?"

"Eh, no, it's nothing. Just some photos and letters gone missing."

It has been quite a while since Sophia has lived at home. She lies back on her single bed and stares at the ceiling. "Here I am," she whispers to herself, "back where I started." She ponders over the missing items. It was in this bed that she wept when she returned from London after Liam died. Liam Taylor. Tears spring to her eyes. . She had met Liam at a party in Trinity.

For the first time in eleven years, she does not fight the memories.

That party. She sees herself and Claire walking into it armed with a bottle of cheap white wine. The place was crowded, the air heavy with smoke, loud music blaring out. What was the song? She can't remember. Claire might remember. She remembers walking down the stairs, about to leave as none of their friends were there. Then she collided with Liam on the stairs.

"Going so soon?" he had said, his voice clear over the heavy boom of the music.

Claire was edging down to the next step. Bodies pushed past. Sophia remained a step above him, their faces level with each other. She seemed riveted to the spot.

"Yes, we are!" Claire shouted as she continued down the stairs.

Sophia stood looking at him, as he flicked his long black hair back. She remembers thinking what beautiful blue eyes he had.

"Why don't you have a beer?" he suggested, handing Claire one from his six-pack.

And that was how it had all started. They met on the stairs. Claire and Sophia were leaving; he had just arrived with his friends. It is all coming back so clearly to Sophia, now. He had turned away from Claire and smiled at her, a slow familiar smile like he had known her all his life.

"What's your name?" he asked, his eyes never leaving her face.

Now Sophia closes her eyes and whispers his name: "Liam!" She strives to conjure up a picture of him. What would he look like now? That photograph she had got through the post – would he really look like that? And who had taken the trouble of doing it and sending it? She leans out of her bed and opens her old jewelry box. Inside is a concealed drawer where she had placed a photograph of Liam and herself. Claire had taken it one day in Stephen's Green. Tears blur her vision.

She remembers herself and Liam walking hand in hand from that party in Trinity back to Liam's flat in Rathmines. They had stayed up all night talking. She can't remember what they talked about – conversation just flowed easily between them.

"Please, Liam, make this stop. I just feel I'm losing it," she mutters. She wipes her eyes and sees the young happy faces of herself and Liam smiling out at her. She can't help but smile through the tears – he was such fun – vibrant, trusting, innocent. Sophia puts the photograph back.

Going to London was Sophia's first real adventure away from home. Claire had gone with her on the Dun Laoghaire to Holyhead ferry. They got drunk, sick, then drunk again. They were offered any amount of lifts to London and accepted one from a lorry driver who looked OK. They went as chambermaids to a hotel on Russell Square. They thought they were so grown up then. She had no idea what was in store for her. That summer should have been the best in their life and it turned out to be a nightmare.

She rings Claire on the mobile. She needs someone to share the bad part with; it was too much to endure alone.

Later she comes downstairs. Carmel is in the kitchen. It's clear she's been crying.

"Sophia, do you really need to go back today?"

"I do, Mammy. I've arranged to meet Claire before the evening train to Sligo."

"But your sister, Christina, has seen so little of you these past few days. She'll be disappointed."

"I know, Mammy, but I really must go. Don't go crying on me, now. You'll set me off. I'll come back at least one weekend a month, I promise."

"Just have this last cuppa with me," says Carmel, wiping her eyes.

Chapter 41

Marianne is sitting in a café across the road from Gavin. He is wearing a cream trench coat and his hair is gelled back. From the distance, he looks attractive. It's up close that he becomes a disappointment. His eyes bulge out of his head like a cartoon character's. Marianne learned from Jim that he is the manager of a gym. She was tempted to join but for the fact that he knows her. Sometimes he sprints across the road, heedless of the traffic, to have coffee in this café. Marianne has often watched him doing this. She wonders if he gets a thrill out of defying death. Perhaps he is aware that she is watching him and is doing it to show off to her. "Look at me – Gavin, the poor boy from the terrace – see what I can do!" Gavin likes to spend his time in the company of young attractive females. Jim told her that he was having an affair with a blonde girl who worked in the gym. Some nights he stayed at her place and he didn't bother going home at all.

Marianne is toying with the idea of getting Jim to take photographs of Gavin with this girl and sending them to his wife. Something stops her from doing it. Surely his wife must already know that something is going on. Perhaps she could try and befriend her, like she befriended Carmel. She could follow her and find out what supermarket she goes to. It's easy, she's done it before. All she has to do is get to know Carmel's routine and start showing up in the same places. Maybe they would get talking. It might be nice to let Sophia have a rest for a while, let things go back to normal. Life is so unpredictable.

At the outset she didn't plan on becoming friends with Carmel and there were times when she found it hard work. In other circumstances, it could have blossomed into a friendship but it existed on deception, obsession and the degeneration of a lonely woman's mind.

But Marianne could not let go now. She felt on the outside of a shining light that would help her talk directly to Liam. Soon, through Sophia, they will talk.

She is about to leave the café when she sees Gavin approaching. He pushes the café door open, his face almost split in two his smile is so big. His big bug eyes scan the café but he doesn't seem to notice her. Marianne pretends to look in her bag. When she looks up, he has her back to her. He is laughing with the girl behind the counter.

She is careful to look away as he makes his way down towards the table where a blonde girl is sitting. He kisses the girl. They are sitting two tables away from her.

"Gavin," the girl says.

"Hi, babe."

Marianne picks up her bag and slowly makes her way to the door.

"Are you coming tonight?" the blonde girl is asking.

She doesn't hear his response. Marianne feels enraged that he can be carrying on like that when he has got a beautiful wife and two adorable children. He doesn't deserve them. It is obvious that he has never learned to count his blessings. She wonders again what would happen if his wife found out. If she was provided with proof that he was having an affair, would she do something about it?

Chapter 42

"Claire, over here!"

Sophia had arranged to meet Claire opposite Slattery's pub, across from Connolly Station. It's clear that we have different ideas on what the word 'opposite' means, she thinks as she tries to gain Claire's attention from across the road. Sophia is on the Talbot Street side. She does not want to go to the station bar as it is usually bustling at this time. She has already picked a quiet coffee shop where she will attempt to lead the discussion with Claire. Matt and Liam. Light and darkness. Hope and reminiscence.

"Sophia," Claire lurches to the footpath as the traffic lights change. They embrace – a little tentatively, at first. They stand back, do it again. True friendship, a bond renewed instantly.

Over coffee and apple-tart, Sophia quickly moves to the point.

"Claire, are you dating Matt?"

"No," says Claire, calmly and firmly. "No, I'm not."

Sophia exhales with relief. "But you were dating him – you were dating him recently?"

Claire shakes her head. "No, I never was."

Sophia believes her. She feels overjoyed. This is the best news she has heard in a long time. It was enough to lose Matt without losing her best friend too. "I knew! I just knew you wouldn't do that to me! Christina – the bitch!" she says, with rage and smug satisfaction.

"Don't blame Christina," says Claire. "I suggested it. She was to make you jealous but I guess she overdid it. And I'm not going to apologise for it. It needed to be done. You were down in Sligo with some smarmy American. Matt was in complete despair – he couldn't understand what you had done."

"So, Matt's on his own," says Sophia, oblivious to Claire's admonishment.

"I didn't say that. I said he's not with me. Sophia, don't be such a selfish cow, always playing safe so you're the last one to be hurt. Ask him if he still wants you, take that risk!"

"I dunno. He might say no …"

"Oh God, are you listening at all? If he has any sense, he'll say no. But since when did common sense mix with love?"

They fall silent and drink their coffees, suddenly aware that a man reading a newspaper is eavesdropping on their conversation. He gets up and leaves. Sad, if the best part of your day is listening in on other people's conversations.

"Claire, don't call me stupid on this now, I'm really serious. Do you believe in the supernatural?"

"Ghosts and that, no. Why?"

"It's Liam, Claire. I'm convinced of his presence. He's all around me, I know it."

"Emm – this is why you went to Sligo, at least part of it."

"Claire, do you remember the letters he wrote to me? The photos. I kept them at home in my room in Mammy's house. They're gone."

They fall silent again and lurch into the past together. Liam, lying prone on the ground. Screams in the street, sirens wailing. The crowd spilling out from the party. The police roughly pushing them back into the hallway, cordoning potential suspects off so they could not escape. The police interview rooms were busy that night.

"God, Sophia, it is awful to think of it. Liam, alone on that rooftop before he died. He was out of it. It's easier to think of it as an accident." The tears are coming freely now, only Claire is able to talk through them. "He loved you, Sophia. Don't keep beating up on yourself. There's no ghost. He's at peace now. The photos and letters, they'll turn up."

"Yeah," Sophia says, composing herself and wiping her eyes. "I don't know how I got through that terrible time. People helped a lot, I suppose. Gavin was so brave, going to tell Liam's parents . . . I just couldn't face it at the time. I couldn't do it, just couldn't."

"You were in a bad way, Sophia. I admire Gavin for doing that. God knows, he hadn't much more going for him."

"No, he hadn't."

"Have you no homes to go to, girls? It's six o'clock. Closing time for us."

They race frantically onto the platform, almost knocking over the ticket man at the gate.

Sophia is on the 6.15 to Sligo as the train rumbles down the tracks.

347

Sophia steps out on the platform at Sligo. The return train journey was uneventful. She is amazed that she slept most of the way. Her sleep was interrupted once at Dromod and she pulled a face when she recognized the same ticket collector as before. This time, the ticket was produced in an instant.

"Not losing them any more?" he said soullessly, while moving on.

Sophia walks towards her apartment. She is on O'Connell Street and the streets are beginning to fill up with young revellers. It is Saturday night. She tenses as she hears quick, purposeful footsteps coming up behind her.

"Simon," she says, with relief. "You really shouldn't come up on people like that."

Simon is in his twenties and teaches languages at the college with Sophia. He must be six foot six, easily, thinks Sophia as she looks up at him in the street. "What is it, Simon?"

"I heard you were ill, and I just thought I'd say hello and fill you in on some developments at the college."

"Developments? Let me guess now, they wouldn't be industrial relations issues, would they? Simon, I'm part-time, temporary, I need this job right now. Leave me out of it."

"Ah, c'mon, Sophia. Listening to it won't harm you."

Sophia is aware that the lecturers are coming under increasing pressure from management to take a more active part in preventative measures against alcohol and substance abuse and unwanted pregnancies. Mary Leahy is leading the management charge, Simon leads the resistance.

"OK, but we can't stand here in the street, talking about it. Where to?"

"Share a pizza and some wine up the road?"

Sophia follows him wearily, reasoning that the wine and his droning will prepare her better for sleep.

"Sharon Da Vincenzo, a second year student."

"Sharon Da Vincenzo," she repeats. "Ah, yes – Sharon – I'm with you now. Italian father, Irish mother. Father is on the board of management. What about her?"

"She's pregnant."

"Simon , no disrespect, but you haven't brought me in here just to tell me that. It's unfortunate, but that's life. There's contraception advice everywhere. What has this got to do with the lecturers?"

"Sharon has made an allegation that somebody

popped Rhoprynol in her drink at a student function. She doesn't know who the father is. She's sticking to her story and her dad is going up the walls. That means Mary Leahy gets it and then we get it."

"Mmm. Hasn't this come up before? Young ladies claiming amnesia and rape, particularly where they don't know the father?"

"Yeah, there was a case in America, where they did a DNA once the child was born. The chap was nearly in the slammer before the girl's memory resurfaced and she withdrew the allegation."

"So, what now?" said Sophia, trying hard to feign interest.

"Come to a meeting, next week. We'll be pushing for more trained counsellors on campus."

"OK, you win. Are you not going to eat any pizza?"

"Eh, I'm not really hungry, you finish it."

"Well, pour yourself some wine, at least."

"I don't drink alcohol. Ouch, why did you do that?" says Simon, holding his foot where Sophia had stomped hard.

"Simon, you are driving me to the apartment door, then you are going to turn homewards and get yourself a life."

As Sophia pours more wine for herself, she wonders if she might seek her old job back.

"Damn Simon Wetherall," says Sophia tipsily as she enters the apartment. She switches on the desk lamp in the living-room and collapses tiredly onto the sofa.

She giggles to herself as she pictures herself at the pizzeria. She had been treated to a full bottle of wine and eaten most of a pizza and he had just sat and watched. All six feet six of him. And attractive, built like a prop forward on a rugby team. He wouldn't be out of place in the Harbourmaster, would he? He'd need to change his dress code though. A nice Hugo Boss shirt, Armani chinos. Probably lives with parents, she muses.

She is dozing for a few minutes when she remembers that she pilfered Ben's classical CD *Claire De Lune* as she left the schoolhouse for the last time. Why not, wasn't she entitled to it? As a memento of the schoolhouse, not Ben. Where did she put it? In the hold-all, that's where.

She staggers forward in the dim light, groping for her bag on the ground. "It's open, I don't remember doing that," she says, rummaging in the bag. "Ah, there it is, got it – I'll listen a little before

I go to bed."

The soothing music is playing in the background and Sophia lies back on the sofa. The week's events swim up to her imagination as she tries to rationalize her life. She drifts slowly into an alcohol-induced coma and the dreams start.

The judge is looking sternly at her as, one by one, the witnesses come forward.

Daddy: I'm floating on a cloud, my lord, looking down from heaven. She forgot to replace her brake-pads.

Gasps of disapproval.

Mammy: She left me widowed, then went away.

Further gasps.

Christina: She has not been a good sister to me or aunt to my daughters.

Boos.

Karen Redmond: She ruined my marriage. My boys do not have a father.

Stone-throwing.

Matt: She was my first and only love, my lord, and she left me.

Send her down. Send her down.

Liam: I was an only child, my lord. I died because of her.

Sophia awakens, sweating profusely. Her head is

pounding, her throat dry. God, it's 8.30 am. There are Alka Seltzer somewhere – in the kitchen, maybe.

Trembling with cold, she drops them in her glass. The fizzing starts and she waits for it to subside. It is then she notices the cup, tea bag floating at the top. A few harsh breaths, a few shallow breaths, as she struggles to stop her racing brain. Her legs are still shaking and she's not sure if they will support her or not. She would like to run from the apartment but she is drawn, magnetized, towards the signs. The opened hold-all bag. Her book has been moved. Into the bathroom. Her make-up! She rushes towards the bedroom, opening the door with a burst. Her eyes open wide and she collapses towards the floor, retching wildly and vomiting on the floor. Coming to her knees at the end of the bed, she looks gradually upwards. In the middle, her black panties neatly laid out. On the pillows, her black bra. Propped up on the pillows, a picture of Mary Magdalen. Written on the wall above, in her red lipstick: *WHORE HARLOT – HELL SHALL BE THY DAMNATION!*

"Help me, help me, somebody help me!" Her piercing screams echo loudly in the ghastly room.

Chapter 43

Marianne is back in Kells again. It's been months since her last visit here. New housing estates are sprouting up all over the place. Cranes are outlined against the blue-grey sky. Liam wouldn't know the place if he were to come back for a fleeting visit. Her son has been dead for eleven years. Her heart sinks at the thought. Coming back isn't a good idea and yet she feels she has to. Her solicitor had advised her to rent the place but she couldn't bear to. She didn't want other people living in her home.

Closing the wrought-iron gates of her home behind her, she drives up the avenue. She can sense the neglected air of the place. Her stomach does its usual little nervous dance. Slowly, she gets out of her car and walks up the stone steps towards the solid door. She is in no hurry. Their beautiful Georgian house stands solidly and almost proudly against the harsh morning. She puts the key in the door and opens it. She stands in their grand elegant hall, and her mind drifts. She conjures up an image of a young boy running down the stairs. "Mammy, you're home!" she hears him say. Slowly, she turns and sees Stephen coming out of the living room, the newspaper in his hand. His reading glasses on his nose. "You're back," he is saying and he comes to greet her. Liam is running towards her now, his upturned face full of love and expectancy.

At her feet are a pile of letters, mostly junk mail. She had asked her solicitor to check on the place occasionally. By the postmark on some of the envelopes, it looks like it has been quite a while since he bothered. Standing in the cold hall sends a shiver up her spine. They converted their dining-room into a bedroom when Stephen had come home from the hospital to die. The dining-room door is ajar now and she can see the two single beds. Shafts of bright light are streaming into the hall from the window on the landing. Marianne makes her way down the hall into her kitchen. She turns on the central heating. Her eyes fill up with tears and everything shimmers around her. Taking, a tissue from her coat, she wipes her eyes. She looks out her kitchen window at her neglected garden. Her heart sinks even further. Right at that very moment, she wants to kill herself. She leans onto the worktop for support.

"Help me," she says in a defeated whisper.

She had driven euphorically from Sophia's Sligo apartment but on arrival her euphoria was quickly replaced by a nauseous feeling. Now there is despair and depression, exacerbated by guilt. She is in crisis as she reflects on the emotional and financial costs of her escapades. Ah, finance. She could make some nice improvements to this house with the money she had given Jim. Emotions, feelings, what of them? She reflects on her Christmas and the way, Christmas Eve excepted, she let go. She might still be down there with David, Emma back in London. David would have had to adjust by dropping the "auntie" bit. What other "adjustments" would have taken place? She stops herself suddenly. These thoughts are disloyal in this house.

Outside, she sees birds hopping around as they look for food. She feels terrible. She forgot about the birds – she always fed them birdseed each winter. They had a bird table set up down the garden. She always made sure that Liam helped when he was young – she wanted to teach him to be kind and compassionate.

She climbs the stairs and walks into each bedroom. She remembers Emma dressed in one of her evening dresses, her face made up as she paraded around the house. It brings a smile to her face. Marianne has forgotten so much. So many little memories have become eroded with the constant waves of grief that hit her over and over again. Wearing her down. In her own bedroom she looks around her with a sense of detachment. It doesn't feel like her bedroom any more. This big house doesn't feel like a home any more. Yet, she can't bear the thought of selling it. She walks downstairs, thankful, at least, that the place hasn't been vandalised.

Just then, her mobile starts ringing and she takes it out of her coat pocket. She smiles through her tears. It's David.

"Are you OK?" he asks when he hears her croaky hello.

"I'm in my house in Kells, brooding, I suppose," Marianne says, trying to minimize her grief for his ears.

"Marianne, you only need to pick up the phone. I would have gone with you if you wanted."

"I know and thank you, David, that's very kind of you. I guess I need to do this, I need to make some decisions."

"OK – we could meet, though, talk this through."

She smiles, pleased that he wants to see her.

"My camera club is having an exhibition in my local library on Friday night," he goes on.

"Oh, good for you!"

"Yes, it should be good. Would you like to come along?"

"I'd love to. I'll call you later in the week about it.

She reproaches herself for the feelings that come up when she talks to David. He is doing this because of the commitment he gave to Stephen, she reminds herself.

What of the mystery woman in the photos? Her romantic feelings are suppressed as her eyes drift over the beautiful, but bleak, setting. The chasm of despair opens wide again.

Chapter 44

"There you go, now. Drink this down."

Sophia is in the armchair of her elderly neighbour's apartment. Mrs Smith has wrapped a warm blanket around her, and has made her some hot cocoa.

"You gave me a terrible fright, my dear, I didn't know what to think. We live in terrible times."

"I can hardly remember – what did I do?"

"You were hammering on my door. I couldn't see you through my spyhole. You were on your knees. I took a risk and there you were on the ground."

"Did you go to my room?" She is finding it difficult to speak, her teeth still chattering.

"Yes, but the door was shut. I didn't try to go in."

"I don't remember closing the door."

"It must have swung shut when you ran out."

"What time is it?"

"Eleven o'clock. You've been sitting on my chair for near two hours. Why won't you let me call the Gardai? What happened to you? Has someone been beating you?"

Sophia shakes her head, thinking feverishly. She does not remember asking the old lady not to call the Gardai. She needs time to think. "Do you mind if I phone Pat, the landlord, from here? He will get me back into my apartment."

"Go ahead, but I'm frightened, and you won't tell me what happened. You have no marks. You have been drinking, haven't you?"

"Yes, I'm very sorry. Please don't tell the landlord when he comes."

"OK, but I'm old. I am not able for this. No repeats, and quit that drinking, won't you? You could have been hallucinating."

The landlord opens Sophia's apartment door.

"Thank you," she says, darting in ahead of prying Pat.

He follows her into the living-room, eying her suspiciously. "This is the second time I've had to do this in a week. I'm not happy about it. Is something going on?"

"No. What do you mean a second time?"

"First your mother, then you."

Sophia looks at him puzzled. "My mother?"

Keys jangles in his chubby hands and he starts to laugh. It rises from his great belly and comes oozing out of his florid face in big bellowing guffaws. She is a lovely lady. I met her when she came to your apartment."

"When was that?"

"The beginning of the week – she said she wanted to collect some stuff for you."

"My mother didn't come to Sligo. She was with me in Dublin." Sophia feels herself starting to panic. "What did she look like?"

He laughs nervously. "You mean it wasn't your mother?"

Sophia feels her legs weaken beneath her. "No, my mother was in Dublin all week with me," she repeats, her voice loud and harsh.

"She was so convincing – I was sure she was your mother. You just can't trust anyone," he shakes his head in disappointment.

Sophia feels her stomach muscles tighten with panic. Her mind is racing, a single question running through it. Who is it? Who is this Real Live Person?

Should she be pleased that it's not a ghost but a real person? Sophia takes a few shallow breaths and manages to ask. "Could you please tell me what she looked like?"

He coughs and Sophia moves a little away from him. "Silver hair, with a pleasant face. She was dressed very elegantly."

"I see," Sophia says, still at a complete loss. "You let a complete stranger into my apartment. When I came back here, I suspected that someone might have been in there but I wasn't sure. I thought these were secure apartments."

The landlord jangles his keys. "How was I to know it wasn't your mother? She told me that it was urgent, that you were in hospital, that she had to get some stuff for you."

"I'm going to phone the Gardai," Sophia says taking out her mobile phone.

"Look, this is my fault. I'll tell you what I'll do for you. I'll get you a new apartment and tomorrow you can move into it."

"Tomorrow?"

"It's the best I can do."

"I want to move out straight away."

"This will never happen again, Ms Jordan, trust me," he is saying but she is hardly listening to him.

"She sounded so sincere. Such a wellspoken –"

"Look, I'm phoning the Gardai and you had better get me a new place to stay at once as I am not spending another minute in this place."

"Of course," he mutters his pig-blue eyes narrowing contemptuously at her. "The only apartment I have is a two-bedroom. It's across town and double the rent of this one. If you like the view of Ben Bulben first thing in the morning, it's made for you."

"But you can't charge me double rent! This is your fault!"

"You'll just have to sign a new lease agreement," he says.

"I'm not paying you double rent – I can't afford to."

"Excuse me," he says as his mobile starts to ring. He turns his back to her and starts to talk on the phone.

When he finishes Sophia says, "Look, I'll ring you later on this evening, maybe in the morning. I'll let you know my decision."

"All right, but don't leave it too late."

"By the way, did the lady have an accent?

"She was Irish, nothing special, a bit like your own."

"Age?"

"She'd have passed for fifty, but she could have been more. I get it, you're having an affair with someone! I saw him around here, with his fancy car." He turns to go. "Bye. Don't forget my offer."

Chapter 45

Marianne has her coat on and she is about to go out the door to her yoga class when the doorbell rings. Her mother hated having visitors coming to the house. The way she got rid of them was to put on her coat before answering the door. It was her way of getting out of entertaining anyone. Even the parish priest got the same treatment. In her mother's eyes, everyone was equal. In the village where Marianne had grown up her mother was considered a little odd. Marianne had overheard two neighbours discussing her mother's odd behavior while she was hiding behind their wall. She had grown up ashamed of her mother.

No doubt it's someone selling something or a Jehovah Witness, Marianne thinks as she opens her front door. She is pleased with herself that she is wearing her coat, as she has never tried out her mother's little trick before. She unlocks the door and is about to say that's she is on her way out, when she sees Gavin standing there.

"Hello, Marianne," he says.

Marianne always considered him an insolent young man. Her mother would have called him "a bad egg".

"Can I come in?" he says as he walks past her into the house.

Marianne is dumbstruck. She tries to think what would her mother do at a moment like this. She stands holding the door ajar.

"We can carry this conversation out in the hall if you wish?" she hears him say to her and he grins at her.

She gestures for him to go into the living-room and, slowly, she closes the front door. The air is suddenly scented with his aftershave. She feels sick at the very sight of him. He sits down on her sofa. He is wearing a light grey suit with a very flashy tie. She notices how relaxed he looks.

"Sit down," he says to her.

Silently, she is praying to Liam for courage to get her through this.

Marianne sits at the edge of her armchair, her hands folded in her lap.

"What is this all about, Granny?" he asks, his lip curling cynically.

All Marianne hears is the word 'Granny' and it's like a blow to the stomach. She is instantly winded.

He leans forward and waves his hand in front of her face. "Is there anyone in there?" he says in a sing-song voice.

"What?" she says as she comes back to her living-room with a jolt.

"Why have you been following me?"

Marianne meets his unnerving gaze. Any minute now his bug eyes will pop out of his head.

"My wife noticed your car outside our house," he says with an air of authority. He leans back in her sofa like he is delivering some grand speech. She can tell he is enjoying this. "At first she thought I was having an affair." He grins as he contemplates this and then he turns serious again. "But then she noticed how old you were and she thought no, he's not having an affair with her. She's too old. Then my good wife took it upon herself to get your car registration. We have a good friend who can help out with such matters. She was going to take it a step further, but I intervened. I told her I would pay you a visit. Ask you nicely why you were doing it and tell you politely to stop."

"So, your wife suspects that you are having an affair?" Marianne says, pleased that she sounds so calm. Jim had advised her to stay away from Gavin. Now, she wishes she had listened to him.

Gavin glares at her. "Look," he says pointing a finger at her, "that's my business. I don't want you following me, do you hear?"

Marianne makes herself smile at him. Inside, she is shaking but she isn't going to give him the satisfaction of showing him just how afraid she is. He is scum. He doesn't deserve a family. He doesn't deserve to be alive.

Gavin stands up and slowly walks around her living-room. He picks up a vase that she has never filled with flowers. He lets it slip out of his hand. A bogus look of apology appears across his face. "Sorry," he says.

Marianne remains sitting, her hands folded together on her lap. She would dearly love to get up and slap this man across the face but she knows he is nothing more than a vicious thug. He is enjoying himself at her expense.

"So," he says as he comes to stand before her. "Who else have you been following?"

"No one, just you."

He laughs. "Your house in Kells has been locked up for the past year ever since your husband died. You've moved to Dublin to this place and I am wondering why?"

Marianne attempts to get up. "I have an appointment," she says.

He pushes her back down, quite forcefully. His fingers dig into her shoulders blades. "I'm not finished," he says. He returns to sit on her sofa. "I'm surprised at you, Marianne," he says. She glares at him as he raises his hands helplessly in the air. "You didn't offer me a cup of tea."

Marianne sits with her hands joined together on her lap. Her face is set in unreadable lines.

"Have you lost your tongue?" he says and grins at her.

"I have no milk."

Gavin laughs. "OK, so we'll dispense with the tea and the small talk." He is on his feet again. He walks around the room and then stops as he looks out into the hall. "What have we got here?" he says as he points at the case that is still standing in the hall. He walks purposefully out to the hall and picks up the case. "Off somewhere nice?" he asks with a raised eyebrow.

Marianne remains seated, and holds her face impassively as he opens the case and looks inside.

"Going somewhere for the weekend?" He begins to pull out the clothes. "Ah," he says when he sees the photo album and the three letters bundled together at the bottom of the case. "What have we got here?" His eyes are dancing with delight. "Sophia Jordan," he says gleefully as he reads her name off the envelope. "Sophia," he whispers. He flicks the photo album open, stops at a picture. "Ah," he says and tilts his head. "Don't they look adorable together?"

Marianne takes a few shallow breaths to steady her breathing.

"Talk to me, Marianne," he coaxes.

He sits on the arm of her chair. She steels herself not to flinch, not to show him just how frightened she really is. "I have nothing to say," she replies stoically.

Gavin laughs. "Oh, Marianne, cut the crap!" He glances at his watch and he is on his feet again. "I have another appointment, much as I would like to stay and chat I have to go." He leans closer, she can smell the cigarette smoke off his breath. "Talk to me," he whispers in what seems like an ominous warning.

She feels a stab of revulsion for this man and feels the best thing she can do is tell him the truth so that he will leave.

"Gavin, I was just curious about you, that's all. I rented this house in Dublin to get away from Kells. To start a new life."

"You were always a lousy liar and so was your son."

"Liam was a wonderful young man," she says quietly.

Gavin nods in agreement. "He was a fool. He fell in love with Sophia but she didn't give a shit about him. She was just using him. She dumped him the first chance she got. But Liam was a spoiled little boy; he couldn't take no for an answer. He couldn't get it through his thick head that she didn't want him."

Marianne feels tears shimmer in her eyes. "Get out, you little shit!"

Gavin waves a finger at her. "Now if your son had your guts he just might be alive today."

She reaches out to slap him hard across the face.

Gavin grabs her wrists. "Not so fast, Granny!" His grip is vice-like. "You've been following Sophia too. Haven't you?"

She bites her lip to stop herself from screaming with pain.

"Haven't you?" he whispers.

"Yes, I have."

"I thought as much," he says, still holding her wrists.

"Let go, please," she begs. "You're hurting me."

Gavin laughs. "That's the intention, Granny. Tell me about Sophia."

"There is nothing to …" she almost screams with pain as he tightens his grip on one of her wrists. "You'll break it," she says.

"Talk."

"Let go first." He does and she rubs her wrist. "She is living in Sligo now, she moved there in September. She's lecturing in the college."

"Why were you following me, Granny? What was the plan?"

"I just wanted to see what your lives were like."

Gavin falls back down on the sofa. He slides his hand into the inside pocket of his jacket. He takes a box of cigarettes out. "Filthy habit," he says as he lights up. You know it's Sophia's fault that your son is dead."

Marianne watches him inhale on his cigarette. He puts his feet up on her coffee table.

"Sophia," he says the name. "I liked her, I liked her a lot." He is standing again. "Has Sophia discovered that you've been following her?"

"No, I don't think so."

He is slowly pacing from the fireplace to the door and back again. "I think I'll have to go and see her."

Marianne is looking at the floor; she sees his size nine feet pass by every few moments as he continues to pace.

"Tell me, Marianne, exactly what you've been doing to her?" He stops now in front of her, and bends down until his face is level with hers. His big bug eyes are staring at her intently.

"I just followed her around, nothing more."

Gavin grins. "You're lying, Granny," he says, his voice a thick whisper.

"OK, I went into her apartment a few times and just snooped around."

Gavin laughs. "You're amazing, Granny. I could do with someone like you working for me."

His smoky breath is making her feel sick. She turns her face away from him.

"Go on," he coaxes.

"There isn't much to tell. She left Dublin and moved to Sligo."

"Because of you," Gavin says as he clicks his fingers together. "I love it."

He is moving again pacing over and back. "So,"

he says and stops pacing. He draws deeply on his cigarette. Exhales. "She's moved to Sligo." He starts pacing again. "Has she got a boyfriend?"

"I think she's on her own now."

Marianne watches in horror as he takes the cigarette out of his mouth and stubs it out on her carpet.

"Stop following me," he says and wags his finger at her. His eyes are dancing with delight. To her horror he picks up the photo album and the letters.

"Because if you don't, you'll be very sorry."

"They're mine," she says.

"No, there're not, these belong to Sophia and I'm going to give them back to her. I'm going now – oh, and by the way, I don't want you going anywhere near Kells. You hear me on that one?

"Yes, I live here now."

"You were there, very recently. My parents live in Kells. Convinced their son is doing well. I wouldn't want anyone putting doubts in their minds. Stay away, Marianne … Granny."

The front door slams after him. From her window, she watches him walk down the driveway towards his sleek car. Her whole body shakes with delayed nerves as she runs to her front door and locks it. She looks at her watch. She is too late for her yoga class, not that she is capable of doing anything now.

Her mobile rings, making her jump with fright. She is relieved when she sees it's Carmel. "Where were you?" she asks.

Marianne closes her eyes and says the first thing that comes into her head. "I have a dreadful headache and I just couldn't face yoga."

"We're like yoyos at these yoga classes," Carmel says and giggles. "If you turn up I don't and if I turn up you don't."

Marianne smiles sadly. It's been a long time since she has felt this low. Today she can only describe as a very, very black day. In fact it is so black she doubts it will ever be bright again. All she wants to do is go back upstairs and crawl under the covers and just hide away from the world. Seeing Gavin up close has really frightened her.

She ponders on ringing Jim. Yes, Jim Crerand, private detective. He might be able to help her out.

Chapter 46

In her apartment Sophia showers as quickly as she can in the bathroom and brushes her teeth. She puts on some fresh clothes. She tries to keep her gaze averted from the bed while dressing, but it is so hard. Locking the door, she rushes out into the street. She is tearing herself apart inside, but feels she must report this to the Gardai.

She pictures herself going into the station, and returning to her apartment with a Garda. In her fantasy scenario, there are no Ban Gardai available. Sophia visualizes herself and this young man surveying the evidence in her bedroom. He is red-faced, almost aroused.

"It looks the work of a jealous woman, Ms

Jordan. You say you were having an affair until recently?"

"Yeah, but he's gone back to his wife in America. My landlord says this woman was Irish."

"Do you know that? Did Mr. Redmond say that his wife was American? She sounds the right age."

"It's not her."

"Is this where you did it, Ms. Jordan?" he says, eying the black underwear.

"Did what?"

"Had sex, you and Mr. Redmond?"

Sophia shudders and breaks off from her fantasy. She decides that she will phone the Garda first. She feels that she has been violated enough. She goes into a coffee shop and orders a latte and fruit salad. Her first food today, Mrs Smith's cocoa excepted.

"Hello, Sligo Garda Station."

"Hello, I want to make a complaint, preferably to a Ban Garda."

"There is one available, if you wish to come on down."

"Thank you, I'll be there soon."

Sophia is walking towards the station when her phone rings. She does not recognize the number. Her heart skips a beat as she answers the phone.

"Hello," she says, nervously.

"Soffiaah, it's Ben."

Jesus, what does he want? " Ben . . . it's not a good time, I –"

"Never mind that. I'm here in America. I've made up with Karen."

"Is she with you now?"

"Yeah, she's in bed. I'm out on the front lawn. It's 6.00 a.m. over here. How are you getting on?"

"All right, Ben, I'm sorry but I –"

"Did you speak to Matt?"

"Yeah, it wasn't him. Ben, what's this call about? I'm really busy, right now."

"I'm not sure. Soffiaah, do you remember Christmas Eve?"

"Yes," she says exasperatedly.

"After we made love?"

"Ben, I'm hanging up n–"

"No, don't, this may be important, to you. Remember you noticed a car with its lights flashing? And you called me? I said to ignore it. Then you went to the bathroom, locked yourself in there, started running the bath?"

Sophia closes her eyes. "C'mon, Ben, where is this going?"

"Well, it kept on, while you were in the bath."

"It kept on? For how long?"

"Long enough to worry me. So I took a stroll out and approached the car, got right up close . . . Sophia, are you there?"

"Yes, yes, go on, Ben."

"She got a right surprise when she saw me. Grey-haired, fiftyish, she was. Drove away quite suddenly."

"What! Ben, did you notice anything else? Don't hold out on me!"

"Well, I didn't think much of it then, but in light of recent events …"

"What, Ben, fuck you, what?"

"I took down the registration number of her car, Soffiaah. Do you want it?"

A minute later she has written down the number. "Can I read it back to you, Ben?"

Ben listens and says, "Yes, that's it."

"Why the fuck didn't you tell me all that before now?" she asks.

"I didn't want to alarm you – then I guess I forgot about it."

"Well, thanks, Ben. Bye."

"Goodbye, Soffiaah. I hope I was some help to you."

The line goes dead.

"You'll never know, Ben, You'll never know."

Minutes later, Sophia is running frantically down O'Connell Street towards her apartment. There, she pauses only long enough to clean up the mess in her bedroom. There remains a blurred reminder on the wall, but it will have to wait. She snatches a black suit from the wardrobe, and a white blouse she ahs worn recently. Sitting into her car, Sophia drives onto the congested street. She needs to make a phone call first thing in the morning, but she feels any progress made east in the meantime will serve her well.

Chapter 47

Marianne parks her car at the Shopping Centre in Kells and walks towards the taxis, carrying a large case. There is a large crowd around. Sunday has become a great shopping day. Kathleen would not approve, she smiles. A day of rest and prayer, she would say. At least she is spared the embarrassment of meeting her, the visit being still part of the "to do" list. Recalling her encounter with Gavin, she trembles violently. She rang the gym before she left Dublin to confirm that he was there and not following her. God, this is what it feels like to be stalked, she says to herself. The hunter becomes the hunted. Stopping at the gates of her home, she pays the six euro to a wordless taxi man and walks up the drive towards her house.

An eerie silence surrounds her as she sits in a rocking chair in the living-room, nursing a cup of tea. Damn Gavin Daly, he cannot scare her from her real home. A rented house in Dublin, yes, but this is her sacred ground, her sanctuary. She feels an anger stirring within, bolstered by a renewed power. "See your journey, through, Mum," Liam whispers. "You'll soon have your answers, don't stop now." She closes her eyes. She enhances the picture by giving herself a warrior-queen-like look. She images herself to be fearless and powerful. She is visualizing that she could be such a woman. This new stronger Marianne wouldn't have allowed Gavin to talk to her like he did. She hears the phone ringing out again. "Not today," she mutters. "I just can't answer you today." She looks at the clock: it's six thirty in the evening. She wonders where the saddest person in the whole world is living? Would she qualify or would her story be lost in other more horrific ones? "What can I do to fend this off until morning – protect myself?" she says to herself. "Kathleen, I'll go and see Kathleen."

"Marianne, come in, come in," beams a small plump woman, with twinkling eyes.

She follows Kathleen towards the kitchen, noting

that faith is alive and well in this house. The Blessed Virgin on the hall table, the Sacred Heart above her on the wall.

Talking with Kathleen is exactly what Marianne needs right now. Over many cups of tea, sandwiches, scones and fresh apple-pie, they trawl back over the years together. Laughing, crying, laughing and crying again. Strangely, with Kathleen, it was comforting and restorative. Liam came alive in this room, Kathleen's faith the genesis of his resurrection.

"God, look at the time! Half ten. I'd better go," Marianne says.

"You're going nowhere, girl. I'll make up a bed for you. "

"No, really, I must go. I have somebody to meet early in the morning."

"You're staying, and that's all there's to it. I have an important meeting first thing tomorrow too. I'll have you up bright and early."

"Who are you meeting? Sorry, that came out – none of my business."

"Don't worry about it. I am going to see Geoffrey, my first visit of the day. He'll be waiting for me. We can walk together, the nursing home is on the way to your house."

Chapter 48

"Half past eleven on a Sunday night – you're lucky to get a room," observes the receptionist at the Headfort Arms Hotel in Kells. "Have you any cases?"

"No, just my bag. I was on my way up to Belfast and was delayed with a puncture," Sophia replies.

"There you are. Room 19. Up the stairs and left. Fifty Euro. It's a single room, one person only. We are strict on this. Here's your special card, with instructions for use."

She takes the card wearily. "It's a natural act," she says.

"What?"

"Sleeping, wanting a bed to sleep in, it's a natural act, same as the sex you are thinking of."

"I wasn't …" said the receptionist, red-faced, but Sophia is already on the stairs.

Ensconced in her bedroom, Sophia stares at the Meath registration she had written down.

She picks up her mobile phone, which had rung frequently throughout her journey.

Seven missed calls, four new messages. She reviews them all again in her head. A *"Did you get back safely?"* call from her Mother. She replays Matt's call in her head. *"Uh, Sophia, sorry, this is Matt. I'm sorry I broke our cups, I don't know what to say . . . look, I hope you're OK. Bye."* The tears sting her eyes.

Gavin Daly. Five missed calls. Two messages.

"Sophia, Gavin here, how are you, babe? How many years is it? Give me a call. I need to talk to you – you'll need to hear this too."

"Sophia, C'mon now, ring me, it's important. I know you're in Sligo. I have something that belongs to you. I'm coming down there next week. You ring me, you hear."

Sophia closes her eyes. She is strangely exhilarated, yet exhausted. This is a journey she should have made eleven years ago. She recites the car registration number in her head. She had planned to make a call to a contact next morning but Gavin's sudden emergence had solved all that. She doesn't need to.

She already knows.

Midnight. Country music continues blaring down below. Sophia gets up, goes downstairs and into the street. Returning at 2.30 a.m. she is annoyed that the main door is locked. She rings the bell. No answer. A drunken reveller leaving the place lets her in.

The receptionist emerges inquisitively from the bar.

"Sleep-walking, it's a natural act, isn't it?" says Sophia.

Chapter 49

Next morning, Marianne stretches herself awake in her comfortable bed. She peers out the window at the neat rows of terraced houses. Kathleen is buzzing away downstairs. She washes and dresses, bringing the borrowed nightie downstairs. Fresh baking assails her nostrils.

"What time did you get up?" says Marianne, taking a chair. A bowl of creamy porridge appears before her in an instant.

"Seven. I always get up at that time and bake a fresh brown loaf. It does the day. Half for Geoffrey, half for me. I made two today."

They eat quietly at the table, comfortable in each other's company and the surroundings. Kathleen eventually breaks the silence.

"What time is your meeting?"

"Half past ten."

They part at the nursing home gate, hugging warmly. Marianne walks down the road, and opens the gate of her long drive.

A lone figure stands in the gateway of a house opposite and watches her disappear into her home.

The shrill ring of the phone makes Marianne rush to the hall to pick it up.

"Hello," she says cautiously.

"Marianne, you're there, I've been phoning you all morning. We're supposed to meet, remember?"

"Jim, sorry, of course, where are you?"

"Downtown in beautiful Kells. Where do you think I am? I drove by twice, but there was no sign of you."

"I've been here all along – wasn't it half ten we agreed? Come on up. Park your car on the main road."

Minutes later, Marianne lets Jim into the house.

"What's with the car," said Jim, nonchalantly as they walk towards the kitchen.

Marianne is suddenly vulnerable again. What were the good times she had recently? Christmas with David and Emma, last night with Kathleen, the Art Gallery with David. Westport, no, not Westport, she had nobody to share it with.

Beautiful, haunting, but missing a vital ingredient: companionship ... love. She sobs repeatedly as she brings Jim up to date on her Sligo exploits and her encounter with Gavin.

"I think it's me making the tea, then," says Jim, when she finishes.

Bastard, she feels, why does he have to be so detached and stoic?

Jim places a large antique pot of hot tea on the table, with two mugs and one spoon coming after. Sugar bag follows but no milk as she had forgot to buy some. God, my mother gave me that pot, she muses. She would not have approved. Cups, not mugs. Sugar bowl, jug and two spoons. A tray, even for the short distance from larder to table.

"There you go," said Jim. "Now, can you tell me, what am I doing here?"

Marianne composes herself. "Jim, I've become tired of all this. I want out but I cannot see the way. I am at the jumping-off point, yet something is missing. All of the photos, the intrusions, they were for a purpose but I cannot follow it through ..."

"There was never a purpose, Marianne," Jim said softly. "You're grieving, and untreated it gets progressive and chaotic. You would have continued, maybe even will, until you are caught or collapse under the weight of it all. You're near that point now."

"Ah, a private detective and a shrink to boot," she retorts, sarcastically.

"It looks like I'm not needed here, then, I'll be off." Jim is already standing up.

Marianne's lips quiver, her mind is racing. "No, don't go, Jim. I want you to bring Sophia Jordan to me."

"Marianne, let it go. I won't do it. I'm a private detective, not a kidnapper."

"Please, Jim, you can do it, this is the last thing … please"

A voice in the background interrupts her pleadings. "That won't be necessary, Mrs Taylor. I'm already here."

Sophia Jordan emerges from the hallway, black-suited. A thousand photographs unfolding towards reality, stillness unto life.

Jim sits uncomfortably in his chair. For the first time since Marianne met him, he appears disconcerted, thrown by events. Alternately, he eyes each woman in the eerie silence of the kitchen. He coughs occasionally, then says, "I think you both need to talk, but I'm not sure – Marianne, do you want me to stay?"

"You can leave now, Jim. Do it," she said firmly. "Thanks for everything."

The cold eyes of Sophia Jordan burn relentlessly at him as he backs out of the kitchen.

The door closes softly in the background.

A wordless, haunting silence ensues. Two women, strangers connected by Liam. Two damaged souls. The threat of eruption pervades the bleak setting that was once home to a bubbling little boy.

Eventually, Marianne gets up, fills up the kettle and plugs it in.

"How did you get in here?"

"I've been in this house nearly twelve years ago with Liam, your son. I watched him use a credit card to unbolt a window at the back – he'd forgotten his key in Dublin."

"Liam took the opportunity to bring you here when he knew we were away. He never wanted us to meet."

Sophia sits silently for a while, as if striving to prevent herself from lashing out at the source of her torture. She thinks of Matt, her father, that terrible Christmas Eve when Ben's penis felt like the devil piercing her heart. Mrs Taylor, the devil's mistress, witnessing her pain. Sophia looks at the set of knives nestling in the wooden block.

"Did you kill my father, Mrs Taylor?"

"No."

"Sure?"

"Yes, I was in Westport that week. I had befriended your mother. Your father was buried before I got back."

"Befriended, surely you mean violated, you sinister bitch! My mother. Dragged into all of this."

"Look, I'm sorry, I'll answer any questions that you ask."

"You don't need to, bar one, Mrs Taylor. I've seen it all. Come with me."

Wordlessly, Sophia leads her towards the drawing-room. Marianne's case lies empty on the floor. On a vast antique table, neatly laid out lies the evidence of torture.

Marianne does not see the stinging slap travelling across the dimly lit room. She staggers backwards, her face enflamed.

"Where are Liam's letters to me, our photos, Mrs Taylor? I want them, they're missing. Look at this filth," says Sophia, pausing to tear up a photograph of her and Ben. "Our photos and letters are the only thing of purity in all of this, and they're missing. You're going to give them back to me – they're mine, not yours. You can keep the rest as evidence for the police."

"I haven't got them. I took them, but they're gone. I can't give them to you."

"Liar! Look at what we have here. Nothing but poison that defiles your son's memory. These letters and photos were pure, spontaneous. They were about love. We're looking at the devil's work here. Give me those letters and photos." Sophia, overcome by fury, heaves up the table, overturning its contents on the ground.

Automatically, the women stand back as the table crashes towards the floor.

"I can't give them to you. Gavin Daly came to me some days ago and took them from me."

Sophia pauses for a moment. The telephone calls from Gavin. "Adds up," she says.

Marianne begins to feel an anger burning. Love. She mentioned love. My son died because of her and she uses the word love. Suddenly, her head is spinning.

She hears a voice. It's a mixture of Liam and Kathleen. *"Hold back, Mum, she came to you. She needs to tell you something, she's hurting too."* Oh God, not yet, not yet.

"Gavin told me about you and Liam. You cheating on him the night my Liam died and here you are, getting all moral about these letters. You have no respect for love and this filth, as you call it, is proof of that!"

"Cheating? I was not cheating on Liam. I was not even going out with him at the time! What did Gavin tell you?"

"He said you were having sex with another man when Liam fell from the roof to his death. What do you mean you were not even going out with him? You're a lying whore!"

Sophia is trembling now. She sees a mother visibly aging in the course of a conversation. She is thinking about Matt; she too is looking for compassion and forgiveness. Her father had often preached: "What goes around comes around."

She images the ghost of Liam coming before her, here in this very room, where they had lit a fire and drank wine until they were pissed. *'Tell her the truth, for me,'* she imagines Liam to be saying.

"There was love between me and Liam, Mrs. Taylor, but it was on his side. I didn't love him. He loved me. I couldn't give him that love back, it wasn't there."

"But you came here with him, the letters, he went to London to be with you."

"Yes," said Sophia, still conscious of the voice in her ear: *'Don't prolong it for her, Sophia. I went back to the roof. I can see it now. I've got acceptance. I am at peace.'* Stumbling with the words, she says: "I liked Liam. He was handsome, caring. There was an attraction. We made love twice, once in this house. He followed me to London. I was flattered and liked the attention he was giving me. I told Liam we couldn't continue, he was devastated, couldn't accept it. I suppose I gave him the wrong reason when I said that Claire, my friend, liked him better.

"The night of the party, Gavin was there. We were all out of it on alcohol. There was some drugs going around and everybody was taking them, except Gavin. Doesn't do drugs, our Gavin," Sophia pauses bitterly. "Gavin was on to me, I liked it. It's funny how something that is attractive in youth becomes ugly with experience. He was kissing me and saying 'Come to the mile-high club with me.' Kept repeating it. I remember thinking that I was not going on a plane anywhere, but then Gavin led me upstairs and onto the roof to show me what he meant.

"We were against a chimney block, Kissing, you know. I was out of it, he was . . ." She pauses, feeling embarrassed, and yet she feels Liam's presence in the room and feels she cannot lie. "Gavin was urgently trying to get inside me. I was trying to help him in, I admit it. Liam must have seen us going up to the roof and followed us up. He came at Gavin with a yell. 'You were supposed to be my friend!' he kept repeating over and over again. He gave Gavin a good beating on the roof and then he missed with a punch . . . oh, God . . ."

Sophia's legs feel shaky, she reaches to support herself against the sofa. Suddenly she is sitting down, aided by Marianne.

Nothing is said as they sit close together, tears streaming down their faces. The room is chilly and they huddle close together as they cry helplessly.

"Gavin didn't push him. He never even got to hit him. It was an accident. I was too scared to go between them. Just too scared."

Sometime later, they make their way into the kitchen. Marianne switches on the heat and Sophia takes the dirty dishes to the sink. She feels she cannot leave yet, she needs to stay with Marianne for a while longer.

After an eternity, and several cups of tea, drunk in silence, Sophia speaks.

"Mrs Taylor, shall we go out to the fuel shed together? Build a fire in here? I think we have some things to burn."

"OK, but you go. I want to go to our room upstairs, for a minute. I'll be back down."

Marianne sits on the edge of his bed, caressing it. She smiles through the tears, "Liam. My Liam." Beautiful. Precious. Human. Flawed. "Be at peace, my baby, be at peace."

Marianne treads back downstairs towards the drawing-room. Her heart is heavy, but she feels a small light beginning to burn within. It is painful, terribly painful, but she dare not extinguish it. She has reached the end of this road, but new ones will open; in some ways they already have. She will ring David later, tell him. Maybe he will ask her down in advance of Friday.

"Sophia, are you there?"

"I'm in the kitchen, Mrs Taylor."

"You should call me Marianne," she says as she enters.

Marianne enters. Sophia is facing her, terror in her eyes.

"Sit down, Granny," says a familiar voice behind her. She feels cold steel pressing against her neck.

Minutes pass. Sophia and Marianne are sitting together at the table. Gavin is pacing up and down, tapping a tyre-lever incessantly against one hand, like teachers in bygone times stroked their canes.

He is strutting, as always, but appears fidgety and nervous.

"I underestimated you, Marianne. I thought you might have heeded my warning to you, but you didn't, did you? This is very inconvenient."

"Get out of my home, Gavin. You're not wanted here. You also have things that belong to Sophia, you should give them back." Marianne is surprised at the firmness in her voice.

"Sophia, yes Sophia. Here she comes, eleven years late. Has she confirmed what I told you all these years ago, her on the job, while poor Liam fell off?"

"Yes, Gavin, it was as you said. Now will you go, please?"

"Not yet." He comes close to Sophia, pressing the tyre-lever into her side. "I'd love to finish what we started. We could tie Granny up, maybe let her watch."

"You won't be doing that, Gavin," said Marianne. "You'd have to kill both of us and you haven't got the guts to do that."

"Jeez, you got me spot on, Granny. You're right. I've moved on since then, as you know." He caresses the lever across Sophia's blonde hair. "Sorry, babe, I have more important things to be doing right now."

"How did you know we were here, Gavin?" Marianne continues, while Sophia sits speechless with fear.

"Eh, I didn't. Coincidence. I was collecting a package from the fuel shed and I bumped into our Sophia out there. Gave me a right shock, after all these years."

"Gavin, what are you storing in my shed?"

"Aw, come on, Granny, don't be a spoilsport. How often did I come up here to play with your precious Liam. I know this house and gardens better than you. It has been useful this past year, while you weren't using it."

"You are an evil man, Gavin, an evil man."

Gavin flinches for a moment. "Don't push it, Marianne. I need to get away from here soon. I want both of you to walk back out to the coalshed, no mobiles. I'll be locking you in for a while."

The women walk towards the shed in front of Gavin, hands by their sides. Marianne does not even dare to hope that someone will see them. She and Stephen had privacy in mind when they bought this house. This is the price of it, now.

"In you go. Hand me out that package, Sophia, please."

Sophia silently hands him over a parcel that is roughly the size of a small box of Weetabix.

"Thanks for all your help, Granny, I won't be using your place any longer. Now, I'm going to bolt the door. Someone should eventually come to search for you – let's hope so anyway. But not a sound out of either of you, or by God, I'll come back and kill you!"

Gavin draws the bolts on the door, leaving Sophia and Marianne in the dark.

"I'll take one or two mementoes from your collection, Granny," they hear him say. "I might need them – don't forget both of you need to keep your secrets."

His footsteps retreat.

"Oh, God," Sophia whispers, "we could be here forever."

Then outside they hear a voice raised in a sharp command.

"What –?" Sophia exclaims.

"Quiet!" says Marianne.

And suddenly there is the sound of running footsteps, slammed car doors, a scuffling on gravel, voices raised in violent abuse.

They listen fearfully.

Then footsteps and the bolts draw back.

A tall man in a grey suit smiles in at them. "Are you all right, ladies? Police."

Gavin is being restrained by two plainclothes Gardai. He is swearing profusely. "I've been set up, I been fucking set up – Jesus!"

"Shut up, Gavin!" says their rescuer. "We've been waiting on this day for a while. I have a feeling we'll find more than we got last time. What was it then, body-building steroids?"

He follows the women into the house.

"Are you OK?" he asks.

"Yes," says Marianne. Sophia nods.

"I'll go, then?"

"Yes."

Marianne follows him to the door. The man turns.

"I can make my own way out, unless you want to tell me something."

"I want to ask you something. How did you know?"

"Got a phone-call. A Dublin gumshoe named Jim Crerand, said he had visited you earlier today. Was coming back to check on you when he noticed Mr Daly going in. First bit of information we ever got from the miser. Had conditions. The two women in the house were to be left out of it. So I'll die curious, won't I? Sorry we didn't move earlier, but we need-ed him to have the goods in his hands, so to speak."

Marianne nods goodbye, then goes back to the kitchen. "Are you OK, Sophia?"

"Yeh, I couldn't speak, I was so scared. I always knew Gavin was a supplier. I'm amazed he didn't harm us. He was the reason I didn't go to Liam's funeral. He raped me on that night while we were rehearsing our statements for the police."

Marianne envelops her in her arms. "Hush, it's all over now."

"I thought . . ." Sophia sobs, "I thought he was going to do it again." She composes herself with an effort. "It's the first time I have mentioned it since it happened."

"I'm glad you did. You have suffered too but I didn't realise it. I'm so sorry, Sophia."

Moments pass. Marianne is starting out her kitchen window, looking wistfully at her neglected garden.

Sophia breaks the silence to say. "I want to go home, to Dublin that is. I'll call Matt. He might take me home."

"I have someone to ring, myself. Sophia, how will we deal with all the questions?"

"Let's light that fire and blow the answers away."

Chapter 50

Sophia saunters down towards the Financial Services Centre. Walking across the site, she enters the Harbourmaster Bar. She sees Claire at a table and walks directly over.

"Sophia, look at you. You look great."

"You look good too, Claire."

"Thanks. So tell me all the news before Matt joins us."

"I'm starting a new job next month."

Claire's face brightens.

Sophia continues. "Lecturing in my old college."

"How did you cope with spending the past three months at your mother's house? Did you not want to kill her?"

"Funny, no. It's been a peaceful time. Oh, she had

lots of questions but she can see how I've improved and settles for that. But not Christina – she's desperate for information. But were I to give her a full chronicle of events, she'd explode altogether with news. She's going to have to wait."

"Orders, ladies?"

"Two lattes, for now," says Claire. "My nose is bothering me about one thing though. You and Matt. You're not back living together."

Sophia giggles and then becomes more serious. "It was a conscious decision, by both of us. We need this courting period, Claire. Matt was very hurt and I had a lot of stuff to deal with. It's been lovely, going to films and plays – do you know, he kisses me at night on Mammy's doorstep!"

Claire is looking at Sophia, wide-eyed. "I think you're trying to tell me that you and Matt haven't, oh, my God, done it during the last three months . . ."

"Exactly. We're putting it on hold."

"Until when? I've never heard the like of this."

"Soon, very soon, now."

"Christ, he'll be like a rampant stud. I fear for you, Sophia, that your heart won't stand it."

"What will it make me like, if he's like that?" asks Sophia mischievously.

A pause, and together the two girls break into song: *"Like a virgin – for the very first time!"*

The barman looks over, quizzically.

"Seriously though," says Sophia, "we're off to Kerry this weekend."

Claire shrieks with laughter. She's thrilled for Sophia and Matt.

"We're going Friday morning," Sophia is saying. "We want to get there early, but we have two mugs we need to buy first."

Chapter 51

Marianne kneels in silent prayer at the graveyard in Kells. Tears fill her eyes.

"Liam, Stephen, forever a part of me, forever with me. Goodbye, my loves, I'll come back soon."

David awaits her at the gate. He is family, but she needed these few private moments. He opens the gate for her. There has been a lot to do over the past few weeks, putting Marianne's home in Kells on the market.

"Tell it all to someone," Marianne's counsellor had said. Marianne had chosen David. He was a willing listener.

Marianne is leaving for Leitrim today and stops by at Kathleen's while David secures the house.

"So, you're off," says Kathleen, almost crushing her friend with a hug and then holding her back to look at her. "My, you've improved these last few weeks. Have you seen anywhere you'd like to buy, put your feet up?"

"I mightn't need to buy. They say there's more bachelors in Leitrim than anywhere in Ireland!"

"Aye, and one of them is not even there at the moment." They both laugh joyously. "Off with you now, my girl, and don't forget to call me."

David pulls up at the gate and they drive off.

It's Leitrim, then.

Marian whispers. "David, what are we going to do, if Greg comes home in August, as promised? We'll be a bedroom short."

David looks over at Marianne with concern.

"We'll manage . . ." He clears his throat and then continues, "Are you saying that, eh, last night, was a once-off?"

"Joking. I hope not! Ah, it's good to be alive again!"

The miles roll by.

"David, there's just another thing. The lady in the photo? We never wrapped up on that one."

"I did. Let's just say her husband persuaded me against continuing. I'm happy he did, now."

The End

If you enjoyed *It Started With a Wish*, don't miss out on Kathy Rodgers' *Misbehaving*, also published by Poolbeg.

Here's a sneak peek at Chapter One . . .

Chapter One

It was lunch-time and it was like rush hour in my head. I had a list of things to do and less than one hour to do them. I was in my local supermarket, like I am every day. I grabbed a basket and made for the baby aisle. Usually I tried to do a big shop once a week, on a Saturday morning, but it never worked out that way. I was always back shopping again the next day.

"Write a list," my husband Gary suggested, when I moaned to him that I knew the supermarket better than I knew my own home. At least I had a better chance of finding what I was looking for in the supermarket. Yet I was grateful for his suggestion. Those days Gary and I couldn't hold down a conversation for two minutes without one of us yawning. We blamed it on parenthood. Other parents reassured me that it got easier as the kids got older.

A quick glance at the checkouts made me grow more irritable – each one had a queue. Even the express looked sluggish today. In the distance I could see my mother-in-law. I turned down an aisle to avoid her. I hadn't time for a quick chat. Kathleen would want to know if Jack's ear infection was better? Did he sleep the night? Did he eat his breakfast? That's the one thing Kathleen has in common with my mother: they need to know everything.

I stopped halfway down the aisle, bewildered. They'd moved the contents of the aisle. It used to be the toy aisle; now it had pots and pans grinning down at me. My armpits were damp with sweat. Outside it was cold and raining, inside it was like a tropical forest. I felt cheated. A loyal customer like me should be informed when they're going to move things. Didn't they realise how confusing it was for me? I raced up the aisle. There was no need for me to glance at my watch and find out the time. The clock in my head was tick-tocking the minutes down for me. All I had to do was keep in time. I'd done this a thousand times. First, I'd run into the supermarket to do a quick shop and get a sandwich.

Then, I'd do some other errands before dashing back to work with only seconds to spare.

I headed for the baby aisle and thankfully it was still there. I picked up a packet of nappies. I still had to go to the bank. And, I had to collect a prescription for my baby. Another sleepless night loomed ahead of me. That's the thing about me: I'm good at predicting the worst outcome.

Gary and I weren't childhood sweethearts, but we grew up together. We never engraved our names on a tree or kissed when no one was looking. I let Gary have a peek at me doing a pee when I was five. He was curious as to how girls actually did a pee without a willy. Then, Gary had to go off and play cowboys and Indians with the boys, while I stayed with my best friend Eleanor and made tea in my white and red tea set.

My feet took me back to the sandwich-stand. I scanned the selection on display: chicken, tuna, ham. I read the labels and tried to make a "quick" decision.

Right now I could be in the pub with the girls from work having our usual Friday lunch of chicken curry and chips instead of standing in Tesco.

"Hi, Michelle," a voice said from behind me.

I turned around and saw Amanda in her school uniform.

"Hi, Amanda, how are you?"

"I'm fine. I've got a French test this afternoon and I'm not looking forward to it," she said, a slight tremor in her voice. Her mother minds my son for me, while I spend my day answering calls from customers.

Amanda's mother had told me she'd ring me if he didn't settle down for her. All morning I'd waited for her call and, when it didn't come, I called her hoping he'd be missing me so much that I'd have to leave work. I wanted to be with him and I longed for a few hours of blissful sleep.

"See ya," Amanda said.

"Did you go home for lunch?" I couldn't help myself, I had to ask.

Amanda shook her head. "I tried to do some study." She walked away from me with a chicken sandwich, her head full of thoughts of the dreaded test.

The tuna sandwich looked like the healthy option, so I picked it up. Being sleep-deprived I'd forgotten that I didn't like tuna.

My life was just busy, ordinary busy. Filled with the everyday things of being mother to a baby boy and wife to Gary.

A familiar face smiled at me and I smiled back as the woman walked past. I live in a small midlands town. It's like a goldfish bowl: you're bound to bump into the same people again and again.

"Michelle," a voice said.

I turned to look. My heart missed a beat. He was standing inches away from me.

I stood motionless. The tuna sandwich slipped from my hand into the basket.

"Michelle."

My mouth dropped open. Inside I could feel my chest tightening, I couldn't breathe. It felt like I was under water. I was aware that things were going on around me, but everything was a blur.

"Damien," I managed to say, and then I gulped for breath. It felt like I had plunged into the deep end and I needed air quickly or I'd drown. "Hi," I muttered. The muscles in my face stretched into a weak smile. The sort of smile you saved for people you don't like, but have to be friendly to.

It was five years since I'd inhaled the Damien smell, that heady mixture of expensive aftershave and body odour. It excited me, made me go all tingly inside.

His soft blue eyes never left mine.

He broke into my thoughts by saying, "It's good to see you." A dreamy smile formed on his handsome face.

Damien's voice opened up the past. Its soft sensual timbre made my heart race. He hadn't changed. If anything he looked better, but then, you don't meet many attractive men in my local supermarket. At least I'd given up looking – after all, I was a married woman.

"It's good to see you." I echoed his words as I couldn't think of my own. I'd been well-schooled to keep my feelings to myself, a family tradition that I've never managed to shake off. I felt stupid, as I stood there tongue-tied and breathless.

At work we have steps that we go through to deal with difficult customers. I longed for Agent Clarke to pass the clipboard to me now. Rosemary and I liked to call ourselves agents. We worked for a company called Express Couriers. It was up to us to help our customers with any problems they had. We labelled ourselves Agent Clarke and Agent Kenny, just for the fun of it.

Damien towered over me. I noticed his face was lightly tanned. I avoided making eye contact. I couldn't help but notice threads of silver woven through his light-brown hair. A part of me longed to reach out and touch him, to see if he was real. Instead I looked down at my list. Yoghurts, milk, bread.

Silence fell on us. I knew he was looking down at me with those blue eyes that always had the effect of making my legs go weak. The shopping list made no sense. I felt like I was being transported to another place, to a time when I was a different Michelle.

"Shopping?" Damien said.

I nodded and then filled the silence by saying, "Yes."

"I know this is a shock . . . me turning up like this, but I needed to see you." He moved closer to me as he spoke.

I ventured to look up from his chest and meet his eyes again: they were the same devilish eyes, full of mischief. Dormant feelings surfaced. A feeling of warmth spread through me, making me blush. Was I falling in love with this man all over again? Could someone from your past just walk into your life and tilt it so that you lost your direction? My thoughts swayed.

I was sure of one thing, that I was certain of nothing. It dawned on me, then, with brilliant clarity, that things would never be the same again. The floor seemed to move beneath me, then steadied itself.

"I know it's been a long time," he said, in the cultured tone that once was as familiar to me as breathing.

Five years, I wanted to say. Five years, one marriage and a child later, you turn up – like a bad penny, as my mother would say.

"I – I –" I heard myself stammering. I wanted to cry and laugh at the same time. My hands gripped the shopping basket for support.

"I can explain. Perhaps we could have lunch together?"

A long time ago I'd closed my mind to Damien. I'd locked the door to that part of my life. I never thought about him, dreamt about him, wondered what he was doing now. Nothing. It was like he'd never existed, that our time together had never happened.

By some accident my mind was playing tricks on me. I'd opened the wrong door. This was not Damien, this was   me – having a nightmare in the middle of the day. All I had to do was pinch myself and I'd wake up.

I reached out my hand and touched his arm. He was real – I was not dreaming.

"I have to do my shopping." I replayed the

words I'd said to the girls thirty minutes ago: "I haven't time for lunch. I'm going to have a sandwich at my desk."

"Michelle," he said, his voice almost a whisper, as if he was afraid of other shoppers hearing.

I loved the way he said my name – it was like a caress. I quelled a longing to reach out and touch him again.

"I know you've got a new life and the last thing you want is to meet an old lover, but I need to see you."

Two girls from work passed by.

"Hi, Michelle," they said in chorus and then they sped down the aisle giggling.

"I know you're married," he said.

Those simple words conjured up a picture of my son and Gary. A family portrait, but I was missing.

"You've got a son," he added.

"Yes," I found myself saying. A tingle of joy ran through me. At least I could still speak.

"Jack," he said.

I attempted to smile, but the muscles in my face were frozen. Damien smiled for me.

"Michelle, I was thinking it was you!" came a familiar female voice.

I smiled feebly at my mother-in-law Kathleen.

She turned to look at Damien.

He picked up a sandwich and walked purpose-fully towards the magazine section.

"How is Jack?"

"Fine," I said.

I glanced at my watch, saw the time, but couldn't make myself move from the spot. I was way behind schedule. I should have collected Jack's prescription already and be on my way to the bank.

"Michelle, you look terrible," Kathleen said. For once her eyes were full of sympathy for me. I knew she'd never considered me good enough for her only son.

"I don't feel well."

I stole a glance at Damien. He was standing at the magazine-stand. The cream raincoat that he wore might have looked ordinary on another man – on him it looked tailored and perfect.

"Michelle . . ."

I heard Kathleen say my name. I felt irritated and found my face falling into a frown as I turned to look at her.

"Is there anything I can do to help?" she asked with an arched eyebrow. She had a pleasant face and, unlike my mother, she always seemed to be smiling.

I attempted to tune into her wavelength. I needed to get rid of her as fast as I could. Delving into my bag, I pulled out the prescription.

"You could collect Jack's prescription from the chemist for me."

She took the prescription from me. "Of course, I'll drop it in this evening."

That was the last thing I wanted Kathleen to do because she always forgot to go once she'd "dropped in". I saw her face brighten, then she turned and headed for the exit.

He was gone. I looked around and he was nowhere to be seen. Not at the magazine-stand, not at the express checkout, nowhere.

My head was spinning. I wanted to cry. Where the hell had he got to? And what did he want with me? I didn't need this, not now, not today.

I had shopping to do, a job that I had to get back to and baby Jack to think about. I was stopped in full flow as I watched him materialise with a bunch of flowers in his hand.

"For you, Michelle," he said.

For some unexpected reason my heart swelled with joy. This was the Damien I had fallen in love with. He bought flowers not as a peace offering or to negotiate with, but because he wanted to.

"Thank you," I said. Tears were filling my eyes, making him quiver in front of me. "There . . ." words failed me. "There . . ." I attempted to speak but couldn't.

"Let's go somewhere quiet. We need to talk."

I shook my head. "I can't."

"Michelle, I'm really sorry about this. I've handled it so badly. I should have phoned you or written to you, but I was afraid that you'd turn me away."

Habit made me look at my watch.

"I have to go – if I don't I'll never make it back to work on time."

Damien nodded.

I picked up my basket. My legs shook uncontrollably as I joined the queue for the express checkout. For once I didn't care if it took forever. He stood alarmingly close behind me.

An aching started in my belly and ran all the way down to my toes. I wanted this man. I inched myself a little away from him. He moved closer. While not actually touching, it was enough to excite me.

A part of me wanted to turn around, look into those electric eyes of his and ask him, 'Where are you taking me?'

"Hi, Michelle."

"Hi, Susan." I smiled at the girl on the checkout. She lived two doors down from me. She eyed Damien curiously. Quickly I moved away from him.

"Terrible day out," she said.

I nodded. I saw her stealing another glance at Damien. He was used to it, thrived on it. In fact, he'd probably die if women didn't stare at him.

"See ya," Susan said.

While I was pushing my nappies into the carrier bag, Damien was paying for his sandwich. A great sense of shame and guilt rose inside me. Even though I'd done nothing wrong. But I wanted to. I longed to. My fingers trembled as I picked up my shopping and ran for the exit. I ran all the way to my car. When I gave a quick look back, I realised no one was chasing me and felt disappointed.

The flowers scented the car, reminding me of when I was a little girl. I loved to pick buttercups and daises when I went to visit my granny. As I inhaled the sweet smell, I was again watching my brother Vincent running down the hill. His supple body moved speedily and with little effort, skipping over the long grass. It's a picture I've always held in my mind.

"You can't catch me!" he shouted and laughed at me.

I waved at him and started to run down the hill, knowing I wasn't as fast as he was, but enjoying it all the same.

Right now, that is what I wanted to do: run. I didn't want to think about my past with Damien or my present with Gary. And the last thing I wanted to do was go back to work.

Deep down I knew that I'd see Damien again. My stomach rumbled nervously. If I was honest, I knew I wanted to see him again. I wanted to sit down and listen to him, to hear his refined voice and be seduced by whatever he had to say. My head was spinning with the crazy picture I was dreaming up.